P9-ARM-991

THE
BEACH HOUSE
ON
Amelia Island

SEVEN SISTERS
BOOK ONE

HOPE
HOLLOWAY

Hope Holloway

Seven Sisters Book 1

The Beach House on Amelia Island

Copyright © 2023 Hope Holloway

This novel is a work of fiction. Any references to historical events, real people, or real locales are used fictitiously. Other names, characters, places, and incidents are the product of the author's imagination, and any resemblance to actual events or locales or persons, living or dead, is coincidental. All rights to reproduction of this work are reserved. No part of this publication may be reproduced, stored in or introduced into a retrieval system, or transmitted, in any form, or by any means (electronic, mechanical, photocopying, recording, or otherwise) without prior written permission from the copyright owner. Thank you for respecting the copyright. For permission or information on foreign, audio, or other rights, contact the author, hopehollowayauthor@gmail.com.

Cover designed by Sarah Brown (http://www.sarahdesigns.co/)

Introduction To The Seven Sisters Series

Meet the Wingate women, seven sisters who are all unique and unforgettable...but they all share inner strength, abiding love, a few quirky traits, and the ability to support each other through every challenge. This family is founded on love and laughter and a sisterhood unlike any other.

The series consists of seven books with recurring characters, continuing stories, heartbreaking and hopeful moments, later-in-life romance, a touch of mystery, and lots of happy tears. All of the books will be available in digital, paperback, and audio formats.

Visit www.hopeholloway.com for release dates, covers, and sneak peeks into the series!

The Seven Daughters of Rex Wingate

Born to Charlotte Wingate

Madeline Wingate, age 49
Tori Wingate, age 45
Rose Wingate D'Angelo, age 43
Raina Wingate, age 43

Born to Susannah Wingate

Sadie Wingate, age 35
Grace Wingate Jenkins, age 33
Chloe Wingate, age 29

Chapter One

Raina

Why was there an open suitcase, fully packed with her husband's clothes, on the bed? Was Jack going on a trip she didn't know about? Or was...

Raina squeezed her eyes shut.

Was he serious about a separation?

"Hey," she called, walking across the spacious bedroom toward his bathroom and walk-in closet. "I came home early."

As she passed the bed and glanced at the contents of the suitcase, her heart dropped. That was...a lot of clothes. Not a quick trip. More like a lengthy escape.

On a sigh, she dipped one shoulder to slide off her laptop case and handbag, then the other to drop the messenger bag her assistant had filled with files and contracts. From inside one of them, her phone buzzed, but she ignored it, shaking off her suit jacket and tossing it on the bed.

Worry curled like a smoky tendril in her chest.

He *wouldn't* leave her, would he? Yes, he'd been

furious that she'd opposed his latest acquisition, and they'd argued.

But a married couple who shared a thriving real estate firm could be expected to have a disagreement from time to time. Good heavens, yesterday morning, hours before that fight, they'd been...intimate. Wasn't that the normal ebb and flow of a sixteen-year marriage?

He wouldn't give up on them because of a business dispute...would he?

"Jack?" Raina called again when he didn't answer, stepping into the vestibule that led to his personal area in their shared bedroom.

The "two baths with separate dressing rooms" in the main suite had been her husband's brainchild when they'd gutted and redesigned the luxury home in the upscale Coral Gables community known as Cocoplum. Jack said he'd sold enough multimillion-dollar homes to Miami's uber-rich to insist the feature was a must-have for couples who wanted personal privacy in their posh primary suite.

And, of course, he was thinking about resale, since selling expensive homes—even his own—was always top of mind to Jack Wallace. And Raina, who'd been raised and mentored by a real estate genius, had agreed.

But sometimes that dual bathroom made her feel distant from him. She missed the true intimacy of brushing their teeth together like they did when they were first married, back when they shared a sink, big dreams, and so many toothpastey laughs and kisses before bed.

When had those halcyon days disappeared? When had it become as much about their business partnership as their marriage? It had happened slowly, insidiously. Staleness had crept in, and laughs and kisses had somehow become fights about...acquisitions.

"Maybe it's time to rethink this partnership, Raina."

His words from the argument echoed in her head, each one a gut-punch.

"Are you in here?" she called again, inhaling the mist of a shower and an oaky aftershave he'd recently started wearing.

But there was no sign of her husband, just a wood-paneled walk-in closet that definitely looked emptier than the last time she'd been in here. Tension crept up her spine as she remembered how angry they'd been last night, the last time she'd seen him.

Not only had they gone to sleep angry, but they'd gone to work that way, too. At least Raina had. Jack had been down in the home gym when she'd left this morning, and too lost in his workout and screaming loud music to say goodbye.

She figured she'd see him at work, and they could rethink the acquisition, with spreadsheets handy to drive home her point that buying that small firm wasn't a smart move financially. He always responded to a good spreadsheet and the bottom line.

But he never came into Wallace & Wingate, the real estate company they co-owned, and his assistant said he was working from home. Sensing something was really wrong, Raina had left the office and come back here in the middle of the afternoon.

To find his half-packed suitcase.

"Oh, you're home." Jack's voice floated in from the bedroom, making her dart out to find him sliding a pair of sneakers into the side of the suitcase, vaguely aware of her phone buzzing again.

Right now, everything else could wait.

For a minute, she watched him, waiting for him to look up to meet her gaze.

But his only movement was the rise and fall of his shoulders, which seemed broader lately from his obsessive working out. His light brown hair was a little longer, too, which was a change. He never liked it to so much as brush his collar. And...she blinked in surprise at his long, tanned fingers as he struggled with the zipper on the storage pocket.

"Why aren't you wearing your wedding ring?" she asked the moment the question popped into her head.

He looked up, his dark gaze sharp. "I took it off to work out and..." He shrugged. "I forgot it."

"And why are you packing?"

His expression shifted to one of exasperation and maybe a little disbelief. "I told you last night that I need... time. And space. And a new perspective. So I'm leaving."

"Leaving? For...a trip?" But even as she said it, even as her voice rose in uncertainty, she knew. She *knew*.

"For...a *while*." He yanked at the uncooperative zipper that didn't budge, grunting like Jack did when things didn't go exactly as he wanted them to. Which was rare. From the moment she'd met him at a statewide real estate conference in Orlando, she discovered that Jack Wallace had a way of getting what he wanted.

And that day he'd made it infinitely clear that he wanted *her*. The feeling had been heady, the romance had been a whirlwind, and before she knew what happened, they married and she moved from Amelia Island to Miami to dominate the real estate world together.

Before meeting him, Raina had been on track to take over her father's business, Wingate Properties, but Jack detoured that—*"We can build our own empire, Rain!"*— and they'd been down here doing just that for sixteen years.

Was he willing to walk away from that history?

"You understand that, don't you?" Jack asked.

Raina blinked at him, not sure if she'd missed a question while she was meandering down memory lane, or if he meant she understood "a while."

She didn't.

She took a step forward, digging for composure. "If it means that much to you, I'll stop fighting you on the Godfrey acquisition. It's not worth you leaving over."

"Good, because the deal is inked, Raina, and it would cost a fortune to get out of it. But I'm still leaving."

Her heart shifted. "Jack, please. We can figure this out."

"Can we?" he shot back.

During that beat of time, she heard a chime from her phone, this one indicating a call that she ignored.

"Yes," she said, taking a step closer. "If you can put business aside for one minute and think about us. About this marriage and our future. Our family and—"

"Family?" he scoffed. "We are *not* trying again, so don't even suggest it. You were a train wreck after the last one."

She closed her eyes with a shuddering breath. The first miscarriage was heartbreaking, but she was still hopeful. The second one was shocking, and she was scared. The third, a year ago? It nearly broke her.

"I won't. I'm done."

"And don't start with the adoption stuff. We've been at this baby thing for a stinking decade. At our ages, the only way we'd get a kid is to buy one in some foreign country. It's too much."

She swallowed, not really willing to delve into *that* fight again when this one was so immediate and that suit-case was so...packed.

"Why are you doing this, Jack? Really?" she pressed. "This is more than an acquisition, more than the miscar-riages. What's at the heart of all this?"

He lifted a shoulder, considering the questions. "I'm just not sure what I want to do with what's left of life," he mused, picking up a T-shirt from the top of the pile and refolding the sleeves.

"What's *left*? You're forty-five. That's *mid*life, I hope." She frowned. "Is that what this is? A midlife crisis?"

He stared at the suitcase for a few long heartbeats. "Maybe. I just need to find my passion again."

"You lost it?" she asked, hearing the phone buzz again.

He tipped his head toward it. "That could be a client."

"They can wait," she replied. "What kind of...of passion are you looking for?" Wasn't *she* his passion? And their business? Their lives?

"I don't know," he said so softly she had to take a few steps closer to hear him. "I want new opportunities, new...stuff. That's why I wanted Godfrey. She—the owner—has some kind of wild connections to the richest of the rich in this town. I want some of those forty-million-dollar listings. Don't you?"

She sighed, knowing she was dragging them back to the *other* thing they fought about, but she didn't want to dance around it.

"What I wanted was...a family," she admitted.

"I know, I *know*," he said, clearly sick of the subject. "You want a big happy *clan* like the Wingates, with a million kids and all those...events."

He made her family sound like hell. Of course, every time she dragged him up to Amelia Island for a birthday or holiday, he made it clear the whole thing *was* hell for him. He claimed he felt like an outsider in her family of seven sisters, no matter how they tried to include him.

"Not a million kids," she murmured. "I would have settled for one."

He looked at her, a question in his eyes.

"What?" she asked when he didn't say anything.

"I don't know, Raina. You used to be such a...dynamo.

You made things happen, got the best sales, closed every contract. You were a ball of fire and I loved that."

She could barely swallow. "Past tense?"

"No, no. Raina, please," he said quickly. "It's probably me who's changed, not you. Midlife. You're right." He breezed by her to go into his closet. As he passed, she got a whiff of that scent again, which smelled like...defeat and exhaustion.

She dropped on the bed and almost answered another call coming in, but she couldn't get sidetracked now. She had to fix this.

"Jack." She pushed up and followed him into the closet, where he stared into a dresser drawer, his back to her. As she took a step closer, she realized he wasn't looking for clothes, but reading his phone.

"Where are you going?" she asked.

He tucked the phone back into his pocket. "I'm renting that house on Old Cutler Road that we just listed. They agreed to a six-month lease—"

"You're renting a house? Ten minutes from here? For six months?" She heard her voice lift in disbelief. "Why?"

Very slowly, he turned from the dresser and scowled at her, that "don't you get it" expression all over his face. "Because I need some time and space, Raina."

"So...we're separating?"

"Call it what you want."

What she called it was...wrong and ugly and, yes, a failure. Was there anything Raina Wingate hated more than failure? Than a problem she couldn't solve?

"I need a break, a clear head, and place to live and think," he said.

"And...work?"

"I can run my part of our business from home, or..." He lifted a shoulder. "We can break up the company."

"The company *and* our marriage?"

"Raina, please, I..." He just shook his head and walked out, back into the bedroom, leaving her standing alone and broken.

She pressed her knuckles to her lips, fighting back the urge to cry out. Why did this seem so easy for him? Because the idea of a separation just killed her.

"Your phone is blowing up," he called to her. "You might want to get it."

She took a steadying breath and walked back into the bedroom, trying not to stare at the sight of him conquering the zipper to finish packing.

Wordlessly, she opened her handbag to find her vibrating cell phone.

"Whoa," she muttered as she read the list of calls and texts, which looked like the seating chart at a Wingate family dinner, with the names of all six of her sisters. "It's my mother calling, and not for the first time."

"Step," he corrected. "She's actually not your mother and I don't know why you always call her that. You don't call her 'Mom' so—"

"She raised me since I was three," she said, touching the screen and wondering why he was being so incredibly difficult. "Hey, Suze, it's not a great—"

"Your father's had a stroke."

"What?" All the blood drained from her head. "Is he okay? How bad?"

"He's...not good. Way worse than the TIA he had last time," she said. "This one is..." She hesitated long enough for Raina to feel her heart crawl into her throat, her legs quivering as she dropped on the edge of the bed.

"His words are slurred," Susannah said. "And his whole left side is...is...not working properly. I found him in his home office, just slumped on the floor. Called 911. We're at the hospital on Amelia Island now."

"Oh my God." Raina's heart slammed against her chest, everything else in her life forgotten as she refocused.

"What's wrong?" Jack asked, coming closer with a frown.

"My dad," she whispered. "He had a stroke. A real one this time."

He flinched. "Yikes."

She ignored the reaction and tried to listen to Susannah, whose voice was reed thin with nerves. "The EMTs kept saying time was of the essence with a stroke," she continued.

"Was Gabe on duty?" Raina asked, hoping her brother-in-law, a Fernandina Beach firefighter and EMT, had been in the ambulance.

"No, but they were all very good. And today is critical. After that? I don't know. I just don't know."

Raina closed her eyes, trying to process the impossibility of Dad not being able to talk or move or...run the world. Or at least run the Amelia Island-based real estate company known as Wingate Properties.

Jack towered in front of her, staring down. "Is he..."

"In the hospital being treated," she told him, then returned all attention to her mother. Step or not, she loved Susannah and her heart hurt for how scared she must be.

"Who's with you?" Raina asked, already rethinking her whole day and week and, well, life.

She could get up to Amelia Island, at the very northern tip of the state near the Georgia border, in under six hours if she hauled it. And haul she would.

"Madeline's here with me, and Rose," Susannah said. "Grace will be here in a few minutes, and Chloe's on her way from her office in Jacksonville."

"Good, good." That covered the local daughters. "Can Tori come down from Boston?" she asked.

"She's getting on a plane this afternoon. And I spoke with Sadie, but it's six hours ahead in Brussels, so she's not going to do anything until we know more tomorrow. She might not be able to get away, but she will if...if..."

If he doesn't make it, Raina finished silently, the very idea making her heart crack.

"I'm coming up, Suze," she said.

"You don't have to..." Her mother's voice faded, because they both knew she most certainly *did* have to. Nothing could stop her.

"And I'm staying for...*a while.*" At the echo of Jack's words, they held each other's gaze.

"But your work—"

"Will survive without me," Raina told her. "But we need to be together while he gets better."

Because he had to get better. He *had* to.

"Oh, Raina," Susannah's trace of a Savannah accent came across weak with relief. "Yes, I want as many of my girls here as possible."

She smiled at that and wished Jack had heard that. He always insisted on calling Susannah her stepmother, but only because he never really understood their close-knit family. His had been anything but.

"Of course, Suze," she said softly, knowing that this was taking her away from Jack—the opposite of what she should be doing—but no matter what was happening in this home, she had to help her family. "I can keep an eye on Dad's business, too, since he'll be...laid up."

"Thank you, Raina. Thank you."

She finished the conversation and hung up while Jack started asking questions that she couldn't answer.

"All I know is he's had a stroke and it's serious." Her whole body trembled at the words. "I can't believe this," she added in a whisper.

"He's going to be fine," he said, sounding cavalier but no doubt just trying to make her feel better. "Rex Wingate is immortal."

"God, I hope so."

"You're going up, I take it?"

"Of course." She stared at him, waiting and secretly hoping that he'd say he'd go, too. But she already knew that wasn't going to happen.

"And you'll manage his business?" he asked.

She shrugged. "I don't know about managing it, but I'll make sure no contracts fall through the cracks."

Jack gave a dry laugh. "So you get to run the old man's company after all. What you always wanted."

"Are you serious?" She pushed up and shook her head. "My seventy-five-year-old father had a stroke, Jack. This isn't about taking over his business, it's about helping him."

"So you could be gone a while?" He sounded...hopeful, which felt like someone threw a handful of salt on her wounded heart.

"Long enough that you don't have to rent that house on Old Cutler," she said, walking toward her own closet to pack her own suitcase to take her own trip.

As much as she longed to have him at her side for whatever lay ahead, she knew what she had to do. If she dragged him into this Wingate crisis, it would just delay what was eating at him. Dad's stroke gave Jack the time and space he said he needed. Then, when she came back, they'd work this out. She hoped.

"Then I'll be here," Jack said.

"Yep." She stepped into her closet and let out a long, achy groan. "You can just stay here, Jack," she whispered. "And...find your passion."

And she would go home to the family she loved and needed so much right now.

Chapter Two

Susannah

Hold it together. Hold it together. Be a Wingate and hold it together.

But Susannah's fingers trembled as she said goodbye to Raina, hoping she sounded more in control than she felt.

All seven of her girls frequently joked that Susannah's gravestone would read, "She kept up appearances." She wouldn't be ashamed of that epitaph.

One of the ways she did that was by exercising control, a trait that got her through every difficult situation she'd faced in her sixty-one years of life. After a childhood of abject poverty, then as the second wife of Reginald "Rex" Wingate III, a mother to his four small girls, and then three more of their own, Susannah had faced her fair share of difficult situations.

None quite as bad as this, though.

She squared her shoulders and marched down the hall, determined that no one—not the nurses, doctors, her daughters, or the patient himself—would ever imagine that she was so scared of losing Rex that just the thought of it made her knees weak.

First, she stopped in the bathroom to freshen her lipstick and run a comb through her short blond hair, making sure that even in this time of crisis she looked polished and proper.

Then, she texted her daughter, Tori, to give her the access code to the beach bungalow in case she and Kenzie, Susannah's teenage granddaughter, got in too late to come to the hospital. After that, she called Rex's new assistant, Blake...whatever his last name was...to bring him up to speed and ask him to keep the news very quiet until they had a prognosis.

And finally, she stopped to get coffee for Rose and Madeline, her angels of mercy sitting in that harshly-lit waiting room.

By the time she breezed into the area just outside the ICU, she spotted them huddled close, holding hands, whispering to each other.

Before they noticed her, she took a moment to tamp down all her emotions and get strength from these two women she loved and admired so much. Yes, they were *step*daughters, like Raina and Tori. Her four older girls called her "Suze" which, as children, had become their version of "Mom" for her, and it stuck. But they were as much hers as Grace, Sadie, and Chloe, her three biological daughters.

The seven Wingate sisters were Susannah and Rex's greatest joy, and, in times like this, their greatest source of love and support.

Starting with Madeline, the oldest at forty-nine, only twelve years younger than Susannah. A perfectionist by nature, Madeline was the Rock of Gibraltar who could create a breathtaking one-of-a-kind wedding dress from nothing but satin and lace, yet had never worn one of her own. She was dependable, punctual, loyal, and easily Susannah's closest friend.

Next to her was Rose. Who could compare? Although she was Raina's twin, Rose was also the classic middle child, and the glue that held the seven sisters together with her inimitable light, warmth, and unconditional love. Had a cross word or negative thought ever slipped out of her lips? Not likely.

These were only two of the seven remarkable women she'd raised, and she would need all of them in the days ahead.

"I have wonderful news," Susannah announced, sailing in with the coffees extended toward them.

"He's getting out of ICU?" Madeline asked, brushing back some dark bangs that had fallen over her eyes.

"He's talking and walking?" Rose stood as she asked the question which, even for Rose, was ridiculously optimistic.

"Raina is coming," she replied, giving them each the correct coffee made exactly the way they liked it. "And she's staying...for a while."

"Bless you, Suze," Madeline whispered.

"Really?" Rose's brown eyes, always such a contrast to her pale blond hair, widened with a joy that Susannah certainly hadn't seen today. Nothing made Rose happier than time with her twin sister.

Susannah settled in a chair across from them, smoothing the linen skirt she'd worn for the fundraiser luncheon that she'd never made it to today. Not after finding her husband collapsed on the floor in his home office.

"How long is 'a while'?" Rose asked.

She shrugged. "As long as she can. She said she'll look in on Dad's business and make sure things are running smoothly while he recuperates."

Susannah knew "recuperate" was almost as optimistic as Rose, but she refused to say out loud the fact that Rex could barely form a sound, let alone a sentence, and he'd surely be in a wheelchair for the foreseeable future. *If* he made it through these critical hours.

"So six of us will be here. That's good." Rose fell back into her chair. "Sadie keeps texting from Brussels on our group chat, saying she wants to come, but she's worried she wouldn't be able to come back in six weeks for Chloe's wedding."

Susannah felt the blood drain from her head at the words. "The wedding. I forgot about my own daughter's wedding."

"Don't think about it, Suze." Madeline reached out to her. "This just happened. We don't know how bad it is. We can't get upset about things we can't change and it's too soon to panic."

Susannah nodded, but...would Rex even *be* there for

his youngest daughter's wedding? It was unthinkable that he might not.

"Is Jack coming up with Raina?" Rose asked.

"She said he'd stay back and run their business." Which was kind of a relief to Susannah. Raina's husband always made her feel like he'd rather be anywhere but in their midst, no matter how much they'd tried to fold him into the family.

And, truth be told, Rex was not a big fan of Jack Wallace, probably because their son-in-law had persuaded Raina to move to Miami and leave Wingate Properties all those years ago. None of Rex's other daughters were in the real estate business and he'd probably have to sell the company if he ever wanted to retire.

Not that he wanted to retire...unless God just made that happen for him.

It had gutted Rex when Raina left, because he'd always treated her like the son he didn't have. After all, she was Regina, his namesake.

She closed her eyes, thinking of how many times she'd heard the story, and how it never failed to move her. Charlotte Wingate died on the delivery table, the victim of an amniotic embolism that took her life an hour after she gave birth to the second of her twins—a baby she had no idea she was carrying. Rose came first and then the doctor had shocked them all with the news that "there's another one!"

Rex had exploded with joy, certain that this would be Reginald the Fourth. And when he was handed yet another girl, he called her Regina and assured Charlotte he couldn't be happier.

That must have been one of their last conversations, and right now...with Rex hanging on in the ICU, she knew exactly how he must have felt that day.

"I knew Raina would come up," Madeline said, yanking Susannah from her reverie. "I just didn't think she'd stay for more than a day or two."

"This is a family crisis, Madeline," Susannah said softly, twirling a gold bangle. "She'll be here tonight and she'll stay with me as long as we need her to."

"Well, if anyone can jump into Dad's shoes," Rose said, beaming with love and pride, "it's my twin sister."

Susannah hoped so. "He did seem preoccupied lately, so there are probably big deals brewing."

In fact, the night before his stroke, she'd awakened at two a.m. to an empty bed and found him alone in his office downstairs, staring out the window to the blackness of the Atlantic Ocean at night, lost in thought.

Of course, he insisted it was nothing to concern her.

Was the trouble also the catalyst for the stroke that had that ambulance flying down Fletcher Avenue this morning with Rex surrounded by EMTs?

Just then, she heard feminine voices and fast-moving footsteps in the hall.

"Oh! Grace and Chloe are here." Susannah stood and rushed to the door.

Peeking down the hall, the sight of her two youngest daughters hustling closer lifted her heart. Chloe broke into a run, arms outstretched, flaxen hair flying. Still her "baby" at twenty-nine, Chloe turned heads and stole breaths. In less than two months, she'd be a bride, and Susannah knew there'd never be a more beautiful one.

But...would Rex be able to walk her down the aisle?

Biting back tears at the thought, she folded Chloe into her arms and held tight, looking over her shoulder at Grace as she reached them.

The most reserved of her daughters, and the most introverted, Grace was no stranger to tragedy like what had struck today. In fact, she'd endured far worse when she became a grieving—and pregnant—widow four years ago.

With a moan of appreciation, Susannah widened her hug to include Grace in it, soaking up the support from two more of her daughters. Rose and Madeline joined them and for a long moment, all of them huddled in the hall.

"Mrs. Wingate?"

The man's voice broke them apart.

"Yes?" Susannah turned to see the man she already recognized as the ICU head nurse. "That's me. I'm Susannah Wingate."

"Would you come with me to talk to Dr. Singh, our attending neurologist? He'd like to speak with you about your husband's condition."

"Oh, yes, but not Dr. Verona? That's who he saw after his TIA."

The nurse nodded and gestured her toward the hall. "You'll see Dr. V tomorrow when he makes his rounds. For now, Mr. Wingate is in the care of the neurologist on call at the hospital, and all he wants to do is give you a quick update."

"Okay, thank you." She glanced over her shoulder at her daughters. "Um, can I bring…"

"Just you, if you don't mind," he said with a smile. "Small office."

"You go." Madeline gave her a nudge. "We'll all be right here."

"Don't worry, Mom," Chloe said, giving her one more squeeze. "We're together. We're here for you."

"Yes, yes." Susannah knew that together, they could handle anything. Anything at all.

Clinging to that thought, she followed the nurse, sensing that she was about to find out just what it was they'd have to handle.

Chapter Three

Rose

"I come bearing gifts."

Rose turned at the sound of Gabe's voice outside the waiting room, and with just one look at the man she married, everything was better. The tension in her chest eased, the endless wait for another word was forgotten, and the worry that strangled her all day lifted from her heart.

And her ravenous hunger was about to be satisfied by something in one of the French-fry and grilled cheese-scented bags from the Riverfront Café that hung from his arms. Life—even in its worst moments—improved when Gabriel D'Angelo was in the same room.

Surrounded by her sisters, who greeted and thanked him and pounced on the bags, Gabe's insanely blue eyes sought her out, locking on her and sharing that secret smile he saved for her.

He added a wink just to make sure her stomach did a flip and she smiled back, as in love as she'd been as a teenager when she met him on the first day of high school.

She hung back and watched him dole out the bags and hugs to his sisters-in-law and Susannah, waving off their thanks and asking first and foremost for an update on Rex.

"He's doing well," Susannah assured him. "The doctor said we did everything right in getting him here fast, and the medicine they're giving him has already dissolved the blood clot."

"I'm sorry I wasn't on duty, Suze, but you had some of our best medics in that ambulance," he said, his voice rich with pride in his colleagues at the fire station. "Speed is everything with a stroke."

"I'm so grateful," Susannah said. "And the doctor told me they have to run more tests but there is a good chance they'll move him out of the ICU and into a room tonight. I do hope that's true, because I want to stay with him overnight and I can't do that in the ICU."

"You want me to run back to the beach house and get you a bag?" he asked. "I'm sure you didn't pack before you called 911 this morning."

She smiled at him. "If they move him, I'll get a ride home and take a shower and pack for a few days. Thank you, dear."

He nodded and gave her another hug, then lightly elbowed Chloe, who was standing next to him. "There's a veggie burger in one of those bags," he told her. "Unless you're finally off that nutso vegetarian kick."

"Not a chance." She gave him a smug smile. "The day Hunter proposed, I promised him I'd be meat-free." She wiggled her diamond-laden ring finger. "Can't let my man down, can I? Thank you for remembering, Gabe."

"Turkey and Swiss," Grace cooed as she opened a sandwich with her name written on it. "My favorite."

"But no mayo," he said, pointing at her. "Your daughter said, 'It make Mommy tummy hurt.'"

She shuttered her eyes. "Oh, Nikki Lou. Out of the mouths of three-year-olds. Is she doing okay?"

He tipped his head and winced a little. "She misses you, but don't worry, Grace. She's got her bodyguards. Our kids circle that little peanut like she's a princess walking through a party."

"Has she had...a moment?" Grace asked, using one of her many euphemisms for one of little Nikki Lou's breakdowns.

"Nothing serious," he said, tunneling his fingers through his hair, a gesture Rose knew was a dead give-away that he was varnishing the truth to protect someone he loved. "And our girls have her back, I promise."

Rose smiled at that, loving how much her two daughters protected and adored their shy little cousin. It reminded her of how the four older Wingate girls used to look after the three younger half-sisters.

"Where are the kids now?" Rose asked.

"They're downstairs," he added. "No kids in the ICU area, but Zach's in charge, so no worries."

Rose nodded, knowing her fifteen-year-old son was as trustworthy as his father.

"I'm going to go down and see her," Grace said, standing. "Thanks, Gabe."

"Sure, but if she sees you, she might want you to stay." Gabe flicked at the short sleeves of his T-shirt, a habit Rose loved because it unconsciously drew her attention to his impressive biceps, honed from years as a fire-fighter and from being the "muscle" at her flower shop. "Right now, she's smooth and steady and the girls have her distracted with dolls."

Grace sat back down. "Best not to rock the boat then."

Finally done with handling family matters, Gabe wrapped his arm around Rose and dropped a kiss on her hair. Inching her back, he searched her face. "You doin' okay?"

She sighed into his strong body and subtly nudged him toward the door, where they could talk privately. "Yeah. Come out here."

Arm in arm, they stepped out of the waiting room into the wide hallway, which was hushed and empty at the moment.

"How's he doing, really?" Gabe asked, still holding her. "Susannah's put her 'all is perfect in Wingateland' spin on everything, of course. Is it true?"

"This time I think she's right," Rose said. "The attending doctor told her it was a serious stroke, but could have been much, much worse. He'll talk and move normally again, with a ton of physical therapy, which they'll start very soon."

He nodded, considering that. "You do know that this is a very critical time for a stroke victim. Another one could..." He swallowed, obviously not wanting to say the quiet part out loud. But Gabe was an EMT, and no stranger to stroke victims. "Another stroke could kill him, Rose," he finally whispered.

Her heart fell. "Do you think that's likely?"

"The first twenty-four hours are the trickiest, and if they're talking about putting him in a room, then he's responding well to the meds, likely Dipyridamole, which is great. But even after that? Short term? He needs to be careful with his body and his stress level."

"And long term?" she asked.

He just angled his head. "He can't wimp out on the PT or he'll never get out of a wheelchair. The doctor will talk to him, I'm sure."

But would he listen? "I can't even imagine my father as anything but...a force."

"He'll be a force again," he assured her. "But it'll take time."

"I know, I know. But there is a silver lining," she told him with a sly smile.

"There always is with you, Miss Rose-Colored Glasses. What good did you find in the bad?"

"Raina's coming up," she said. "She's on her way now and she's staying."

His brows lifted. "For how long?"

"Indefinitely, I think. Dad is not going to be back in the saddle for a long, long time."

"What about her company?"

Rose shrugged. "Raina and Jack share the workload. I'm sure he'll cover. And," she added, "I'm selfishly so happy I could cry. I can't wait to see her. She hardly ever comes up here and when she does, I feel like all Jack wants to do is leave."

"You want her to stay with us?" he asked.

"I would, but Susannah might need her more, at least at the beginning of all this. She's got the whole third-floor guest suite at the beach house and it makes sense for Raina to stay there. But, oh, I am hoping to get some good long conversations with her."

"Stay there tonight," he suggested without a second's hesitation.

"Tonight?"

"Didn't you say she's driving up now? When is she going to get in?"

"Eleven or twelve. Way too late—"

"For what?" he asked. "Susannah just said she's sleeping at the hospital, but even if she doesn't, you should go to the beach house. You can be there when Raina arrives, crack a bottle of Rex's best cabernet, and have yourself a twin night into the wee hours."

For a moment, she didn't know what to say other than how much she loved him. And she'd probably said that several times today already. "Are you sure?"

"Rose, I can handle the kids. I don't have a shift at the fire station for forty-eight hours and I can switch with someone if I have to. As far as the shop tomorrow, I know there's a shipment of Easter stuff coming and I'll unload it and do inventory, and we have staff for the orders that come in. Spend this night with Raina. Your dad's in the hospital and you need each other."

It all made sense and was so tempting, but she still

felt a frown pull, almost as strong as the desire to do exactly what he was suggesting.

"Zach has PE tomorrow, so he needs a change of clothes in his backpack."

"He's fifteen," Gabe said. "He should know how to handle that or stink in AP English, which would be a real turn-off to Tiffany Kaplan."

She laughed. "He told you about her?"

"No, Ethan ratted on him. And speaking of, our boy got an A on that science project. Ethan's pretty proud of himself today."

"Of course he is," she said on a sigh, filled with an indescribable love for her sweet eleven-year-old boy. "And the girls?"

"They're upset about Grandpa, no matter how much I played it down, so Nikki Lou is a good distraction. But, whoa, can you spell high-maintenance? That kid is a handful. One minute she's screaming, the next she's on another planet."

"I know. I better go home tonight, because Avery won't sleep if I'm—"

He put his finger on her lips. "I got this, babe. This is Wingate time and you can't leave Raina alone. Wait—is Tori coming?"

"She's on a plane now and, oh, this week is Kenzie's high school spring break, so she's coming, too. They land in Jacksonville in a couple of hours, and are planning to rent a car and stay in the bungalow," she said, referring to the much smaller two-bedroom cottage that was on the same property as Susannah and Dad's beach house.

"You could see her tonight, too."

She nodded, so tempted. "And she'll be right next door if Raina needs anything."

"Raina needs *you*. And you need her." He lifted her chin and, like always, she got lost in his eyes, reaching up to run her fingers through his soft, dark hair.

"I do like that idea," she admitted.

"Good. Stay there, Rose. Please."

She melted a little more into his arms. "Okay," she relented. "You win. I'll borrow Suze's PJs, and she always has extra toothbrushes."

"Perfect." He lowered his head and kissed her lightly, but she clung to him and pulled him closer for a longer connection. "But I'll miss you."

"I love you, my angel Gabriel."

He chuckled at the name she'd hung on him way back in the early days, when she knew a truly good man even as a teenager. He'd never changed and they'd never, ever so much as kissed anyone else.

"And I love you, Rose." He kissed her again, gave her a squeeze, and held her for a few heartbeats. "I'm praying hard for Rex. I cannot fathom this family without him."

She groaned into his broad chest. "No one can."

They parted and he stuck his head into the waiting room. "Bye, all. Love you, ladies! Tell Rex to give 'em hell."

He exited to a chorus of, "We love you, too, and thank you for dinner!" Rose leaned against the wall and watched him walk down the hall, still the finest man in a pair of Levi's and a fire department T-shirt she'd ever seen.

When he reached the stairwell, he looked back at her and blew a kiss, because, of course, he knew she'd be watching.

As she turned around, she sucked in a soft breath, coming face to face with Chloe, who'd caught the whole exchange.

"Yeah, yeah, I know," Rose said lightly. "We're ridiculous."

"Actually, I think it's beautiful."

She was surprised at the wistful note in her youngest sister's voice, but before she could dig deeper, a nurse came bounding down the hall with the wonderful news that Dad was being moved out of the ICU and into a room.

She'd never tell anyone but, deep in her heart, she gave all the credit to Gabe, because he walked in the light. Good things seemed to follow Gabe D'Angelo wherever he went, and wherever he went, Rose would follow.

TORI'S FLIGHT WAS DELAYED, Susannah had left with her bag to spend the night in the hospital with Dad, and Raina was still a half-hour away when Rose found herself in the unfamiliar situation of being completely alone at the beach house very late at night.

Was anyone ever alone in this place? To her—to all

the Wingates—Susannah and Rex's waterfront show-stopper was a physical magnet, drawing all of them for comfort, laughter, food, and family.

This expansive home hadn't been where the Wingate family had grown up—that was a sizeable Victorian in town where Rose now lived with Gabe and their four kids.

Dad had owned this oversized beach lot for decades, with only the small bungalow on it, as a getaway to spend weekends. Then he and Susannah had built the three-story stucco and Spanish tile home, and moved in when Chloe was still in college.

In the ensuing years, the beach house had become exactly what they'd intended—a central gathering place for a large and growing extended family. Today, ten years later, it was a home in a sense to all of them. It was certainly the site of every family party, all the holiday events, and a whole lot of summer Sundays spent barbe-quing and relaxing.

Just a few weeks ago, Susannah had hosted Chloe's bridal shower here, and in a week...well, no. There might *not* be a big Easter dinner this year. And she didn't even want to think about Chloe's wedding, not that the reception was to be held here, but still. One major life event at a time.

Her heart dropped at the thought of how they could possibly carry on without Dad. Could he survive this medical setback? Rex Wingate was a man who loved his whiskey and wine, cigars and classical music, and lived every one of his seventy-five years like it was his last.

"Another stroke could kill him."

Rose pushed Gabe's warning out of her head and wandered around the first floor, passing her father's office door with no desire to enter the room where he'd had the stroke. She glanced into the two guest rooms, one with bunk beds and plenty of space for kids to crash. Then she stepped into the oversized game room with a pool table, massive flat-screen TV, and a sectional that fit darn near all of them. Next to the fireplace, there was also a small bar, and a long table Susannah had set up just for toys and crafts for her grandchildren.

Of course, the kids all loved this space and on so many Sundays, it echoed with laughter and love. Grannie Suze and Grandpa Rex's home was certainly a place where they made some of the best memories of their lives.

Rose never wanted that to change.

She headed upstairs to the main living floor, turning on a few lamps to make it welcoming for Raina. It was dark now, but in the daylight, sunlight poured through the windows and warmed every corner.

The centrally located kitchen looked cheery and white, with a ten-foot island that was the site of so many toasts and appetizers before dinner parties. Off to one side, a massive dining table that seated twelve sat under an imposing chandelier, all of it facing out to a large living room with a wall of French doors that, in the daylight, offered a breathtaking ocean view. The master and a small office were on this floor, too, but the crowning glory of this house was up on the third floor.

A set of stairs led to an impressive guest suite every

bit as spacious as the main bedroom. There, next to the fireplace, stood one last staircase, a spiral that led to a square turret that sat like a wedding cake topper, offering unobstructed views of the whole of Amelia Island and the Atlantic ocean.

Raina would be comfortable there, she knew. And Tori would be right across the path in the bungalow; no doubts she'd be a frequent guest while Raina was here. The three of them were very close and although Rose hated the reason, she'd love having two of her out-of-town sisters closer for a few days.

Satisfied that the main living area was bright and welcoming, she walked to the French doors and opened one, tapping a light switch to spill a golden glow over the ocean-facing deck. Of all the areas for fun, family, and laughter in this home, this oversize patio was by far Rose's favorite.

It ran the length of the house and was at least thirty feet deep. In the middle, a long wooden walkway crossed the sea oats and small dunes, ending in a gate with steps to the beach. Off to one side of the deck, another set of stairs led to the large pool in the side yard, and the bungalow just beyond.

Spacious and welcoming, the deck had multiple seating areas, umbrella-covered tables, a firepit, a summer kitchen, and a long rail to perch on and watch the sunrise in the morning and the moonrise at night.

Her father loved it out here. When that moon spilled a silver glow over the water, he could often be found in one of the rattan chairs, listening to Beethoven or Bach on a small speaker connected to his phone, puffing a cigar, and counting his blessings.

He had to be able to continue that. He *had* to.

As she squeezed her eyes in yet another fervent plea for his recovery, her phone hummed with a text.

Raina: *I'm here.*

The simple text seemed a little...short. But then, she must be exhausted from the drive.

Rose darted back inside and rushed downstairs to the garage, opening the door only to be blinded by Raina's headlights as the gate opened. Like every other Wingate-owned property on Amelia Island, the beach house was protected by a wrought-iron gate braced by brick columns, a simple W emblazoned on the ironwork.

"Finally!" she exclaimed, rushing out when the car stopped. Impatient, she opened Raina's door and threw her arms around her beloved sister.

As she did, she dragged Raina from the front seat so she could give her a proper embrace, then drew back and looked at her sister, expecting to see what they used to call the "opposite mirror" when they were young.

The fraternal twins looked stunningly similar in the shape of their features, and their expressions. But Rose had pale blond hair and brown eyes, and Raina had nearly black hair and eyes a little lighter blue than Gabe's.

And right now, those blue eyes were puffy and rimmed red, her skin blotchy from crying.

"Oh, no, Raindrop!"

In her arms, Raina gave a quick laugh at the old nickname. "Oh, yes, Rosebud."

They sighed softly, and Rose rubbed Raina's back. "He's going to be okay. I told you he's out of ICU. That's huge. You gotta have faith, honey."

"I know, I know." She sniffled and wiped her nose. "I talked to Suze and she's super optimistic, and Madeline, too. It's just...upsetting."

"Very much."

"Have you seen him?" Raina asked as she walked to the back of her sedan and popped the trunk to get her bag.

"Briefly. We weren't allowed in while he was in the ICU and his room is private, but really small. Madeline is setting up a visiting schedule for tomorrow."

Raina rolled her eyes with a soft laugh. "Of course she is."

"And Suze is going to sleep in a recliner in the room, but that's love, huh? I would if it was Gabe, and you would if it was Jack."

She looked up, the unforgiving light from the trunk highlighting her expression, which was nothing short of ravaged.

"If we were still married," Raina muttered.

Rose frowned, giving her head a shake. *"Excuse me?"*

Raina stared at her, silent, pain darkening her whole expression.

"Raina? What do you mean?"

She gulped so hard Rose could practically hear the lump in her throat.

"What is it?" Rose asked, coming closer to take her hands. "Is something wrong? I mean, more than Dad?"

Raina nodded, clearly fighting tears.

"Is it Jack?"

Another nod and a stifled moan.

"What happened, Raina?"

"He wants to separate," she managed.

"What?" Rose's heart dropped, but the news somehow didn't shock her. Ever since she'd had that last miscarriage, Raina's marriage seemed to teeter on the edge of unhappiness. "It's just a bad time. Stress and business and all you two have been through."

"I don't know, Rose. I feel like I'm losing him," she murmured, squeezing Rose's hand. "And, honestly, God bless Dad's timing. I've never needed you more."

"Well, you have me. Come on in and tell me everything. Dad's also providing the wine."

Rose managed a smile as she hoisted her bag from the trunk to the driveway. "Good, 'cause I need a gallon."

Chapter Four

Tori

"And we have arrived." Tori let her head drop back with a groan of satisfaction as she pulled up to the beach bungalow. "One small step for mankind and a few major trip-ups by the airlines."

"And one giant step for the Victoria Wingate and Mackenzie Hathaway show, Florida edition."

Tori whipped around to see the phone blocking Kenzie's face as she, of course, memorialized every waking moment of their lives. "Do you mind not making a TikTok out of our personal day of travel hell?"

"Tell me about the guy at the rental car desk again, Mom. You were hilarious when he told us all he had was a van. I knew I should have recorded that."

She looked skyward. "I can't recreate a diatribe. That was stress- and travel-induced. The drive up from the airport relaxed me. Even in this underwhelming minivan."

Kenzie shook her head, having none of it. "No, come on, Mom. Tell me that whole thing about how a van is for work and your mom van days are behind you. That whole, 'How did that happen?' thing. Go ahead. I'll edit it really cute with music."

She reached across the van console—how *did* that happen?—and put her hand on the phone, gently lowering it. "I'm done, baby. I'm fried. I woke up this morning expecting to cater a dinner party for twenty with my menu planned and my schedule actually in shape for once. Then the phone rang. Now, fourteen hours later, I'm in a Toyota Sienna a thousand miles away and my dad's in the hospital and...yeah, no. Recordings are done for today. I'm calling it."

Kenzie sighed, finally abandoning the phone to tighten the scrunchie holding back her long dark hair.

"I'm sorry, Mom. I keep forgetting how worried you are about Grandpa. He's going to be fine. That was said at least six hundred times on the 7 *Sis* group chat, and, yes, I was reading over your shoulder in the airport."

Kenzie was right. The texts had been flying fast and furious today, but the messages were almost all positive.

"I just wish we hadn't had to spend three endless hours in Charlotte. Then I could have gotten to the hospital tonight, and I know I'll feel better after I see him and Suze and my sisters."

"We'll go tomorrow," Kenzie assured her. "But I'm kind of glad we can go to bed now. I'm wiped."

"Agree." She pushed her door open but stopped to take a deep lungful of salty Amelia Island air. "Oh, my. I'm home," she whispered on a sigh.

"Looks like Grannie Suze is, too." Kenzie, already pulling up the back hatch, pointed to the mammoth beach house about fifty yards from the bungalow. "I thought someone on your group text said she was spending the night with Grandpa."

"She is." Tori squinted at the lights on the main floor and back deck. "Oh, Raina must be here. She didn't answer any texts because she was driving." She looked at Kenzie, lifting her brows. "My sister's alone. Want to go see her?"

Kenzie thought about it, then shook her head. "Honestly? I'd love to see Aunt Raina, but I really want to crash. You go. Are you up for it?"

A minute ago, she would have said no. But the siren call of the sister she so rarely saw and the house that hugged every Wingate who walked into it was mighty strong.

"Let me put the bags inside and I'll text her."

They used the code to get in the front door and tapped the lights on in the small living area and kitchen. It wasn't large, but Susannah's elegant touch could be felt everywhere, from the shiplapped walls to the gleaming sand-toned hardwood floors and the cushy white sofa made for afternoon napping in the sun.

"I always love this place when we stay here," Kenzie said. "And bonus: No pesky brother I have to share a room with."

"Aw, I miss Finn. He's so weird and fun."

"Ha-ha. You're funny, Mom. That's like saying, 'Aww, I miss the plague. It's so deadly and pleasant.'"

Tori snorted and dragged her bag toward the bedrooms down the hall. "I'm sorry he's stuck at home, but he would have been a thirteen-year-old nightmare with all the delays. Plus, Dad would have had a cow if Finn missed a baseball game this close to the end of the season."

Trey's endless prodding to get their son to love that sport—just because Trey played all the way to the minor leagues—was a source of consternation for all of them.

"You're right," Kenzie agreed. "Finn is better off with Dad and Heidi-Ho."

Tori smiled at the name her always-irreverent daughter had hung on their father's girlfriend. "Well, it's a shame you weren't both on spring break at the same time, but hopefully my father will be better or well enough for us to go home in a week."

"I'm not complaining," Kenzie said as she stepped into the smaller of the two bedrooms. "For one thing, all you were going to do this week was work. My friends are off with their families on Instagram-worthy vacations and now I'm on one of my own."

"Thank you for being such a good sport, Kenz," Tori said. "It's not exactly spring break vacay, but I love your attitude."

Tori let go of her suitcase and pulled out her phone to text Raina, but not before she put her hands on the narrow shoulders of her favorite human on the face of the Earth.

No, a mother wasn't supposed to have favorites and Tori loved her son, too, beyond description. But with each day, especially after the divorce five years ago, soon-to-be-sixteen-year-old Kenzie had grown into a dependable, hilarious, rock-solid pal. A pal who deserved a better spring break her sophomore year of high school and a mother who was around more.

"I swear, when we get back, I'm going to work less."

"Mom, don't be silly. You have a successful catering company in suburban Boston. And you're a single mom. Of course you're busy."

"I am woman, hear me roar," she joked.

Kenzie's eyes flashed and in a split second, the iPhone was out. "Again, please. Only sing it this time. Maybe actually roar."

"I hate it when I have to kill you," Tori said, looking down at her own phone. "Let me text my sister." She tapped the screen and sent a simple note.

Don't tell me you're not awake. I see the lights. Want company?

A second later, she got a text, but this one was from Rose.

Rose: *I'm here with Raina and please COME NOW! Warning, some landmines ahead.*

Tori replied with a thumbs-up, assuming they were just as upset about Dad as she was. Unless "landmines" meant he'd taken a bad turn and no one had told her yet.

"You sure you're okay here alone?" she asked Kenzie, trying to keep her voice light and not give away her worry.

"Of course. I'm just going to sleep anyway. Go. Hug your sister."

"Sisters," she corrected. "Rose is there, too."

"Ooh, fun. Go get some R&R time." She gave Tori a

kiss. "I'll see you in the a.m., bright and early. I'll make breakfast."

"Out of...what? Suze didn't have time to shop."

"What a slacker," Kenzie joked. "Whatever. We'll figure it out."

Still smiling at how much she adored her daughter, Tori changed into sweats and a T-shirt, stuck some flipflops on her feet, and slipped out the door, freakishly excited for the reunion.

She had a great life in Wellesley, and a terrific business. But few things on Earth made her as happy as running along the sand toward the beach house, rounding the pool area, and taking the steps upstairs to fall into the arms of her sisters.

More than any of the others, Raina and Rose had been there for Tori during every crisis of her life. When she found out Trey had cheated, and when she filed for divorce, and when that divorce was final, and when she launched Tori Wingate Catering as a newly-single woman.

Culinary school had led her to Boston, and love had kept her there. But during any moment—good, bad, or otherwise—her heart was right here on Amelia Island.

She walked across the deck toward an open French door, listening for the laughter that always rang out when the two sisters she was closest to were together. The twins were two peas in a pod with an enviable relationship, but they never excluded anyone from that bubble, especially Tori, who was just two years older.

They'd always been a threesome that could get

through anything together. Madeline was more mature by nature and forced to be maternal after their mother died.

Then Dad met Susannah when Tori was five and the twins were three, and none of them ever knew life without a mother again, and there was plenty of laughter in the family.

But she didn't hear any of that now, likely out of deference to Dad's sickness.

"Hey, girls," she called lightly as she reached the door. "I'm here."

"Come on in, Tor," Rose called, but her voice was strained and quiet, making unease wrap around Tori's chest.

She stepped inside, looking around the softly lit living area and finally spotting the two of them curled up on a giant sectional, wine open, two glasses in front of them, Raina currently wrapped in Rose's arms.

She stood stone still, taking in the scene, when Raina looked up, her face tear-streaked and wrecked.

Tori just stared at them, waiting to hear the words she dreaded most: *Dad died.*

"You can tell her," Raina murmured.

Rose gestured Tori closer. "Raina and Jack are... having some issues."

"She's pulling a Rose," Raina said on a sniffle. "It's worse than that. We might be separating."

Tori fell on the sofa with a thud. Not what she'd feared but, wow. Nearly as bad. Divorce was not, as she knew all too well, for the faint of heart.

"Oh, wow." Tori whispered through fingers pressed to her lips in disbelief. "What's going on?"

"I don't know," Raina said glumly. "He needs passion or purpose or more houses to sell or...I don't know."

"He's having an affair."

Raina gasped. "No! No, no."

"You're wrong, Tori," Rose insisted. "That was Trey, but not Jack."

"I'm sorry, really, Raina," she exclaimed, and meant it, leaning forward to take Raina's hands. "That was wrong of me and I'm just...I don't know. What's that called? Projecting? Reliving my own hell."

"He's not..." Raina grimaced. "Well, he has started working out a lot and wearing a new cologne."

Oh, boy. Tori hid her immediate reaction, shaking her head. "Means nothing."

"He does seem to be having some kind of midlife crisis," Raina said. "He said he needs time and space and...passion."

The words punched, far too familiar for Tori. But she refused to drag Raina into that dark place a woman goes when her husband cheats. The poor thing had been through enough today.

"He's just...restless. Men get that way."

"Oh, Tori!" Raina broke out of Rose's clutch and slipped across the sectional to hug her other sister. "I miss you."

"Same, sister." Tori hugged Raina and gestured Rose closer, knowing this was not a job for one woman, especially one who still nursed the wounds from an acrimonious divorce. They needed all the happy juice that poured out of Rose.

They hugged for a few seconds, then Tori leaned back, looking from one to the other. "God, you two scared me. I thought it was Dad. Any news?"

They both shook their heads.

"Suze just texted us goodnight, and she said he's done nothing but sleep," Rose said.

"And she already has the nursing staff changing her chair, adjusting their schedule, and reporting in hourly," Raina added. "They surely know that she's the captain now."

"They'll rename it the Wingate Wing by tomorrow," Tori cracked.

Raina snorted a laugh. "Have a wine, Tor, and keep us smiling. We busted open a Silver Oak because Rose thought the label was pretty."

Tori lifted the bottle from the table and checked the year and vintage, fighting a smile at what they'd chosen. "Pretty? Yeah, pretty expensive. Nice choice, Rosie."

"Please tell me it isn't a four-figure bottle," Rose said, already in the kitchen to get Tori a glass.

"Three," Tori said. "But the first one is a two, so, well done. Pricey, but Dad will never notice."

Raina sighed and picked up her glass. "Thanks, Dad," she whispered. "Blame Rose for pilfering the two-hundred-dollar wine." She took a deep drink and sighed. "I hate dumping my personal garbage on top of all this family has been through today."

"That's what families are for," Tori said.

"Here." Rose gave her a glass. "Fill 'er up and tell us what's new in Boston."

"Nothing. At least, nothing like this." She poured her wine and lifted the glass to Raina in a silent toast. "Tell me everything, and let me assure you this is a bump in an otherwise happy road. Unless he has actually filed, taken a bunch of money from your bank account, and can't account for missing hours of the day, it's not what I—a veteran of the divorce wars—would call serious."

Raina cringed. "He hasn't done any of those things. But don't say divorce. I can't... I'm not ready for that word."

Tori just nodded, determined to keep her personal history off the table. She might be jaded when it came to men and marriage, but both of these women were firm believers in Happily Ever After. And she hadn't spent the day in travel hell to throw cold water on them.

"Did this just happen, or have you been talking about it?" Tori asked.

"We've been growing apart," Raina admitted. "And he's so...ambitious and hungry and always looking for more. He closed a deal to acquire another smaller firm that I didn't agree with. I didn't think it made sense financially or for our company, and the woman who runs it seems like a little shark. But he thinks she has some magical touch and gets all the multimillion-dollar listings."

Even as she said the words, they didn't sound right to Tori. "Are those reasons to break up or...reassess how you are living your lives?"

"I don't know," Raina said with a groan. "I'm certainly not ready to throw in the towel."

"Don't," Rose said. "You have to try. You can't give up a sixteen-year marriage—and a successful business—without a fight."

"That business has just taken him away from me, not made us closer. He puts it before everything." Raina took a deep drink and then put the glass down. "You guys want to know the honest, ugly truth?"

"That's what I'm here for," Tori said.

"I think he was relieved when I had the last miscarriage."

They both stared at her, and even Rose, the sayer of all things nice, didn't have a rationale for that ugly truth.

"I do," Raina continued when they stayed silent. "In fact, he wasn't that excited for any of my failed pregnancies."

"Raina," Rose said gently. "I'm sure he just has a hard time showing emotion."

Raina gave her a "get real" look. "He only cares about work, and me being pregnant didn't help the bottom line."

"I doubt he thought of it that way," Rose insisted, but Tori didn't doubt that. But then, she had been married to a Class A jerk. Rose had been with one man her entire life, and he was pretty much a saint.

Raina thought for a long time, staring into her wine glass before looking up at them.

"I don't know," she finally said. "I look back at when I fell in love with him and married him; it was because I thought he was so much like Dad. A real estate genius, a man with vision, a force of nature. He's nothing like Dad. Nothing."

"But you do still love him, right?" Rose asked.

"I do," Raina answered without hesitation. "But I'm confused. I mean, he says he's looking for passion. Aren't I enough? And what about my passion? I wanted a family more than anything." She looked from one to the other, her eyes full. "You have six kids between the two of you and I—"

"Don't," Tori said. "Don't compare. I lived through a hideous divorce and now I share custody and have to see the man I married shacking up with Heidi-Ho."

Raina snorted. "That name's gotta be a Kenzie special."

"Who else?"

"I love that girl," Raina said. "And Finn. And your kids, Rose. And Nikki Lou."

"There you go," Rose said. "Seven of the world's greatest nieces and nephews. Which I know," she added quickly, "isn't the same."

"But they are wonderful," Raina said. "And before you ask, he put the hammer down on adoption. It's so hard to get a baby, he refused to foster or go to another country. We've covered it and his decision is made. I'm telling you, girls, he doesn't want kids. Which is...well, not fine, but it is what it is. Plus, I'm forty-three, so there is that."

"But he's the one threatening to leave," Tori said, trying to piece it all together. "Since it looks like you're not having kids, you'd think he'd want to settle down into a fabulous life without mountains of debt, constant worry, and sleepless nights."

"I thought we'd travel more," Raina said. "But then we bought that giant house and he wanted to renovate it top to bottom and now he wants to buy another real estate firm. Why isn't he ever satisfied?"

"Oh, honey," Rose cooed. "Does he know you feel this way? Have you been completely honest with him?"

Raina nodded. "What should I do? I'm not ready to give up."

Tori leaned forward. "Take this time that you're here to really think about what you want, and let him get a little taste of life without you. He might hate it."

"Or not," Raina said glumly.

"He'll hate it," Rose insisted. "I know I do."

"Same," Tori added. "The minute I breathed the air on this island I realized how much I miss it here."

"I do, too," Raina said. "But he would no sooner live on Amelia Island than he'd live on the moon. He's not a small-town man."

Rose sighed, then regarded Tori. "What's keeping you from coming back?"

"My life, my business, and that shared custody." Tori leaned back, rocking her wine glass as she thought about it. "The kids' lives are up there now, and I don't know. That ship has sailed and landed me in Boston."

Rose looked from one to the other. "Well, I know I sound like Dad, but I'd love you both to come home. Sadie, too."

Tori snorted. "Talk about not being small-town girl. Our little sister is as continental as they come. She's enamored with life in Europe."

"Not so enamored right this minute," Rose said. "She called me earlier and, whoa, she's upset she can't be here. But she had to move Heaven and Earth and the entire Belgian chocolate industry to get a week off for Chloe's wedding, so she has to make a choice, this or that."

Tori groaned, so grateful she didn't have to make that choice. They all sat silent for a moment, each taking a sip of wine.

"I'm just glad I'm here," Raina said. "And six of the seven of us can be here for Suze and Dad."

"Yep," Rose agreed. "There's no guarantee of a tomorrow. Didn't we learn that today?"

Tori sighed and nodded. "I, for one, do not want to think about life without Rex Wingate in it."

"Don't even say it," Raina added.

Rose leaned in, putting a hand on both of their legs. "All I'm saying is you should live where you want, near those you love, and not make compromises." She added her warm smile. "At least we've got this little slice of time together, to support and love each other."

"Amen to that," Raina agreed.

Tori tapped her glass to theirs. "And here's to Dad. And poor Suze, who loves him so much she's sleeping on a recliner at the hospital."

After they toasted, Tori settled back and looked from one to the other. "Now, tell me everything I missed during the marathon hospital day. Start with every word the doctors said and fill me in."

No surprise, that conversation led to another and another and another. They talked until the bottle was empty, their hearts were a little lighter, and when Tori slipped out to go sleep in the bungalow, the very first peach glow of sunrise hovered over the horizon.

She stood between the two structures for a few seconds, sand in her toes, salty air on her face, and the comfort of the last few hours clinging to her as she felt... something. Some emotion that came from deep inside and wasn't easy to describe.

Exhaustion? Yes, beyond. Worry? So deep, for her whole family. But it was something else tapping at her heart. She narrowed her eyes and stared at the water and sky, letting herself just taste the moment, as if it were a new recipe and she had to figure out what one ingredient was overpowering the rest.

Homesick.

She was aching with homesickness. Not for the house in Wellesley she'd fought so hard to keep in the divorce. Not for anything in the Boston area, where she'd lived for well over twenty years now.

She was homesick for *this*. The tangy morning air of Amelia Island, the white sands of the beach, and the bone-deep comfort that came from being surrounded by the women who made her who she was.

But this wasn't home anymore, and like Rose had said, she'd just have to accept that and soak up what she could while she was here.

Chapter Five

Susannah

S usannah opened her eyes and tried to turn her head, only to freeze mid-motion from the pain shooting down her back, her whole body locked into a permanent fold.

The recliner.

The hospital.

Rex.

At the thought of her husband, she shook off sleep and forced her eyes to open, but even in the darkened room, they burned. Too many tears, too little sleep.

"Rex?" she murmured, like she did every morning when she slid closer on silky sheets to pull her husband's warm body into hers.

But today, she turned in a wretched and unforgiving pleather hospital chair. Instead of seeing Rex's profile with his strong patrician nose and white hair trimmed close to his head, she saw a man in a hospital bed who looked helpless and still and...darn-near dead.

She watched his chest rise and fall nearly impercepti-bly. But it was enough to know the oxygen being pumped into his nose was working. The machines were beeping softly, and he was still alive.

"Oh, Rex," she sighed his name and pushed up, glancing at the wall clock to see it was nearly seven. Had she slept at all? Maybe a few hours, no thanks to the nurses who marched in here every hour, turning on blindingly bright lights to cheerfully take vitals, check meds, and promise to see them again soon.

Taking a deep breath, she ignored the aches in her body as she peeled out of the chair and stepped toward the bed.

"Hey, there," she whispered, putting a hand on his shoulder, which felt strong and broad, like Rex. But his face was...not Rex. With tubes in his nose, his normally tanned skin ashen, his strong jaw hanging slack.

The fact was, he barely resembled the handsome man in his late thirties who'd come into the Riverfront Café when she was a brand-new waitress who'd just moved to Fernandina Beach.

She smiled, thinking of how that man had walked out without paying his check. Even though he'd left a healthy tip, she'd run out after him and chewed him out right in the middle of the street...only to learn he *owned* the place. And half of the other buildings in town.

Had that been the moment she'd fallen for Rex? When he'd slyly pointed to the street sign as he said his name...and she realized he was the *Wingate* of Wingate Way? She liked to think it wasn't his money that attracted her, despite the fact that she didn't have two nickels to her name. It was his smile, his essence, and his power.

All of which were missing right now.

"Are you awake, sweetheart?" she asked softly.

The response was the faintest grunt, hardly loud enough to hear.

"You're out of the ICU," she said brightly. "Do you remember coming up here? I came back after you were moved. The nurse was so nice to let me sleep here..." Her voice faded out as his eyelids fluttered faintly, then he was still again. "Rex?"

Nothing.

She leaned on the railing and looked at his body, which was darn-near corpse-like. He really did look dead, and the very thought rocked her.

Although she had known from the first that this day could—and would—come. Was it today?

Was this the inevitable loss, the dark and unwelcome time when Susannah Wingate would have to make the transition from younger wife to older widow?

Even that first day, when he asked to take her to dinner to make up for how distraught he'd made her, she knew there were things to think about with a man fourteen years her senior. First, she worried he might be married.

When she'd learned he was a widower, she'd been concerned he might have children and that could complicate things. Well, yes, indeed, he'd told her during that first dinner date. He had four girls, and they were very, very young. Four! That seemed...impossible.

Then she met the sweet angels who stole her heart almost as easily as their father had. With each passing day of a truly whirlwind courtship, she'd convinced herself that the age difference didn't matter. She didn't have a mother to ask, and her father, a gutter-drunk living in a hovel outside of Savannah, certainly didn't care what she did or who she loved.

Her only concern as she fell hard and fast in love was that a man of thirty-eight wouldn't give her children of her own. But when Rex told her the story of losing his first wife within an hour of her giving birth to twins, he'd cried. Not just because she was gone—though it was clear he grieved her loss—but because he so desperately wanted more children.

Of course, he longed for a boy.

At that point, the deal was sealed. She promised to give him those babies. She promised to be his loving wife who would wear the Wingate name with endless pride, honoring his proud history of a family deeply rooted in this town. She promised to love, honor, cherish, and, yes, obey him until death parted them.

"Oh, Rex," she whispered as a tear rolled down her cheek. "I'm not ready for that bit of the vows. I truly am not."

She'd kept every promise, however, except the one about the son. She gave him Sadie, then Grace. But after the dicey and dangerous delivery of Chloe, Rex had up and gotten a vasectomy.

"I'll never risk your life for my dumb ego," he'd said. She understood, because he'd lost one wife in childbirth, and he refused to lose another.

But she *would* have had a fourth child, for him. She'd

do anything for this powerhouse of a man who'd changed her life and given her everything.

"Rex?" She tried again, putting her hand on his chest to feel his heartbeat. There it was, faint but going.

"Hello again, Mrs. Wingate."

She turned to see a tall, dark-haired man in scrubs holding a computer tablet, his warm blue-eyed gaze on her.

"Hello..." She felt a frown form and tried to place him, but she was certain he hadn't been in the ICU yesterday. "I'm sorry, I don't remember meeting you."

"Dr. Verona," he said, extending his hand. "Your husband's neurologist. We met briefly after his TIA when you came to my office."

"Oh, yes, of course. Dr. Verona." She returned his handshake. "I forgot they told me you'd come on your rounds today."

"I'm sure you barely remember yesterday," he said with a kind smile that crinkled the corners of his eyes. With a few gray hairs at his temples, she put him in his late forties, a handsome man with a lovely bedside manner.

He inched to the side to look at Rex. "Is he awake?"

"Not yet." She turned to Rex, her heart dropping to see his eyes were still closed despite the chatter around him. He never slept through a conversation when he could be in the middle of it. "I've been here all night."

"Good, that's good. I like when they let a spouse sleep here." He took a few steps closer, glancing at the tablet again. "I'm going to talk to him for a bit. And do an exam."

"Yes, of course." She stepped back to the recliner, vaguely aware that she wore sweatpants and a pullover top, and her mouth felt like a desert. But she perched on the chair and watched as the doctor pulled out a pen light, lifted Rex's lids, and peered in.

"Can you wake up, Rex? It's Justin Verona, your neurologist."

No surprise, Rex didn't budge.

Unfazed, the doctor tapped his chest, felt his hands, and scribbled with a stylus on the tablet.

"Should he be awake?" Susannah asked softly.

"He's awake."

She stood. "He is? Why aren't his eyes open? Are his lids paralyzed? Is he?" She pressed her knuckles to her lips as that reality hit. This was Rex! He couldn't live as a paralyzed man.

"Rex." The doctor gently moved his shoulder. "Open your eyes, sir. Your wife slept in a chair and you should look at her, if only to thank her."

His eyelids fluttered, making Susannah whimper softly. "Rex?"

He gave a grunt, fighting to open his lids, and finally, he did. He stared straight up at the doctor.

"There you are," Dr. Verona said. "Can you look at your wife?"

She started to step closer, but the doctor held up his hand. "Let him. Move your eyes, Rex. Show me you can."

Very, very slowly, his dark irises moved to the left and his gaze landed on Susannah.

"*Ooze.*" It was little more than a growl and a vowel, but she pressed her hand to her chest, overcome.

"He said my name," she whispered. "Suze. He said my name."

In the scheme of things, it was nothing. Right now? She felt like he'd stood up and waltzed with her.

A slow smile spread over Dr. Verona's face, too. "That's what I want to hear." Taking Rex's hand, she assumed he was going to feel for a pulse, but he just held it in one of his, more like a son than a doctor.

"You know you've had a stroke, Rex?" he asked. "Much more serious than the last incident that had you in my office."

He managed to nod his head up and down, barely a centimeter, but the tiny movement made Susannah's heart soar.

"He isn't going to die," she murmured under her breath.

Dr. Verona angled his head, then gave her a quick smile. "Not if I have anything to do with it. You have too much to live for, right, Rex? Kids? Grandkids, I assume? And I haven't lived here that long, but I see your name all over Amelia Island real estate signs, so you must have a thriving business."

He responded with a grunt, but Susannah knew all that was behind that sound. She could just imagine what Rex was thinking.

"You bet your backside I do, son. Three generations of Wingates buying and selling this island."

Which meant...he *was* thinking. His brain worked!

"Did you hear that, Rex?" she asked, coming to the other side of the bed. "You're going to live."

Half of his mouth, just the right half, lifted in a smile.

"You have some mild paralysis," Dr. Verona said. "The PTs will beat that out of you."

Mild? Susannah clung to the word.

Rex shifted his gaze to the doctor, a question in his dark eyes. Susannah saw him work to form a word, then he gave up.

"Can you explain to me what happened to him?" Susannah asked, sensing that might be what he would ask if he could. "And can you tell me how to keep it from happening again?"

The doctor nodded slowly, finally letting go of Rex's hand, thinking for a moment, maybe choosing his words carefully.

"Short version without a lot of medical jargon? Rex had an ischemic stroke, and that was confirmed by yesterday's CT scan."

Still too much medical jargon. "Isn't that what he had last time?"

"The last one was a *transient* ischemic stroke, and I told him then that it can be a precursor to something worse. This time, instead of a mild restriction of blood flow to his brain, he's had one far more severe."

"Oh, I didn't know. He wasn't even sick. I went in to

say goodbye before my luncheon and..." She swallowed at the memory of finding Rex slumped on the floor.

"You did everything right, Mrs. Wingate. You got him here within the critical 'golden period' and they were able to give him the tissue plasminogen activator..." At her look, he held up a hand in apology for the terminology. "A clot-buster. Very important."

"Is that the worst kind of stroke, this ischemic one?"

"No, it isn't. A hemorrhagic stroke is far worse, which essentially means a blood vessel has burst and the prognosis is rarely good."

She winced. "Could he still have one of those?"

"Unfortunately, yes. But to avoid that, we need to figure out what caused the first one. Based on his blood work and medical history, he doesn't have any blockage, or too terribly high blood pressure. He isn't a smoker, is relatively healthy—"

"Uh, he likes his cigars, so he does smoke."

"Sorry to say this but..." He tapped Rex's chest. "You've smoked your last stogie, my friend."

Rex grunted with just enough force to make Susannah smile. "He didn't like that," she translated. "Any other changes he'll need to make?"

"In general, his life is going to change and so is yours. Physical therapy and rest are all he'll do for the foreseeable future. Whatever he was doing when he had the stroke, he should stop."

"He was working in his office."

"Might be time to consider retirement, Mr. Wingate."

Rex's eyes flashed, then closed.

"Stress is not your friend," the doctor continued. "I'm going to order a few tests, prescribe your PT and some other medications, and I'll be back at the end of the day to check on you."

He wrote on the tablet again, then gave Susannah a look, angling his head in the direction of the hall to speak privately.

"I'm going to walk the doctor out," she said to Rex, who still had his eyes closed.

She followed Dr. Verona into the hall. "Yes?" she asked.

"First, Mrs. Wingate, do you have questions you didn't want to ask in front of him?"

She took in a soft breath, so grateful for this man's style. "Will he walk and talk again?'"

"Absolutely. In the early days, it will feel like a mountain he'll never climb. But I remember Rex as being a very robust and resilient man, and the fact that he's still working at seventy-five tells me he's not a quitter."

"Not in the least," she confirmed.

"In ten days or so, you will see a huge change. He'll stop slurring, and with his right side fully functional, he'll start to feed himself. Once he gets sick of that chair and with the right PT, he'll start walking again. First on a walker, then a cane, then on his own. Just prepare yourself— this takes time and patience and love."

"I have all of those."

He gave a big smile. "Then he's a lucky man. But," he added, leaning in to make his point. "That 'no stress' order is not given casually."

She nodded. "I understand."

"Because all of the walking and talking and therapy isn't going to happen if he has another stroke, which he is very much in danger of right now. This is the most tenuous and critical time, which is why we'll keep him in the hospital. The next one could be far worse."

"How long do we have to worry about that?" she asked.

"Two weeks is the hot zone, then the danger drops exponentially. I'm keeping him here for about a week to ten days, for testing, evaluation, and the start of what will be very, very taxing physical and occupational therapy."

"And then?"

"Many patients go into a rehab center, but I far prefer home. If you can arrange your home in a way that he has a minimum of stairs and all the therapy equipment he needs, he can go there. Is that possible?"

"Absolutely," she assured him, already picturing how she could redesign the first-floor game room to accommodate that. "How long will he need to do therapy?"

"It's hard to say, but he's in generally good health, so without another incident and with complete support and cooperation, he could be close to one hundred percent in six months."

Six months? Susannah reeled. "Our daughter is getting married in less than two months."

He smiled. "Then we have a goal. He may be in a wheelchair, but he can take her down the aisle."

"Really?" She felt her eyes fill with tears, a mix of joy

at the news and heartbreak for Chloe, who wanted her day to be perfect. Well, if Rex was there, it would be.

"Someone from PT will be here in a few hours to get things started."

"Today?" It seemed preposterous that Rex would do physical therapy the day after his stroke.

"For a planning session," he said. "But we must start tomorrow, with very small movements. Your job in the meantime is to let him rest, but when he's awake, talk to him. No TV. No phones. Just love, attention, and patience."

"Visitors?"

"Of course, bring his family in here. And any movement is encouraged. Remember, he's not paralyzed, but the left side was affected," he said. "I will do some very specific scans to see what part of his brain was involved. You may have trouble communicating with him for a long time, but you two seem to have the kind of relationship where you do that telepathically. That's a blessing." He smiled and held her gaze. "It won't be an easy road, Mrs. Wingate. But I'm certain you'll be up to the task."

"I'll try," she said, and never meant anything more.

He nodded and looked back down at his tablet, turning away. Just as he did, someone came careening around the corner, smacking right into him and nearly spilling coffee everywhere.

"Tori!" Susannah exclaimed when she realized who it was.

Tori jumped back so the spill didn't hit her. "Yikes!"

she cried out, shaking some spilled coffee off her hands and looking up at the man she'd plowed into.

Behind Tori, Kenzie stood with a box of donuts and a smirk. "Smooth move, Ex-Lax," she murmured.

"Excuse me, ma'am." The doctor retreated a step, glancing down at the huge splash of brown coffee on his scrubs.

"Oh my God!" Tori gasped as she realized what she'd done. "I am so, *so* sorry."

"Not at all, it's fine." He brushed at the spill, laughing softly as he looked up and met her gaze. "I've had worse things spilled on me while making my rounds."

Tori's fair skin blushed hard, making her cheeks almost the color of her strawberry-blond hair. "I'm so...*oh!* Clumsy. I was in such a hurry to see my dad and...I..."

"Ah, the daughter who is getting married?" His voice rose in question.

"No, no, that's Chloe. I'm Victoria, er, Tori." She went to shake his hand then realized she held the cups. "Not able to shake your hand and apologize enough."

Susannah stepped in, taking one of the cups. "This is Dr. Justin Verona, Dad's neurologist. This is my daughter, Tori Wingate. And my granddaughter, Kenzie." As she made the introduction, she reached for Kenzie. "Who gets taller and more beautiful every time I see her. Hello, Mackenzie. How was your trip?"

"Not as embarrassing as the one Mom just had," she joked. "Why don't I have my phone out when life gives me the best content?"

The doctor gave them both a smile, but his gaze barely flicked to Kenzie, settling directly on Tori.

"Dad's doctor?" Tori rolled her eyes. "And I tried to mow you down and cover you in coffee. Eesh. How is he today?"

"Your mom will fill you in," he said, smiling. "I'm going to..." He looked down again at the spill. "Go amuse my next patient."

"I am so sorry."

He just held up one hand. "Not to worry, Tori." Then he turned to Susannah, who apparently had been completely forgotten in the exchange. "I'll see you later today, Mrs. Wingate."

"Thank you, Dr. Verona."

With that, he walked off, leaving Susannah staring at Tori...and Tori staring at his back as he walked down the hall.

"Did you burn your hands, honey?" Susannah asked.

"Oh, I got fried, but not by coffee." She finally turned, her color still high, leaning in so Susannah could hug her. "What an entrance, huh?"

"Never dull with you two." She wrapped Tori and Kenzie into her arms. "I didn't expect you here this early."

"First time ever in my life," Tori quipped. "We were hungry and there wasn't—"

"Food!" Susannah gasped. "I can't believe I didn't stock the bungalow fridge."

"Seriously, Grannie Suze," Kenzie gave her a playful elbow nudge. "You're slippin', lady."

She laughed and gestured for them to come into the room. "He's awake and the doctor has one order: no stress. Just talk to him, and let him rest when he wants to and...no stress."

"Gotcha. Then I'm glad he missed my last stunt." Tori went first into the room. "Hey, Daddio. How's the greatest guy on Earth?"

Susannah hung back, letting out a sigh that she might have been holding since the doctor arrived, vaguely aware of Kenzie's arm around her.

"Don't worry, Grannie Suze. You will not be alone, whether you want to or not."

She smiled at her granddaughter, who really was an inch taller, a beauty with mahogany hair and impossibly dark eyes. "For that, my sweet Mackenzie, I am grateful."

Chapter Six

Raina

"**M**adeline has spoken." Raina held up her phone to Rose, who was just finishing her coffee and getting ready to leave the beach house after they'd cleaned up from last night's wine and gab fest. "There is officially a schedule for when we can visit Dad. Why am I not shocked by this?"

"Because our oldest sister is Organized with a capital O, and that room is small," Rose said. "We don't want to overwhelm Dad. Tori's there already. Did you see her text? Suze has turned it into a stress-free zone. Not so much as a wayward whisper of anything that will worry him."

"But I can't go in until this afternoon? I drove up from Miami last night to see my father." Raina threw up her hands. "How can I not be first on the list?"

"Because Madeline always has a method to her madness and she has you and me there at the same time," Rose said cheerily.

"It's all right. I mean, I guess I could drop in on

Wingate Properties in town today and see if it's running smoothly."

"I'm sure it's fine, Raina. Dad did hire a new assistant not too long ago. I've met him a few times and he's very efficient, so you don't have to run in and work."

"Well, I admit I'm not dying to jump into Wingate business, but maybe I'll peek into his office downstairs and see if anything looks like a fire that needs dousing. And then I'll be at the hospital, just waiting my turn outside the door."

"I'll see you there." Rose stepped closer and gave her a kiss on the cheek. "You look better than when you got here," she added. "Did you hear from Jack?"

"Two extremely brief texts." And the truth of that hit her right in the solar plexus. "I'm going to take a run on the beach and I'll call him." She searched Rose's face, marveling at how it was still like looking in a mirror that only had the hair and eye color wrong. "Thanks. You helped me last night. And you're right, Rose. I'm not ready to give up on him."

"Then don't! You're going to get through this. In fact, it might end up being the best thing that ever happened to you two."

She rolled her eyes at Rose's endless optimism. "Not if we're almost four hundred miles apart for too long."

"Can he come up for a weekend?" Rose suggested.

Raina shrugged, already knowing that wouldn't be his idea of a good time. "I'll see." Then she gave her sister a nudge. "Go. I know you're dying to get in to your shop and make glorious flower arrangements."

"I'm dying to see Gabe and he's not on duty today, so he'll be at the shop after getting the kids to school."

"Gah. He is perfection."

"Can't argue with that," Rose agreed. "And Coming Up Roses is busy these days. Everyone is. Madeline is booked for the next year with wedding and bridal party dresses and Grace said The Next Chapter is having the best year ever."

"I'm happy for you," Raina said, visualizing Wingate Way, about a mile from where they were, in downtown Fernandina Beach. Dad didn't own every building on the street that ran parallel to the Amelia River, but he owned most of them. And many of those buildings housed Wingate-owned businesses.

Raina knew each building from Wingate House, the inn at one end of the street, down to the Riverfront Café. In between was Rose's flower shop, Madeline's dress business, and Grace's bookstore, along with other small businesses, eateries, and gift stores.

Across the street was Wingate Properties, housed in an old bank built by their great-grandfather. Raina had spent a good many hours in that historic structure, learning the business that was in her blood.

But before she went to stroll down memory lane, she needed to talk to Jack and see where things stood.

"I'll get down there, I promise. But I do want to take a run and call Jack." She crinkled her nose. "Maybe not in that order."

"Agree. Call him ASAP." Rose backed up and blew a kiss. "Love you, Raindrop."

"Love you back, Rosebud."

A few minutes later, Raina tried Jack's cell, but got his voicemail before it even rang. Okay, time to run.

She tied on her sneakers and pulled on a cotton T-shirt over her sports bra, heading out to the beach. April was still off-season on Amelia Island and the wide white sands of Fernandina Beach were relatively empty.

For most of Fletcher Avenue, the portion of A1A that ran along the coast of the island, the beachfront property was almost exclusively private homes. There were a few parks and waterfront restaurants, and those areas of the beach could get a little more crowded, especially in summer.

But on a clear, sixty-five-degree spring morning, she could look left and right from the top of the beach house walkway over the dune and see five, maybe ten, people.

She tucked her phone in her pocket and adjusted her wireless earbuds, ready for some good running music, but as she did, Siri announced a call from Wallace & Wingate.

"Thank you, God," she muttered, even though she thought Jack would call from his cell, not the company line.

But a girl could hope, right? Hope that her very own husband was calling.

"Good morning, this is Raina Wingate," she answered professionally, on the off-chance it was a client.

"Hey, girl. It's me."

At the sound of her assistant's voice, Raina felt her heart thud in disappointment. Not Jack. "Hey, Dani."

"What happened to your dad? A stroke? Seriously? Jack told us you blew out for a while. How is he?"

Raina abandoned the run, dropping down on the top step to stare out at the frothy surf spilling over the sand. "Yeah, he had a stroke. I haven't seen him yet, but I'm going to the hospital soon. I was going to call you in a few minutes."

"Is it serious? How long will you be gone?"

"It's serious, but could have been worse, for whatever that's worth," she said, not bothering to put a Rose Wingate positive spin on the situation. She was too close to Danielle Alvarez, who was as much a friend as an assistant. "He's going to be okay, but it'll be a long journey back."

"Holy cow, I'm so sorry, Raina. That's awful. How's your mom? Your whole family?"

"I got in late last night and have only seen two of my sisters. I'll know more when I go to the hospital, but you can kind of plan on me being out of the loop for a while."

"That's what Jack said."

So he'd talked to Dani, but hadn't called Raina?

She tamped down another wave of disappointment and tried to concentrate. "I can be reached and can do remote work if I need to, but I'd like to pass off as many projects as possible," she told Dani. "You know all my open listings, so do me a favor and start doling them out to the right agents."

"Jack already had me do that."

"Oh. Okay." They usually worked a little more independently, but she appreciated him stepping in. "Great. I have two closing this week—"

"Jack said he'll handle them. Or Lisa will."

"Lisa?"

"Godfrey? You know, of Godfrey Luxury Realty? The company we just bought."

"Oh, it's...finalized?" The word caught in her throat. "I didn't know that was official-official, you know?"

"Oh, yeah, Raina. Jack filed the paperwork with the state and she's..."

"Picking up my listings," Raina finished.

"I guess with you out of town indefinitely, it made sense."

Not to Raina.

"And we're all celebrating over lunch," Dani added, unintentionally digging the knife in a little deeper.

"Oh. That's...nice." She swallowed. "Where?"

"He asked me to set up a twelve-thirty reservation at Caja Calliente."

Well, that made sense. Sort of. The Coral Gables Cuban restaurant was no place for a business luncheon, but perfect for a company celebration. Caja was a joint. Noisy, fun, delicious, and Raina and Jack used to go there for date nights years ago. Too many years ago.

"Cool," she said, even though it was anything but. "Can I talk to him?"

"Not a chance," Dani said. "He's deep in negotiations with the Jimenez brothers."

"Oh my God!" Raina threw her head back with a soft cry. "I totally forgot they were coming in this morning."

"Of course you did, girl! Under the circumstances, you're allowed to forget."

"But I wanted to drop the price on the Brickell property and he doesn't know—"

"Yes, he does. I filled him in from the voice memo you sent after your last meeting. Relax, Raina. We've got this. You take care of family."

But the Jimenez brothers were a huge client—her client. "How are Rodrigo and Emil taking the news?"

"From what I can see? It's going to be a while."

Raina closed her eyes and pictured their ultra-modern office, bathed in sunlight. Behind a glass wall, her office and Jack's were side by side, completely visible to any employees or agents working at desks in the middle.

Suddenly, her world seemed a million miles away, along with her husband. "Just tell him I called," she said. "And in the meantime—"

"In the meantime, you just forget Wallace & Wingate," Dani insisted. "Your focus is your family. From everything you've told me, your dad is a force. I'm praying for him."

"Thanks, Dani." But her mind drifted to Lisa Godfrey, a shark of a real estate agent who had built a small but thriving shop from the ground up. She was barely thirty-five and reminded Raina of herself about eight or ten years ago. Hungry, unstoppable, a dynamo.

All the things Jack loved in a woman.

No. No. A thousand times *no*. She wouldn't even go there.

"Just be sure Jack calls me before he goes to that lunch," she added.

"Okay, but I'm telling you, Raina—"

"I know, I know. My family first." She glanced over her shoulder at the empty beach house. "I promise."

"Good girl. Talk soon!"

She hung up and squinted into the morning sun and felt every ounce of will to run fade out of her body. All she wanted to do was get in the car and drive right back home and fix *all the things*.

Well, she couldn't. And family did come first—this family.

She pushed up and, after a second's hesitation, she walked back into the house, and trotted downstairs to the first floor to Dad's home office. After all, it was the promise she'd made to Suze.

At the door to the office, she frowned, her gaze moving over the heavy cherrywood desk and dark shelves, the entire décor so *not* done by coastal design-loving Susannah. He'd insisted she leave this room alone, and his deeply masculine touch could be felt everywhere.

Her attention fell on the floor, to the black and maroon Oriental carpet with one piece of paper on it in front of his desk. He must have dropped it when he...

She bit her lip, not wanting to think of her father doubled over as the blood stopped flowing to his oh-so-mighty brain. She didn't like to think he had any weakness, and had spent her life modeling herself after him.

On a sigh, she bent over and picked it up when she caught a whiff of something that smelled like...smoke?

Dad would never risk smoking a cigar in here, would he? Besides incurring the wrath of his wife, it was just not like him.

Still, the scent was strong and coming from somewhere in the room. She straightened and sniffed, turning around to try and find the source. The room was dimly lit with the shutters closed, so she went to the windows to snap them open. As soon as she got closer, she noticed the plantation-style shutter wasn't closed completely and something was between it and the window, on the sill.

Pulling open the shutter, she blinked in surprise at a large pile of ashes on a plate. What the heck? Had he burned something and wanted the smoke to go outside?

They weren't cigar ashes, not by a long stretch. It was paper...with typed words too burnt for her to read. Well, she'd wondered if there were any work fires that need to be put out, but she hadn't meant it *literally*.

"How about an old-fashioned shredder, Dad?" she muttered to herself. "Much safer, cleaner, and smarter."

She examined the only piece of paper that wasn't completely burnt and tried to see what it was, but there was no way to tell. The only clear word on the paper was "page 5" at the top and the words *ignature req* still visible.

Signature required, she presumed. Was this a contract he was burning?

Frowning, she glanced down at the paper in her hand that she'd found on the floor, immediately noticing that this was page 3 of 3.

It was blank, though, except for one line that must

have not printed from the previous page. The words, printed in in all capital letters, read *ALL DEBTS ERASED BY RW*.

All *whose* debts erased by Rex Wingate?

Her phone buzzed and yanked her attention to the text on the screen.

Dani: *Jack said all is cool with Jimenez bros. He's off to an appointment for a new listing and lunch. Said he'll call you later. Take care!*

An impersonal text sent via her assistant hurt, but she just wrote back with a quick thanks. Then she cleaned up the ashes, brushing them into the empty trash can while she tried to imagine why Dad was burning things in here.

She stared at the one unburned page again.

ALL DEBTS ERASED BY RW

She slid it under Dad's blotter, hidden from view.

Was this erased debt the cause of his stroke?

RAINA STEPPED off the elevator on the third floor of the hospital, sucking in a soft breath at the sight of Rose and Susannah standing right next to each other, talking.

"Well, hello there, strangers."

"Raina!" Susannah's whole face brightened as she reached out and wrapped Raina in a hug. "Oh, I'm so happy you're here."

"I know I'm early for my time slot, Suze, but I couldn't wait." She drew back and slid a look at Rose. "I see my twin is also ignoring Madeline's schedule and showing up two hours early."

"I had a hospital flower delivery," Rose said, "and decided to bring it myself."

"I'm just glad you're here." Susannah beamed at Raina, looking no worse for the wear of having spent the night at the hospital. Her license might say she was sixty-one, but she could have passed for the oldest of the Wingate sisters, which was a testament to how well she took care of herself.

Her blond hair was styled in a short, sassy cut, she wore just a touch of natural makeup, and was fit and trim in matching joggers and a stylish hoodie. "Grace had to switch shifts because Nikki Lou cried so hard, the sitter called for help."

"Oh, that child." Raina glanced around. "Why are you in the hall and not with Dad?"

"The nurse is in there taking vitals," Susannah said, linking her arm through Raina's. "We'll go in soon. How are you doing? Was it a long drive last night? Rose said you two stayed up late."

She threw a look at her sister. "Rat. Did you tell her about the Silver Oak?"

"Worse, I told Dad and, wow, did I get the evil eye, but not from him."

"Because I said no stress!" Susannah insisted. "Not that I think you girls drinking a bottle of wine bothers him one bit. He's probably quite happy to share. But I can't take chances. I promised Dr. Verona."

Just then, a nurse came by, pushing a cart laden with machinery.

"He's all set, Mrs. Wingate," she said. "Very tired, but I think he'd love to see you before taking his nap." She shifted her gaze to Raina. "Are you another of the seven sisters? Your mom told me all about the family."

Raina smiled and gave Suze a squeeze. "She's a braggie one, isn't she? Yes, I'm number four, and thank you for taking care of my father."

"It's our pleasure, dear."

As she walked off, Susannah ushered Raina down the hall. "They're all very sweet here," she said. "But prepare yourself, Raina. He's not able to talk or move his whole right side. So...go easy on him."

"What else would I do?"

"She's just trying to warn you," Rose said quickly. "It's a surprise the first time you see him."

"And you and Rex sometimes..." Susannah let the rest of it trail off, but Raina could fill in the blank.

They loved each other, but she and Rex could get into it, and fast. It hadn't always been that way, but he was so unhappy when she married and moved away. He'd counted on her to take over Wingate Properties, but Jack had a whole different vision of their future.

They paused outside a patient room that Raina assumed was her father's, quiet for a moment.

"Trust me, Suze," Raina finally whispered. "I won't upset him."

With a nod, Susannah pulled the door open.

"I have a surprise for you, Rex!" she called as they

walked into a tiny vestibule that blocked the view into the room. Stepping in further, Raina slowed at the sight of her dad in a hospital bed, managing not to suck in a noisy breath.

"Hey, Dad," she said softly, forcing her voice not to crack.

His only response was a low, soft groan.

"That's hello," Susannah said. "I've heard him say it to everyone now."

A little afraid of how emotional this was going to make her, Raina slowly approached the bed. It was only about four steps, because no one had exaggerated about how small the room was.

She put her hands on the bed railing and looked down at him, giving him a moment to shift his head a millimeter and trap her in his dark brown gaze.

"Ay...na."

"It's me," she said brightly, leaning over to plant a kiss on his oh-so-pale forehead. "All the way from Miami just to give you that."

He just stared at her, a million emotions in his eyes, nothing but silence from his lips.

"I heard the nurses are all in love with you, and that the PT has already started."

He almost—*almost*—rolled his eyes and the right side of his mouth lifted in a pitiful smile. But talking, she suspected, would be a chore. Her heart squeezed at the change in this great man, at how helpless he seemed.

She managed a shaky breath, having no idea what to say.

"Here, Raina." Rose pushed the only other chair that wasn't the recliner next to the bed. "Just talk to him for a minute. I'm going to make sure my flower delivery got put in the patient's room. Tell him...everything."

She glanced over her shoulder at her sister, but her gaze got snagged on Suze's warning look. *Okay, no stress. I got it.*

"Sure, sure. I'll tell you all about..." Well, not Jack. What else could she talk about? "My firm acquired another little company." A company she didn't want, but she and Dad always went straight to business. It was their favorite meeting place. "We beat Coldwell in a bid," she added, not that she was thrilled with the acquisition, but he'd appreciate the magnitude of the move.

She could have sworn she saw a smile in those eyes, or maybe that was the approval she always sought when they talked about work.

"And we sold a monster out on Star Island a few weeks ago. Our largest listing ever."

Did he really want to hear about this? Work? When he was flat on his back?

"Jack sends his love," she said, doing what she realized she always did with her family: good PR for her husband. "He's going to try and get here soon, but until he does, I'm here for you. I'm going to help you with... whatever you need."

Susannah had walked around to the other side of the bed, where presumably she could direct the conversation and steer it away from stressful subjects. Raina gave her a questioning look. Was she allowed to tell Rex she was going to help with his business?

Getting a nearly imperceptible nod from her, Raina exhaled.

"I'm going to go into Wingate Properties this week," she said, purposely keeping it vague. "So if there's anything you'd like me..." No, he couldn't tell her. "I'll spend a few minutes with your staff, maybe pick up any loose threads that might be hanging."

He just stared at her, more of that impossible-to-read emotion in his eyes. What did he want to tell her? Was there a specific project? Why did he almost look...afraid?

Because he probably thought he might never see the inside of Wingate Properties again, she presumed. The thought made her heart shift and she glanced up at Susannah again. This time, her nod was more enthusiastic, as if she approved of this conversation and was giving Raina permission to carry on.

"So, Dad, I'll be happy to take care of anything you have going on."

His eyelids fluttered and he worked to keep his eyes open.

"But you're tired, so—"

He shocked her by reaching for her with his right hand to give her a squeeze. He might as well have reached into her chest and grabbed her heart, making her fight tears.

"He wants you to stay," Susannah said. "And I'm going to take this call from Madeline. You can keep talking to him, Raina."

"Sure, sure." She inched a little closer, still holding his hand, instantly more relaxed when Susannah stepped away and they were alone. "I popped into your home office and I wanted to ask you—"

He squeezed her hand again, this time with a little more force. Was he trying to stop her from talking or asking her to continue?

"Um, it's okay that I went in there?"

He just stared at her and squeezed again. She was taking that as a yes.

"Anyway, I don't know what you were doing but...I found some papers. Did you burn some—"

One of the monitors beeped, snagging Raina's attention. Was that his heart rate? She stared at it, and it beeped again. And again. And *again*.

As the alarm screamed, Susannah burst back in. "What's going on?"

"Nothing! Nothing." Raina popped up and put her fingers to her lips. "I don't know what happened."

"Oh, God. Rose, are you out there? Get a nurse! Rex, are you okay? Calm down, dear. Deep breaths."

Raina took a few steps backwards, her heart slamming so hard that she could be the one setting off that monitor with the deafening beeps.

A nurse swept into the room and shot out an order, and Raina managed to get out of her way, slipping into the vestibule entryway, looking for Rose, who was gone.

"I need a doctor in 302," the nurse said into a headset. "Patient's BP suddenly elevated."

Behind her, the door shot open and a doctor bolted

in, barely giving Raina enough time to press against the wall and let him pass.

"I'm so sorry," Raina said to no one in particular, pressing her knuckles to her lips. "I was just talking to him."

"Hey, hey, what's happening?" Rose pushed the door open to come in, but Raina launched out into the hall, desperate to leave after causing such trouble.

"I don't know. It just started beeping and..." Tears filled her eyes.

Instantly, Rose's arm was around her, her gentle voice in Raina's ear. "It's okay, it's okay. He's surrounded by good help. Do you want to take a walk?"

"I want to..." Raina closed her eyes and felt the sting of tears. "Cry."

"It's okay, honey. You can cry." Rose wrapped her in a hug, holding her for a minute until she heard another familiar voice.

"What's going on?" Tori asked.

Raina lifted her head. "What else? I stirred up trouble."

The door opened and Susannah came back out. "He's going to be fine," she announced. "They gave him a medication to bring his blood pressure down. They want him to sleep."

"I'm sorry," Raina whispered, reaching for her. "I really am."

"It's okay." Susannah gave her hand a squeeze with trembling fingers. "We're all on edge, Raina, but please, you can't—"

"You don't have to tell me twice, Suze. I'm going to find a cafeteria and get some coffee."

"I'll come with you," Rose said.

"Me, too," Tori added. "Kenzie is on her way up, Suze. She'll stay with you."

"That's good. I don't want to leave until... I don't want to leave."

"You want anything?" Raina asked. "I mean, other than for me to leave."

"Raina! No. Please. I'm just...really scared. And no, I don't want anything." She gave Raina a hug and sent them off.

Flanked by her sisters, Raina walked down the hall, not surprised she was still shaking.

Chapter Seven

Tori

By the time they reached the cafeteria, Tori could sense that Raina had calmed down. Rose had worked her magic, reiterating that Susannah was so on edge that she simply couldn't be held accountable for trying to control everything, including Dad's blood pressure.

"What did you say to him, anyway?" Tori finally asked when they got in line for something to eat and coffee.

"Just that I..." Raina shook her head. "Not important. I just don't think he should talk or think about business."

"Good call," Rose said. "Once he can communicate again, he'll love having you here and will thank you for leaving your company to run his."

"Maybe," she said, sliding a tray from the stack and lining it up behind Rose's. "Although I'm not sure he's forgiven me for leaving and starting my own firm. He'd probably be over the moon to know Jack and I are on the rocks. I should tell him to speed up recovery."

"Don't do that," Tori said. "It's not something anyone would be happy about."

"Plus, you shouldn't send the thought out to the universe," Rose asked. "Stay positive and hopeful this will work out. I am."

"Because your middle name is Positive." Raina smiled at her, then slid a look to Tori on her other side, pausing and letting Rose get a few feet ahead to get some food. "So how was he when you saw him and somehow managed to not set off any alarms?"

"Oh, trust me, alarms were set off, but they were mine, not Dad's."

"What do you mean?" Raina asked.

"My man alarm."

"Your *man* alarm?" Raina laughed. "What's that?"

"That's what screams, 'Run, don't walk!' when you lay eyes on the world's hottest doctor. And not just eyes, Raina. I sailed around the corner, smacked right into him, and spilled hot coffee all over his scrubs. And yet *I* was the one who melted."

"Seriously?" Raina's eyes widened with interest. "Did you talk to him?"

"Not much, but I will. He's Dad's neurologist! Holy smokes, Batman." She shook her head as they moved a few feet down the line. "They don't make them like that up in Boston."

"Dr....Verona?" Raina asked, her expression a mix between uncertain and something else Tori couldn't read. "Have you met him, Rose?"

"Dr. Hottypants is what he should be called," Tori muttered.

Rose turned and her eyes grew big, too, flashing at Tori.

"Am I right?" Tori asked on a laugh. "Some lucky doctor's wife got that sweet package all sewn up."

Rose just stared at her, her complexion paling as she looked over Tori's shoulder.

"Um, Tor," Raina whispered. "You, might, uh..."

Behind her, Tori felt the presence of another person before it actually registered that she was holding up the line and no doubt ticking someone off.

"Sorry." She threw the comment over her shoulder without risking eye contact as she moved along.

"Don't be," the man said. "But you're wrong."

She whipped her head around and came face to face with...scrubs. Coffee-stained scrubs.

Slowly, very, very slowly, she lifted her gaze and met blue eyes dancing with humor.

"And just for the record, no one has sewn anything up." He held her gaze and warmed it with a sly half-smile, long enough for her to want to crawl into the floor and hide...*forever*.

"Oh. Hi." Blood rushed to her cheeks.

"Hi."

"Do you want eggs, ma'am?" the server behind the counter asked impatiently, no doubt not for the first time.

"Yeah. Hi." She had to be six shades of maroon by then. "Uh, no. No eggs. Just...coffee." She managed to throw the doctor a look. "That I will not spill."

"Don't make promises you can't keep, Tori."

She gave a nervous laugh, pushing through the line to catch up with Raina and Rose at the coffee bar, barely able to breathe.

They, of course, were cracking up like this was a high school cafeteria instead of a hospital.

"Faster, faster," she said. "Actually, just buy me some coffee. I'll get us a table."

"Maybe Dr. Hottypants will pay," Raina said dryly, making Rose snort.

"I hate you both. Shut up." She marched away with her empty tray, her eyes locked on a table as far away from this crime scene as possible. She dropped into the chair, stared at the wall, and decided it was a good thing to be in a hospital when you were dying...of embarrassment.

"ALL RIGHT, YOU TWO," Tori warned her sisters, who could not stop replaying her moment from hell while they ate late breakfasts between snarky—and slightly hilarious—comments. "The fun is over."

"I'm sorry, but that was so classic Tori," Raina said. "And I needed to laugh. Desperately."

"So happy I can help," she deadpanned.

Next to her, Rose leaned in and looked at Tori. "If you ask me, the man handled that with grace and humor. I already like him."

"Not as much as Tori does."

Tori narrowed her eyes at Raina. "I thought we were down here to make you feel better, not mock me mercilessly."

"We can do both," Raina said. "In fact, your whole scene made me forget about mine."

Rose reached across the table to put a reassuring hand on Tori's arm. "We can see him from here and you're safe. He's by himself eating a breakfast burrito and looking at his phone."

"And, not gonna lie, Tor," Raina said. "He's what my assistant would call a smokeshow. I mean, if you like them with a bit of silver in the hair and hours in the gym."

"Oh, no. Hate that," Tori murmured.

"And a neurologist." Raina lifted her brows. "Smart *and* successful."

"And single," Rose added. "At least based on the, 'I'm not sewn up,' comment."

Tori groaned, reliving her shame. "I don't even know for sure what he said, because I was busy turning into a ball of schoolgirl mush. Oh, and please, I beg of you on our sisterhood, do not tell Kenzie. I'll never hear the end of it."

"Doesn't she want you to date?" Rose asked.

"Date? Who said anything..." Tori sighed. "Okay, yeah, I can dream. And Kenzie is the world's greatest daughter."

"One of them," Rose interjected. "Alyson and Avery are pretty perfect, too."

"So perfect," Tori agreed as she sipped her coffee. "But as far as dating? Kenzie would be fine. Finn? He's not fine about anything these days. But you know what a thirteen-year-old boy is like, right, Rose?"

"Oh, I do. And I will again in two years with Ethan. It's a challenging age, or it would be if I didn't have..." She let her voice fade out.

"If you didn't have Gabe," Tori finished for her. "It's all right. I don't have Gabe. We can all say it out loud."

"But you *could* have Dr. Hottypants," Raina joked, risking getting her shin kicked.

"Seriously, Tori," Rose said. "Have you been seeing anyone? It's been, what? Five years since you divorced."

"Yes, five years, and no, I'm not dating. First of all, the pickings are slim for a forty-five-year-old woman with two kids and a very time-consuming business. Sometimes I feel like all I do is work and try to keep my head above water with Kenzie and Finn."

"I don't know how you do it," Rose said. "I know Kenzie is probably a huge help, but if I didn't have Suze and Madeline and Grace around? When Gabe has one of those horrible three-day shifts, I would absolutely collapse without help. In fact, he's back on duty tomorrow and I'm already worried."

"I'm here," Raina said.

"And me," Tori added. "But even better, Kenzie is here for a Big Cousin Bash. She can babysit them all—except, I guess, Zach doesn't need a sitter, since they're the same age."

"No, but he could probably use some advice about girls from one he trusts and who isn't his mother," Rose said.

Next to her, Raina looked over Tori's shoulder. "And guess who's coming over here."

Heat crawled up Tori's chest. "Oh, no. He's not coming over. Is he coming over? Does he look...mad? Interested? As good as I remember?"

"Better," Raina said.

Rose laughed and shook her head. "You're awful, Rain. Put her out of her misery."

"It's your sisters," Raina said. "Sorry to disappoint."

"Oh, no disappointment." Tori turned and waved to Grace and Madeline, the sisters she hadn't seen in months, the doctor forgotten.

A moment later, they were adding chairs to the table, hugging and laughing and, of course, Raina had to do a reenactment, but only after she assured Tori that Hotty-pants had left the cafeteria.

As they laughed and teased her, Tori's embarrassment completely disappeared, replaced by a warm comfort that only came when two or more Wingate girls were gathered.

They chatted about Dad—who was fine right this moment, Madeline assured her—and talked about Kenzie babysitting the kids, and whether or not Grace's uber-shy little girl would like that. Finally, they decided yes, and the kids could all go to the beach house tomorrow night while Gabe was on duty.

"That way, we can all be here with Dad," Madeline said.

"No night schedules?" Tori asked her older sister.

"Well, we can't all be in the room at once, but we

can hang in the waiting room. I think these early days, and evenings, we should be here for Suze and Dad when we can and when there's no PT or doctors or tests."

"What about Chloe?" Raina asked. "Wasn't she here last night?"

"And went back to Jacksonville. Coming up is hard for her," Grace told them.

"It's only an hour away," Tori said. "Is her work at the PR firm that demanding? I mean, her father is in the hospital."

"It's not her work," Grace said. "It's her fiancé's. You know Hunter's a resident at Mayo in plastic surgery and keeps insane hours."

"But *she's* not a resident at Mayo," Tori said. "She can come up here and stay at the beach house, right? Or even with us in the bungalow. I miss that beautiful girl and Kenzie flat-out adores her."

"Chloe likes to be home when he gets off his shift," Rose said. "But they're both coming up soon for a pre-wedding flower meeting and a walk-through at the country club."

"Oh, the wedding!" Tori exclaimed. "With Dad and everything, we've hardly talked about it. I hated that I missed the bridal shower a few weeks ago."

"It's fine," Madeline said. "Of course, Suze nailed the whole event. Oh, you know what? With you two here"— she flipped her finger between Tori and Raina— "we can do a dress fitting and I won't have to ship your bridesmaid dresses for final alterations."

"That's perfect," Raina said. "I love that she picked the six of us for her bridesmaids."

"Oh, yeah, we're gonna look like a row of whipped rhubarbs in that color," Tori joked.

Madeline laughed, shaking her head. "It is...pink. But that color suits the style of the dress, I promise."

"I found African daisies and pink calla lilies that are going to slay the bouquets," Rose told them. "The tablescapes are stunning, too. Really, it's going to be a gorgeous wedding. I just hope..."

For a long, long moment, none of them spoke. It wasn't the bridesmaid dresses that worried anyone, and they all knew it.

"That Dad's there," Raina finished for her.

"He *has* to be," Grace whispered. "It would break Chloe's heart if he..." She took a deep breath. "Do you guys think he can walk her down the aisle in six weeks?"

No one answered, because no one knew.

"Well, nothing can mar her big day," Raina finally said. "Even if he has to cruise the aisles of St. Peter's in a wheelchair."

"He certainly knows the way," Tori cracked, since four of his seven daughters had married at the stunning Episcopalian church.

"I suppose Mom could walk her," Grace said. "Although I doubt Hunter would like that."

Tori looked at her. "Hunter? It's not his decision who walks Chloe down the aisle."

Grace shot a look at Rose, as if she needed help.

"Hunter is a traditionalist," Rose said. "He wants

things just so, and they all should be exactly by the book. It's kind of how he is."

Tori considered that, realizing she knew very, very little about the man her youngest sister was marrying. And maybe, she thought with a thud, how little Chloe knew.

"How did they meet, anyway? Hasn't their relationship been mostly long distance?" Tori asked.

"They met when she was doing an internship for a Baltimore TV station when she was in graduate school," Grace said. "He was at Johns Hopkins Med School, but she was living in D.C. Not exactly long distance, but then he started his residency at the Mayo Clinic in Minnesota, and they were apart. When he got accepted into the plastic surgery program in Jacksonville, she jumped at the chance to move down here and be with him, and they got engaged."

Tori nodded. "So this is the only time they were in the same city?" Maybe she never had the opportunity to really know the guy.

"Yep, and I fear they'll be off again when he gets a job," Rose added. "They'll go to whatever city that's in."

"What about Chloe's job?" Tori asked.

"I honestly think he won't want her working, especially if they have kids," Grace said.

A tiny chill meandered up Tori's spine as a hundred old arguments replayed in her mind.

She could practically hear her ex-husband's complaints when he got home from work and she'd destroyed the kitchen cooking for other people, back when she was a fledgling caterer.

"Trey hated me working, too," she said, getting a few looks from them and realizing it wasn't her place to compare Chloe's fiancé to hers, who was, by all accounts, a subpar husband and human. "But a totally different situation," she amended quickly.

"She won't have to work," Rose said. "He'll be a plastic surgeon."

Raina fluttered her hands in fake celebration. "Botox at the friends-and-family discount," she joked.

"Oh, no," Grace said. "I teased him about that once and he...well, Rose is right. He's a huge rule-follower."

Tori looked down at her now cooled coffee, fighting a flashback of her own marriage. Rule-followers were... strict and heartless and cold. At least hers was. Also, rules were for other people...rules about fidelity and such.

She pushed the thoughts away and got on safer ground. "All I know is Dad has to be at the wedding or there will be tears in the pink calla lilies."

"What can we do?" Grace asked. "How can we make sure that happens? I feel so helpless, you know? This isn't in our hands."

They shared looks, silently thinking the same thing. No one knew better than dear widowed Grace that some things weren't in anyone's hands.

"I don't know the answer," Madeline said honestly. "But we will do everything—absolutely everything—to get Dad to Chloe's wedding. Together, as a family, helping Suze, helping Dad, helping Chloe. *Whatever.*"

"I wish you two would always be here," Rose said, reaching her hands out to Tori and Raina. "I feel like anything is possible when we're together."

"It's not that long until the wedding." Grace leaned in with a question in her golden-brown eyes. "Any chance you guys can upend your lives and stay? For Dad? For us?"

Tori glanced at Raina, wondering if she ached to say yes to that question as much as Tori did. Raina looked torn. But Tori wasn't. She loved this place more than any other on Earth.

"I'm not sure." Raina sighed, definitely struggling with the answer. "But I only have a long drive to get home, and Jack is running our company. I actually could, but you, Tori? What about your catering business?"

"I have staff," she said. "They could probably cover the immediate events I have on the calendar, but even more complicated? My kids have school. Kenzie has to go back next week. I suppose she could stay with Trey and Heidi-Ho. She wouldn't love that, but she'd do it if she thought it would make me happy."

"Oh my word," Rose said on a sigh. "You are a terrific mother, Tori."

The others agreed, making Tori brush off the compliment and feel her cheeks warm. "Please, I've been gifted with her. Both of them, really."

"The fact that she'd stay with her dad cheerfully and make it easy for you to stay?" Madeline pointed at her. "That's on you, Mom. Well-raised, well done."

"Thanks, Madeline." She felt Raina's gaze on her and

turned, curious as to what her sister was thinking. She couldn't quite read her expression.

"What an incredible thing it must be," Raina whispered.

"What?"

"To have a daughter like that. A friend. A connection that you made." Raina's eyes misted, making Tori suck in a soft breath.

Tori searched her face, an old ache for her dear sister rising.

"We're all blessed in different ways," Tori said, then leaned in to whisper, "Channeling my inner Rose here."

That made Raina laugh, but then her smile faded. "I just don't know about staying here until the wedding," she said. "It's a long time to be away from home."

"I just want Dad at that wedding," Madeline said. "No matter what it takes. For us to jump in, help, make life easier, we have to change our lives, make deals with the devil, or..."

"Not give Dad stress," Raina added, looking guilty.

"Whatever it takes," Tori and Grace said in unison.

"Then we promise." Madeline held out two hands, which the sisters on either side took, then they held theirs, completing the circle.

"Stating the obvious," Tori said dryly, "but the circle is missing Sadie and Chloe."

"They're here in spirit," Grace whispered.

Holding hands, they shared a look, then all looked down for one second and whispered, "Promise."

Chills danced up Tori's spine, because the silly sister tradition felt so *right*.

"Wow," Raina whispered. "A Seven Sisters Promise. It's been a minute, ladies."

"Too many minutes," Tori agreed. "But we just made one, so we all have to do whatever we can to get Dad to that wedding."

"And down the aisle," Grace added. "It's important."

It was, Tori thought. And she wanted to stay those six weeks so much, she couldn't breathe. Deep inside, she already knew she had to stay. She *had* to.

Chapter Eight

Rose

Before the alarm went off at six a.m., Rose woke with the same silent prayer she'd said every morning before Gabe left for a twenty-four-hour shift at the station.

Please keep him safe.

She always opened her eyes before the alarm on shift days, as though her whole body knew it was about to face twenty-four hours of low-grade tension that would only be eliminated when her husband walked in the door and kissed her on the lips.

Yes, she should be used to it after eighteen years of being married to a firefighter. But the fact was, she knew the goodbye kiss he gave her when he headed off for the station could always be the last.

It was kind of crazy, considering that the Fernandina Beach Fire Department didn't battle that many fires, had very few run-ins with life-threatening situations, and most of Gabe's shifts were spent cooking, eating, cleaning, and sleeping. Still...he was a firefighter and EMT. So he certainly did see some rough stuff on those shifts.

He saved lives with the same competence and ease that he coached soccer, grew tomatoes, fixed broken Barbie dolls, and kissed Rose until she got dizzy.

Holding that thought, she let herself drift back to half-sleep, listening to the quiet overture of dawn bringing their rambling one-hundred-year-old house to life.

The very first wisps of light slipped in through the bay window that formed the corner of the room, allowing her to see the gleaming wood crown molding, the beams along the vaulted ceiling, and the soft floral wallpaper that captured the essence of her truly Victorian home.

Not really "her" home, Rose corrected. It was a Wingate Family home, and belonged to the whole clan, the historic town, and the past.

She never failed to recognize the fact that this seven-bedroom, many-times-restored grand dame of what the Historical Society dubbed the "silk stocking" section of town had been her grandparents' home. After that, with two additions, it became the family home where all seven Wingate girls had grown up.

Then Dad and Suze built the beach house a decade ago, and offered this house to Gabe and Rose.

Madeline had no need or desire for a place this size; Tori moved to Boston for culinary school, then marriage; and Raina had headed off to find her fortune in Miami. None of the three younger girls wanted to deal with it, either, since Chloe was in college, Sadie had moved to Europe, and Grace had lived wherever Nick was stationed.

Rose and Gabe jumped on the opportunity to own such a landmark, and they'd taken excellent care of the home, lovingly decorating it to be perfect for a big family, but always honoring the deep history.

A few years ago, Gabe had added a greenhouse to the back, where they grew flowers, fruits, and vegetables. They'd long gotten used to tourists taking pictures of their gabled and turreted home and lush garden. The entire property had a soul—and maybe a ghost or two, though they were benign—and Rose always woke up grateful to live here.

And even more grateful to live here with Gabe and their four children.

The alarm dinged just loud enough to wake her husband, who responded the way he did every morning before a twenty-four-hour shift. Rose might say secret, silent prayers, but not Gabe. He slid his leg over hers, entwined their bodies, tucked her so close she could feel every muscle. Every move made it abundantly clear that he didn't want to get out of bed and save the world.

But he would, because he was dedicated, hard-working, and about to make captain. Plus, his father, now retired, had been the chief for many years, his uncle had worked at the station, and his cousin was another lieutenant with the same team. Gabe had his own respect for his family name and legacy.

"Morning, angel Gabriel," she pressed a kiss on the solid shoulder she leaned on every single day of her life.

"That night was way too short." He tipped her face

up and looked into her eyes. "But the kids won't be up for half an hour."

She eased into him, warm and willing, then froze as reality hit. "Except I promised Suze I'd be at the hospital to spell her. She wants to go home because the medical device company is delivering the hospital bed and exercise equipment for Dad to use at home."

He exhaled his disappointment, then nodded. "Getting him to do rehab at home and not in a center is really important," he said. "It will make everything smoother and faster for him."

"I know," she agreed. "So, I'll drop the kids off, but I have two early flower orders that I want to get out. And a meeting with a bride-to-be, and a local woman hosting a huge event who needs flowers, and...and...and..." She closed her eyes and squeezed him again for the sheer pleasure of holding this man she loved more than anything or anyone. "Oh, so busy. When will we have uninterrupted time again?"

"Mommy?" Avery's voice floated in from the hall.

"She's six, so...twelve years?" Gabe whispered, easing her away. "Mommy's awake," he called. "Come on in, sweet pea."

She scampered in, her golden hair tousled, her eyes still hooded with sleep. "Can I see Grandpa today?" she asked as she climbed up on the bed, oblivious to the intimacy under the covers.

Well, no more. Rose was instantly in Mom Mode, and Gabe's glorious body would have to wait.

"Soon," she promised Avery, pulling her close for a

morning kiss while she smoothed her wild waves. "Grandpa's going to be home soon and we will visit him all the time. I think seeing you will make him just want to get better faster and faster."

"'Cause I'm his favorite," she said with zero humility.

"You are?" Gabe chuckled. "I think Grandpa loves all his grandkids the same."

"Nope. He told me, I am definitely his favorite." She sat up on his knees. "It's 'cause my middle name is Regina, like Aunt Raina. Also, I'm a better fisher than any girl he ever met, he told me."

Rose snorted and rolled her eyes. "Don't tell Aunt Madeline. She prides herself on her fishing."

"Plus, I beat him at checkers, so he said I'm a genius."

Gabe snorted but Rose tapped her little girl's nose. "A genius doesn't brag."

"It's not bragging. Grandpa says if you're the best, you gotta be the best at letting people know that."

"Sounds like Rex." Gabe rolled over and lifted his phone from the nightstand, peering at the screen. "Dang, I totally forgot I have a probie starting today and he's my problem—er, responsibility."

"What's a probie, Daddy?"

"A young, clueless, wanna-be firefighter, sweetheart. Probie means he's on probation. Do you know what that means?"

"Umm..." She screwed up her little face, thinking. "He likes bees?"

Rose and Gabe choked back a laugh as Gabe threw

back the covers and climbed out. "It means he better not mess up or he's out of here."

Rose pulled Avery closer for another squeeze. "Anyone else up yet?"

"Ethan is. Zach is still asleep, because he was texting last night."

Gabe grunted from the closet where he was pulling out his uniform. "Don't we have a 'no texting after eleven' rule?"

Rose shook her head, knowing that she could only blame her complete and utter distraction with Dad this week on Zach's infraction. "Only for emergencies and maybe a select group of friends," she said.

"Is Tiffany Kaplan select?" Avery asked. "'Cause that's who he was texting."

Gabe groaned as he passed the bed.

"I know what you're thinking," Rose said. "He's exactly the age we were when we met and became boyfriend and girlfriend."

"Eww." Avery made a face. "Boys are ucky. I hate them."

"Don't hate anyone," Rose said. "And don't snitch on your brothers."

"Boys *are* ucky," Gabe agreed. "I recommend you stay away from them for at least twenty, maybe thirty years. In fact, I'll make sure of it."

Rose chuckled. "Good thing my dad didn't say that to you. But, Avery, I mean it. No snitching on your brothers or sister."

"Well, how else would you know that he texted a girl last night?"

"I'd find out," Rose said. "I would see it in his eyes this morning."

"Really? Do they change color when you like a girl?"

"Yes!" Gabe said, making his eyes huge as he wiggled his brows right in front of Avery. "Mine used to be brown. Then I met Mommy."

She giggled and flicked her hand like how could they think she was so dumb, making them laugh.

"And I gotta shave or risk the wrath of my captain."

He disappeared into the bathroom and Rose eased Avery from the bed. "All right, fun's over. Big day ahead."

"What's so big about it?" Avery demanded.

"Well, for starters, you're having a party at Grannie and Grandpa's house tonight with your brothers and cousins and none other than cousin Kenzie is going to babysit."

"What?" She jumped off the bed. "I love Kenzie! I'm tellin' everyone!" She zoomed off as fast as she'd arrived, leaving Rose alone with a huge smile on her face while she laid out Gabe's uniform on the bed.

A few minutes later, Gabe stepped out of the bathroom, freshly shaved and looking delicious in nothing but boxers. "She sounded excited about tonight."

"Of course," she said. "They all love Kenzie. And Tori. Do you think there's any way we can convince her to move here permanently?"

"Tori? Here?" He pulled on the FBFD T-shirt, his

always short-cropped dark hair and clean-shaven face popping out. "Why would she do that?"

"She misses us and raising kids without family is so dang hard. And she could start a catering business here. I do so many weddings, I could recommend her. We could be a team."

He smiled at her, leaning over to give her a kiss that tasted like toothpaste and...that goodbye she dreaded. "Make it happen, Rosie girl. You can do it."

"Maybe." She frowned as he stepped into his pants, and not because he'd covered up. "You are leaving early today."

He let his gaze drift over her long T-shirt and bare legs. "Sadly, yes. I got that probie and something tells me he'll be standing in front of his locker all fresh and rarin' to go well before the shift changes. I'll eat there, so don't worry about me."

She nodded and came around the bed, arms out for him. Without a word, they embraced, long and bittersweet.

Inching back, she looked up at him. "Be safe, my angel."

"Never fear." He gave her a long kiss, one that could never be a peck. By unspoken agreement, the goodbye-before-a-shift kiss was, well, a *kiss*. "I love you forever, Rose Wingate."

"Forever and then some," she whispered.

One more quick kiss, one more hug, one more happy glance, and he was gone.

Please keep him safe.

WITH THE KIDS DROPPED OFF, Rose stopped at her store before heading to the hospital.

She unlocked the back door of Coming Up Roses, breathing in the floral fragrance that hung in the back of the shop, humming to herself while she chose exactly the right flowers for the two pending orders.

The process always gave her peace, which she needed more than usual right now. Finding the right bloom, clipping it correctly, and sliding it into place grounded her. Choosing colors and greens, placing the baby's breath sprigs to add dimension helped her tell a story or deliver a whisper of love to someone.

Get well, be happy, find joy, be blessed, celebrate.

Even when sent for sad reasons, Rose believed that every arrangement—truly every flower—infused the world with hope and help.

"Knock-knock."

Surprised, she spun around to see her twin sister standing in the doorway. "Raina!"

"Shouldn't you lock this door when you're in here alone?" Raina asked.

"This isn't Miami, Rain. What are you doing here at this ungodly hour?"

"I'm going into Wingate Properties to assume my duties as Substitute Rex." She shook her head. "I saw your SUV and couldn't resist."

Rose smiled. "Can you come to the hospital with me?" she asked. "I'm almost done and my delivery truck will be here any minute, then I'm going to take over for Suze."

"Oh, I'd love to but I still haven't gone into the actual office to see what's going on there. I should show my face and make sure it's still running at a profit."

"Gotcha. Could I persuade you to please have a coffee with me at the Riverfront Café?" Rose pressed her hands together in a plea. "I get so little time completely alone with you."

"Done and done, Rosebud."

"Perfect. Let me put these arrangements in the cooler and we can walk right down there. I have some time before Suze is expecting me."

A few minutes later, they enjoyed a rare stroll through a nearly deserted Fernandina Beach. In April, there were plenty of tourists soaking up the small-town vibes, but at this hour, most of them were still tucked into the many inns and B&Bs that dotted the landscape.

They walked along the Amelia River, which was peaceful and calm this morning, quiet as they inhaled the brackish scent of the wide body of water that separated this barrier island from mainland Florida.

"What do you think it would take to get Tori to move back here?" Rose mused, still stuck on the idea she'd discussed with Gabe.

Raina slowed her step. "I can't believe you said that! I was just about to broach the subject with you."

"Don't tell me you're thinking about it?" Rose asked, unable to keep the hope out of her voice.

"Oh, gosh, Rose. First of all, I have Jack and a business and a house down in Miami and..." She sighed. "I mean, I hope I have all those things. If not, make room for Raina."

"I'm not going to hope that happens, because I want you to be happy. Have you guys talked?"

"Barely. But about Tori—I thought I saw a glimmer of something in her eyes when we talked about living here."

"Right?" Rose had seen that, too. "I think she'd be happier with us than she is in Boston, but it would be hard for her to make it happen. She has her business and you know how kids are once they get in high school. It's hard to move them."

"I don't know about that," Raina said. "Kenzie is madly in love with Amelia Island. She said she's always liked it here, and she was asking about colleges nearby, actually."

"Really?" That was encouraging. "Of course, Finn would get a say and I think he's kind of close to his father. At least they do the sports thing together."

"Or he does to make Trey happy," Raina said, then sighed. "Whoa, divorces are complicated, aren't they?"

Thankfully, Rose would never know. "They sure are, especially with kids."

"Or with a profitable business that you share."

Rose gave her a look, hating the sound in her sister's voice.

"Raindrop." She put her arm around her sister's waist. "You're a long way from thinking like that. Have you talked about the, uh, issues?"

"No. Just work and...that Godfrey woman."

Rose laughed. "That Godfrey woman. Sounds like a dark Victorian novel. What does he say about her?"

"That he's handed her all my listings, agents, and open contracts and she closed three deals and brought them—er, *us*—a few major new clients. Blah blah blah."

Rose shot her a look. "You're not really jealous of this woman, are you?"

"A little," she admitted. "She's way too much like me when I was younger and more ambitious. Plus, he spends a lot of time with her."

"Eesh, that's unsettling." The very second the comment came out, Rose regretted it. "Oh, God, Rain. I don't mean—"

"It's okay, it's okay. Kind of refreshing to hear you be honest instead of painting something in a perfectly happy light."

"Everything can be seen in a different light," Rose insisted. "I'm not optimistic because it's phony, but because I choose to see the glass half full."

"No, for you it's bubbling over with champagne and gold dust."

Rose looked at her, not quite sure how to take that.

"Which I love!" Raina insisted, leaning into her. "It's just that sometimes life isn't, well, rosy."

"I know that. But, Rain, are you seriously worried he'd...be unfaithful?"

Rose's last word was nearly lost at the sound of a loud whistle, indicating the arrival of the small train that traveled the tracks between two paper mills on either side of the island.

They waited in silence as it passed, and with each moment, she could feel her sister getting more tense. By the time the train disappeared, they'd reached Riverfront Café, a creamy stucco building with festive green-striped awnings and umbrella-covered outdoor tables, giving patrons a view of the wharf.

"I'm not worried about that Godfrey woman," Raina finally said. "And as far as Jack? Rex Wingate didn't raise a quitter."

"So true," Rose agreed. "You always fight for what you want."

"I want this marriage to work."

"Then you'll have to fight for it," Rose said as they opened the gate and glanced at the tables, which were weirdly empty for a day as beautiful as this.

Inside, it was oddly quiet, too.

"Does this place look kind of deserted to you?" Raina asked, obviously thinking the same thing.

"It does," Rose agreed, looking left and right. "Where is everyone? Where's Bambi?"

"Who's that?"

"The hostess. Oh—there she is. In the kitchen. Hello?"

"Be right there," the woman called. "But don't get your heart set on breakfast."

Raina and Rose exchanged a quick, confused look when a woman in her fifties who'd been working the front of the Riverfront Café for the past year came out from the back.

"Oh, golly," she said, wiping her hands on an apron. "I was hoping no Wingates would come in here today."

Rose inched back in surprise. "Why?"

"Because last time I checked, you owned the place and things are..." She heaved a sigh and brushed back a stray lock of light blond hair that escaped from what looked like a hastily created ponytail. "What's the word on Rex?" she asked. "Is he okay?"

"He will be," Rose said confidently. Although Rex was hands-off with the café, he still owned the place and was the boss. "This is my sister, Raina, Bambi. Have you two met?"

"No, no." She wiped again and held out her hand. "You're the twin, right? I see the resemblance even though your coloring is opposite."

Raina smiled and nodded, no doubt as used to the comment as Rose was. "Where are the customers?" she asked.

"I sent them out. I was just going to make a sign that there won't be breakfast and probably not lunch today. I was going to close, but..."

"Bambi, what's going on?" Rose asked. "Where's Jim?"

She looked around for the manager and head cook who'd run the place for the past six months. Before that, the position had been held by a Greek man who'd worked for the Wingates since all the girls had been little, but Tobias had retired and filling his shoes hadn't been easy.

"Your guess is as good as mine," the woman said. "He called in sick."

"Sick? And no one else is in the kitchen?"

"No one is scheduled and..." Bambi crossed her arms over an ample bosom. "Let me be clear that by 'sick' I mean they poured him out of the Palace at two this morning, more sheets to the wind than anyone could count."

Ouch. Rose dug for the perfect thing to say, but, as happened on rare occasions, she had nothing.

"Can you call in backup?" Raina asked. "Surely you have another line cook."

"Miguel doesn't want to come in on his day off," she said. "The other cook quit on Monday. Jimmy doesn't exactly elicit, you know, loyalty."

Then Jimmy had to go, Rose thought.

"And I don't cook," Bambi added, as if they were about to put her on the line. "So, I'm very sorry. I can get you coffee or tea, and scare up a pastry from yesterday, but..." She shrugged. "No hot food today."

Rose glanced at Raina, knowing they were thinking the same thing—they'd made a promise, and this fell firmly under "Do anything we can to make Dad's life and job and world easier so he can get better."

What would he do in this case? Probably march back there and start cooking.

"We'll try and get you a line cook for the lunch rush," Raina said, pulling out her phone, which was also what Rex Wingate would do. "In the meantime, why don't you make a nice sign and bring out the pastries and...whatever else you have. Everything should be on the house for guests this morning."

Bambi's eyes flickered with a bit of surprise, and respect. "Sure, Ms. Wingate. I'll go get them."

As she walked away, Rose turned to Raina, grateful that she was such a natural leader and businessperson. But her sister didn't know very many people on Amelia Island.

"Who are you calling?" Rose asked, genuinely curious.

"Texting," she said. "A chef who could run lunch with her eyes closed."

"You know a...oh my, yes!" Rose exclaimed. "Of course, Tori! Brilliant, Raina!"

Her sister looked up from her phone, and smiled. "Maybe she'll love it so much, she'll stay and run the Riverfront Café."

"That is...wow. You're so resourceful, Raina. Why didn't I think of that?"

"You would have, but...oh, she's writing back." She held up the phone. "Fingers crossed she doesn't laugh in my face."

Rose held up crossed fingers and then used them to point at the screen. "What did she say?"

Raina read the text with a soft whoop. "She's on her way! And bringing Kenzie to help."

They gave each other a high-five.

"You've got to get to the hospital," Raina said. "I'll stay and wait for her."

"What about going into the office?"

"Well, this café is part of Wingate Properties and if I

know Dad, this is where he'd want me to focus today. You get to the hospital before Suze has a conniption."

"Done and done." Rose leaned close and kissed Raina's cheek. "I love you, Raindrop."

"Backatcha, Rosebud."

Heart light, Rose headed back to her shop, hopeful and optimistic as always.

Chapter Nine

Susannah

Rex was sitting up and Susannah could now understand every word he was saying. He didn't moan as much when the physical therapist came, he was sleeping well, and when Rose came into the hospital for a visit, he was downright cheery. When Grace showed up a few minutes later, he sat up a little and gave her a high-five with his good hand.

Going home couldn't be that far off.

The only disappointment Susannah had that morning was the text telling her the delivery of the hospital bed ended up getting delayed. Grace walked into the hall with her to get coffee, now that Susannah didn't have to get home to meet the truck.

"Oh, Mom, you should get out for a bit anyway," Grace said as they waited for the elevator.

"I admit I was looking forward to it," Susannah said on a sigh. "Raina and Tori have been awesome about bringing me fresh clothes, but I do need some air. Oh, and I need someone to go to Wingate House and bring

Doreen up to speed. But..." She made a face. "That woman is so difficult, I hate to ask anyone to do it."

"I'll go. I've had a box of books in the back of my van for weeks to take over there. You know I like to replenish the library at the inn. I put a sign up for guests take the books if they're in the middle of the read when they check out."

"Would you go there this morning?"

Grace tipped her head and smiled. "If you'll go with me."

Susannah opened her mouth to say no, she couldn't leave Rex, but the idea was awfully alluring. Grace was such a calming presence, and she so needed to get out of this building.

"I'd love to."

"Perfect. We have our bags, so just text Rose and let her know we'll be gone for an hour or so." Grace slipped her arm around Susannah. "Let's breathe the air and have a break, Mom."

Susannah dropped her head on her daughter's narrow but strong shoulder. "Yes, please."

Grace drove them to Wingate House, and Susannah's heart was already a little lighter just being outside.

"You're so strong, Mom," Grace mused as they turned toward Fernandina Beach. "I honestly don't think I've ever known anyone with as much fortitude as you."

"Me?" Susannah scoffed. "Please. I'm crying myself to sleep in that recliner half the time. And as far as fortitude? You got that, Gracie girl. More than any of us."

Susannah slid a look at her daughter. "I've been thinking about you a lot lately."

"Why?"

"Because of what you've been through. Because I'm afraid that Dad will have another stroke—or worse—and you already endured the ultimate loss when Nick died." Susannah studied her daughter's lovely profile. "You carry on with the grace of your name."

Grace smiled at that. "You do what you have to do, Mom."

It was quiet for a beat again, but emotions still bubbled up in Susannah. Of all her daughters, Grace was by far the quietest, a woman who never felt the need to fill the air with words unless they had to be said.

"How?" Susannah asked simply. "How do you do what you have to do when your heart is breaking?"

"Some days are easier than others," Grace replied.

"But you still have hard days." Susannah put her hand on her chest. "I hate to think of you in that pain."

"Don't worry, Mom. I power through it. I actually can go hours now, maybe half a day, when all I do is remember Nick or think of him with a nice feeling. I get busy and Nikki Lou is..." She smiled. "She keeps my mind occupied."

"I'm so glad you have her," Susannah said. "But other times? Do you still—well, obviously you miss him. Do you still cry?"

Grace sighed before answering. "Not that often," she finally said. "But every once in a while, something will hit me. I'll hear a song or smell a cologne and I can't believe he's gone."

"I can't imagine how hard that can hit you sometimes," she said.

"The other day?" Grace gave a dry laugh. "I absolutely lost it. All because of his ring."

"His ring? You saw it somewhere?"

"I don't have it."

Susannah startled at that. "I didn't know that."

"I don't talk about it," she said. "I don't want people to think about how he died and that they never recovered...everything."

Including, Susannah presumed, his wedding ring. She tried never to think of Nick Jenkins dying in a car explosion. She preferred to remember only the tall, easygoing, always happy military man who Grace had married. She loved her son-in-law, and had prayed for him every day he was deployed. Those prayers, sadly, weren't answered.

"What happened?" Susannah asked. "I mean, when you thought about his ring."

"I was looking at mine..." She held up her left hand where a slender silver band with a few diamonds still resided. "And I suddenly got overwhelmed thinking that his is somewhere in the dirt of Afghanistan."

Susannah felt her eyes close, unable to fathom how much that had to hurt. "Oh, baby."

"And everyone says I should take this one off."

"When you're ready," Susannah said. "And not one minute before."

"Thanks." Grace gave her a soft smile. "I might never take it off. Would you? If..."

Susannah looked down at her own diamonds. "I doubt I'd ever take my wedding ring off."

"Well, I don't want to be anything less than Susannah Wingate."

Her heart softened at the compliment, but then she narrowed her eyes at Grace. "Maybe you should."

"Why?"

"Because you're thirty-three years old, honey. If a handsome man waltzes into the bookstore, he'll assume you're off-limits."

"I *am* off-limits."

"Grace!" Susannah shifted in her seat, and got closer. "You're far too young to say you'll never love again."

"Watch me: I'll never love again."

Susannah fell back against her seat, not sure what to say. The very idea that Grace was so closed off was too sad for words. Didn't little Nikki Lou deserve a father? Maybe that balance would slow her toddler temper tantrums. Didn't Grace want to love and marry and maybe have another child?

"And I mean it," Grace said, turning off the main drag and snagging street parking instead of going around to the back lot.

Susannah knew when this girl was done with a subject, so she let it drop as they got out and walked toward the impressive home that rose up over Wingate Way like a blue and cream Victorian sentry keeping watch over all who passed.

Susannah remembered the first time she'd been inside Wingate House. She'd been on a date with Rex and he'd recounted the home's history with pride. She'd simply melted at the idea of having a family with deep roots and an enviable past.

Wingate House had been built in 1910 by the very first Reginald Wingate, Rex's grandfather, a young entrepreneur who'd left New York at the turn of the century to follow the Gilded Age multimillionaires to this area. He made money first as a banker, then in real estate.

He'd gobbled up several of the buildings along the river, adding a brick and iron gate with a W in front of every property he owned. He'd lobbied to rename the street Wingate Way when he built the bank that took up almost a whole block, across from what was now Madeline's dress shop.

His oldest son, Rex's father—known as Regis—had not only owned the newspaper and local bank, he'd also inherited his father's Midas touch with real estate, and was given the house when his father died.

He raised his own family in Wingate House, but in the mid-1950s, Regis and his wife transformed the home into one of the first thriving inns on the island, a position it held to this day.

Every time she approached Wingate House, Susannah still squared her shoulders like a soldier preparing for battle. The gingerbread Victorian was gorgeous and welcoming, but it also was home to the singularly most unlikeable person Susannah had ever met, Doreen Parrish.

"You seem even more tense now than at the hospital," Grace mused.

"I'm never relaxed when I have to face Doreen."

"Dor-mean," Grace said with a soft laugh, using the secret nickname the Wingate girls had hung on her years ago. "But you are her boss, Mom."

"Tell her that," Susannah quipped.

Yes, the woman had handled the day-to-day supervision of Wingate House for close to fifty years. Living in a third-floor apartment, Doreen mostly oversaw the maids —who quit with way too much regularity. She also did the shopping, made the breakfasts, and responded to the needs of their guests onsite.

But every other task involved with running a successful inn, such as billing, inventory, marketing, upkeep, décor, and reservation management, had landed on Susannah's plate about fifteen years ago when the previous manager retired.

"Well, she's old now," Grace said.

Susannah shrugged. "But no less judgmental and nasty. In fact, she might actually be getting worse."

Grace chuckled. "When Chloe and I were little and came here, we used to play a game we called What's Scarier? Being forced to go into Doreen's apartment or to be locked in the Coraline?"

"Definitely the apartment," Susannah said on a laugh. "The Coraline suite might be haunted, but the real terror is on the third floor."

When she'd remodeled well over a decade ago, Susannah had also re-christened each room. Seven were named for the Wingate girls, one for the late Charlotte Wingate, and one for Rex's mother, Adeline. But the grandest suite of all, the Coraline, was a nod to Rex's grandmother, who died of influenza when it swept through the town in the 1930s.

Many a guest had claimed to sense Coraline's presence in the room, which boasted a canopied bed gathered in a crown and a massive portrait of the suite's namesake over the fireplace in the sitting room.

Grace looked up at the third-floor windows. "You gotta admit, it's kind of creepy. Why doesn't she leave?"

"I guess she has nowhere else to go," Susannah said. "She's never so much as whispered about retiring."

As Susannah understood the history, Doreen had cleaned the inn as a teenager, a young girl from a far less fortunate family on the island. Sometime in the late 1960s, when she was eighteen, Doreen had run away from home, but returned a few years later, penniless and desperate for a job. Apparently, Regis had given young Doreen a job as a housekeeper out of pity.

Fifty years later, she was still there—a lonely spinster —and no one had the nerve or heart to do a darn thing about that.

As they reached the steps from the walkway, Susannah gave a sweeping glance to the wraparound porch, which sometimes looked a little unkempt. But today, everything was spotless and gleaming, a perfect entrance for the guests.

"At least it's in tip-top shape," Susannah murmured.

As they stepped inside the grand foyer and paused at

a wide mahogany staircase that led to the second-floor rooms, Grace inhaled deeply.

"She might be judgey," Grace said softly, "but, wow, that smells good."

The heady scent of french toast and poached peaches hung in the air like a welcome temptation.

The house was quiet at this mid-morning hour, with guests off walking the streets of town, enjoying the beach, or taking boat rides up to Cumberland Island. The only sound was the grandfather clock ticking in the hall and...

"Is that the vacuum I hear?" Grace asked. "Or..."

"Someone is humming." Susannah took a few steps past the living room and the closed doors of the bar, frowning. Yes, someone was definitely humming. Was that Doreen?

Together, they headed toward the sound, coming from the kitchen in the back of the inn. They slowed as they approached the kitchen door, hidden behind a back staircase.

And the humming suddenly became...whistling. Then, a few words of a deep baritone voice singing—most definitely *not* Doreen—all of it punctuated by the sound of the faucet and the clatter of silverware.

"Please bring me home, precious Jesus, to you..."

Susannah cocked her head and gave Grace a questioning look. "Would she let a guest work in the kitchen?"

"That would be strange," Grace agreed.

They came around the edge of the door jamb and Susannah drew back at the sight of a man—tall, bald, and broad—wearing a way-too-small apron and working at the sink, looking right out the window, singing his heart out.

"To your home, precious—"

"Um, excuse me?"

He lowered the dishes to the sink as he turned, pinning brown eyes on her.

"Hello," he said with the ease of someone who lived or worked here. "I've just cleaned up breakfast for the guests, ladies, but I'm happy to whip something up for you. And the coffee's still hot."

Susannah shook her head, too stunned to respond. Had they hired someone she didn't know about?

"I'm not a guest," she finally said. "Where's Doreen?"

"Miz Parish is upstairs today, in her apartment."

She hadn't handled breakfast? That was a first.

"And you..."

"Oh, where are my manners?" He wiped a huge hand on the apron and extended it. "Isaiah Kincaid. I'm staying in a room—"

"The Grace," Susannah said, shaking his hand as her nearly photographic memory recalled seeing the name on the reservation list.

"Oh, that's me." Grace came in behind her and he did a doubletake, nearly sucking in a breath.

"You're Grace? *The* Grace?" he asked, his deep voice sounding surprised, as though he expected the rooms to be named for ladies who were long gone.

"Yes, this is my daughter, Grace," Susannah explained. "I remember a Kincaid reservation that requested the Grace. Yes, the room is named for her."

His dark, dark eyes widened as he stared at her daughter for a beat too long, then wiped his hands again. "Hello...Grace." He almost whispered the word; it sounded like the way someone would use the name in a prayer.

"I'm Susannah Wingate," she said, extending her hand. "And we don't normally ask our guests to clean up after breakfast."

"Wingate, like the house?" His brows lifted as he engulfed her hand in one twice its size. "Very, very nice to meet you, ma'am. And nobody asked. I volunteered. Miz Parrish was feeling poorly from the sniffles, and I'm more comfortable in here than the fancy rooms."

Susannah couldn't ever remember Doreen Parish taking a day off in her life, let alone for a cold. But letting a guest stand in for her? That was unheard of. She must be very, very ill.

"My goodness, I had no idea she was sick." Guilt washed over Susannah as she realized she hadn't even communicated with Doreen since Rex had his stroke.

Hadn't Madeline said she'd sent word over here? And checked on new reservations? Yes, but then Susannah just...forgot.

"I think it just came on," he said. "She confessed to me that she wasn't feeling well last night when I checked in. I came down at four-thirty—I'm an early riser, ma'am —and she was feeling so poorly, she took me up on the offer. I know my way around a breakfast menu."

Grace smiled up at him. "Well, based on the aroma, you nailed her signature dishes."

"She just told me what she was going to serve and I put my own spin on things," he said with a dash of humility that sat well on his strong shoulders. He obviously knew his way around a gym, too.

"Well, thank you." Susannah reached for the towel on the counter. "But this is no way to spend your vacation, Mr. Kincaid. We don't put our guests to work—"

"Oh, it's not really a vacation, ma'am. I'm just..." He stole another look at Grace, holding it for a second and confirming exactly what Susannah had been thinking on the drive over—Grace was far too young and lovely to take herself off the market. "Just passing through."

Then she processed what the man had just said. Passing through Amelia Island? That was...not possible unless he "passed through" a bridge over the Amelia River from the mainland.

"And I don't mind helping Miz Parrish out while she recovers. She was so nice."

Wait. Wait. *Nice?* Then she was way sicker than Susannah imagined.

Susannah studied him for a minute, putting him around forty. A handsome Black man with an essential kindness in his eyes, Isaiah did indeed seem at home in this kitchen.

But he was a guest, and this would not do.

"Well, thank you so much, Mr.—"

"Isaiah," he said. "And you don't have to thank me. A woman needed help, is all." Very gingerly, he plucked the towel from her hand. "And I'm happy to finish up here,

Miz Wingate. You can go on up and see her, if that will make you feel better."

Honestly, it might.

"Please," he added in that warm baritone. "I was actually really enjoying myself. What's work for one man is a joy for another."

She relaxed a bit, sensing he had that effect on most people. "All right, Isaiah. We'll break the rules just this once. I'll go see Doreen."

"Do you want me to go with you, Mom?" Grace asked.

Susannah considered that and knew that Doreen would feel ambushed if two Wingates showed up at her door. "Why don't you get the box of books from your car for the library."

"A box of books?" Isaiah asked, turning to Grace. "Would you like some help carrying that?"

"Sure, yes. Thank you. It's only one box, but it's heavy."

It wouldn't be a problem for this man, Susannah thought as she went back into the hall and glanced up the back stairs, still trying to comprehend what had happened here.

Something was not quite right at Wingate House and only one person had the answers.

Susannah stood outside the door to Doreen's apartment and lifted her hand to knock, unable to remember the last time she'd been inside. She remembered it consisted of two bedrooms, a bathroom, a living area, and a small but fully functioning kitchen, but she'd only been in it when there'd been some work to do on the flooring.

She knew the apartment cried for an update and a clean out. Doreen wasn't a hoarder, but she sure liked her *stuff*.

Tapping on the door, she called, "Good morning, Doreen. It's Susannah. I heard you're not feeling well."

There was no answer, but on the other side of the door she could hear some footsteps and the click of the lock turning.

"I'm fine, Susannah," she said as she opened the door a crack. "Can't a person take a day off once in a while?"

Susannah blinked, not that the snarky comment surprised her, but the fact that Doreen's green eyes were red-rimmed and puffy. She looked every one of her seventy-some years, even thinner than usual, with her skin ashen and a network of creases on her cheeks like she'd just gotten up.

Yes, it could have been a cold. But had she been crying? Was she *capable* of crying?

"Are you okay?" Susannah asked, reaching for her.

Doreen inched back quickly, never one to accept the least bit of physical touch. "Of course I'm okay."

"You have a guest working in the kitchen."

"I know that," she fired back. "He wanted to cook so bad, I would have hurt his feelings saying no. I needed... rest. I'm feeling weary. Don't you ever get that way?"

"Every day this week," Susannah admitted. "Please take a few days off, Doreen. We can cover for you."

"I'm covered."

"Has...Diane, is it? Has she finished cleaning?"

She rolled her eyes. "She quit a few days ago."

Susannah sucked in a breath.

"Don't worry," Doreen said. "We got this."

"We?" She gave Doreen a hard look. "You and the guest named Isaiah?"

"He's a godsend," Doreen said softly, using a tone Susannah wasn't sure she'd ever heard before. "He fixed a broken pipe in the Madeline. He swept outside, cleaned the rooms, and breakfast? Well, you can smell how good that was."

"He doesn't work here," Susannah said, slightly aghast. "He's a paying guest, and we have no insurance, or pay or—"

"I'll pay him under the table."

"You'll do no such thing," Susannah said.

Doreen's face fell. "I like him, Susannah. And he wants to stay. He's already asked me for a job."

Susannah swallowed, so removed from this business with her mind completely occupied by Rex. She didn't have time to hire, fire, or manage the staff, and that really was Doreen's job.

"All right," she conceded. "But he's in a room? The Grace? And we're charging him? That won't do."

"He's been out to the cottage in the back and seemed to like it. He could stay there."

Susannah drew back. "It's mostly storage space with a bathroom."

"He liked it and offered to clean it out, so..." She shrugged. "He said he could stay there. It was once a maid's quarters, you know. I lived there before this apartment was available, but well, that's long before you were around."

She loved to remind Susannah that she'd been on the premises much longer than Susannah had been a Wingate.

Before Susannah could respond, Doreen's eyes narrowed. "Why are you here and not at the hospital?"

Only then did she realize Doreen hadn't even asked about Rex.

"Rose is there, and Rex has PT this morning. He's coming home soon, we hope."

"Okay. I was wondering."

"I'm sorry if you've been in the dark, Doreen," she said, and meant the apology. "It's been a difficult week. I thought Madeline was keeping you informed of Rex's progress."

She flicked off the apology. "I don't care. I just wanted to be sure he didn't die."

Susannah startled at that bluntness, though she shouldn't after all these years. Doreen wouldn't know a social grace if it bit her. "No, he didn't," she said softly. "And for that I am eternally grateful."

Doreen's eyes flicked as though...as though she wasn't happy Rex had lived. Surely Susannah misread that, or it was just one of this woman's many struggles with social interaction.

"Okay. Fine." Doreen started to close the door in Susannah's face, but froze, her eyes narrowing. "If Rex died, would you keep me on?"

Susannah nearly reeled backwards. "Doreen, how can you even—"

"Please, don't bother with your sugarcoated talk, Susannah. I'm here because Rex's dad made me a promise. You know it, I know it, and Rex knows it. If my insurance policy keeled over from a stroke, I'd be packing my bags. It's all I can think about this week."

Her...*insurance policy*? That's what she thought of Rex, who'd paid her salary for fifty years?

"Doreen, that's nonsense. The Wingates are a family and we are all connected to Rex's father and his grandfather, and this beautiful inn that you have managed so masterfully for longer than I have known you."

Doreen stared at her like she wasn't buying a thing.

"You absolutely must rid yourself of the idea that we would ever ask you to leave," Susannah continued, not caring if it was "sugarcoated." In this regard, she represented the Wingate family name and Susannah never let that tarnish. "You will live and work at Wingate House until you no longer want to, and at that point, you know we will take care of you. We're indebted to you."

"Well, *you* aren't," Doreen muttered.

Susannah wasn't sure what that meant, but she also knew she didn't want to continue this conversation for one more minute. "You have nothing to worry about, Doreen."

The other woman nodded and sighed. "All right. Bye."

And this time the door closed, and latched.

As she walked back down the stairs, Susannah sighed, certain she'd never figure that woman out. Anytime she mentioned her to Rex, he just shuddered and called her a burden he'd inherited.

As she reached the bottom of the steps, she headed toward the front of the house, pausing at the living room and hearing voices from the library, immediately recognizing Grace's and their brand new employee's low, Southern tone.

"Oh, you were a Marine?" she heard Grace ask.

"Yes, ma'am. Just out after twenty years."

"Really? That's..."

Susannah held back, unable to see or be seen, but she didn't want to interrupt what would surely be a personal conversation. Because of course Grace was about to tell him that her husband had been a Marine, too. That might be tough but—

"Well, thank you so much for carting that box for me, Isaiah. I appreciate it. I better get going."

Or maybe she wouldn't tell him.

"Sure, sure, happy to help."

On the beat of silence, Susannah started to walk in, but froze when she heard Isaiah say, "Could I ask you a question, Grace?"

"Of course."

"Would you be free for a cup of coffee sometime in the next few days?"

Susannah felt her eyes widen as she sucked in a silent breath. *Say yes, Grace! Say yes!*

"No, thank you," she said simply. "I'm afraid I'm just too busy."

"Oh, sure, but—"

"I better go find my mother."

Grace came barreling out of the library, flushed, and that only deepened at the sight of her mother. "Oh. I'm done here, Mom. Let's go. Dad's probably wondering where you are."

Susannah stood silent for a moment, staring at Grace's back as she walked away, then followed her to the car.

As they settled into their seats, Susannah decided she had to know what was going on in Grace's head.

"So, I heard Isaiah ask you out for coffee. He's a nice man. Why did you run off like you'd seen the ghost of Coraline?"

"We just talked about this," Grace said, holding up her left hand. "I'm wearing this ring. He saw it, I know he did. I saw him looking at it. He has no idea I'm a widow and yet he asked me out for coffee. No, thank you. That's no Marine."

"You think he was lying about being a Marine? Because I just agreed to hire him."

Grace shot her a surprised look, then her expression softened. "No, I don't think he was lying, but no *decent*

Marine would ask a woman wearing a wedding ring to have coffee. So, not my type."

As much as she'd like to think differently, Susannah knew it would be a long, long time before Grace ever took that ring off. Maybe never.

Chapter Ten

Raina

After Tori and Kenzie blew into the café and took over the kitchen, Raina headed to Dad's office, finally ready to dive into the task of running his property management and real estate firm.

Wingate Properties took up one whole two-story brick building on Wingate Way, which Jack said was just plain crazy. She could hear his voice as she walked toward the building.

"This is choice real estate in a town with no room for growth!" he'd exclaimed. "Why is Rex hogging it?"

She could see why an outsider would think that. With gorgeous river views, Wingate Way was just off the tourist-filled main street but still able to attract great tenants. A creative developer would repurpose the old bank, bringing in high-end retail or restaurants on the first floor and redesigning the upstairs—which was mostly Dad's private office—into two condos.

Of course, that would have produced a whole lot more cash.

When Jack suggested that to her father, she thought

Dad would explode. Did Jack Wallace have no appreciation for history? he demanded.

Well, Jack Wallace had an appreciation for *profit*. No matter how many times Raina explained that the First Bank of Fernandina Beach was started and built by her great-grandfather one hundred and ten years earlier, he didn't care. Money was left on the table and, in Jack's opinion, that was a dumb place for money to be.

Reginald Wingate—the First—built empires in these walls, and when his son took over and eventually shifted the family business completely from banking to real estate, he'd turned the space behind the eight-foot-diameter vault door into his private office.

Dad had moved his office upstairs but kept the vault door open, and the office inside was a museum-like replica from the past, complete with an old-school phone and typewriter, and pictures of her grandfather and great-grandfather next to Henry Flagler, John D. Rockefeller, and Harry Truman.

"Restaurants and condos?" She gave a little shiver as she opened the main door, sad that her husband didn't see the value of history over cash flow.

She walked through a large two-story entry, warmed by the exposed brick and light pouring in from the second-floor window. A young woman Raina didn't recognize was seated behind a computer, and greeted her with a smile.

"Hello, welcome to Wingate Properties," she said. "I'm Ellen. Are you looking for an agent or information on our properties?"

"Hi, Ellen. I'm Raina Wingate."

"Oh!" She popped up immediately, a smile stretching as she extended her hand. "Raina! I've heard so much about you. We're happy you're here. Although not happy about your father. Any news? Is he still in the hospital?"

"He's doing much better and we're hoping he'll be home soon," she said. "Thank you for asking."

"Of course. We've all been thinking about him." She pressed her hands to her chest. "We love him, you know."

Raina smiled. "We all do."

"We heard you'd be coming in one of these days, so I'm sorry I didn't recognize you."

"That's totally fine. I'm not on Amelia Island very often." Which, right that minute— standing in the sunshine surrounded by memories and history—felt like a darn shame. "His assistant is Blake, right? Is he here?"

"Yes, Blake Youngblood. Let me buzz him down and he can show you around."

"I know my way, if it's easier." She gestured toward the staircase that led upstairs. "Can I just go up?"

"Absolutely, Ms. Wingate. Or is it...Mrs. Wallace?"

"Just Raina, please." She gave a quick wave and headed up the massive staircase, stopping at the top to take in the open area, her heart melting at the sight. For so many, many years, this had been her happy place.

As they grew up, the four older Wingate girls had all found their passions—Rose wanted to be in a garden, Tori in a kitchen, and Madeline at the sewing machine. But Raina wanted to be right here, reading the old-school

MLS listings in a physical book that arrived every week like a little pile of gold.

She'd loved listening to Dad "wheel and deal," as he used to call it, greeting clients, and combing the local newspaper for new houses to sell. This was where she learned to love the business of helping people sell their greatest assets or buy their lifelong dreams.

She'd spent endless hours at this office while still in high school, working part-time, and as an intern during her summer breaks from the University of Florida, where she earned an MBA in five years.

She'd studied for her real estate license exam here, wrote up her first contract in this room, and received her first commission check from a very proud papa right in front of that window.

In her early twenties, she'd worked at a desk that was still there—although no one was seated at it now—and had enjoyed the first blush of true success when a development at the south end of the island selected her as the exclusive agent for all their new homes.

At twenty-five, she attended a real estate conference in Orlando and, suddenly, her trajectory, her priorities, and her life changed. That was where she met Jack Wallace, a Miami real estate agent brimming with unbridled ambition, a charming personality, and heart-stopping good looks. Almost instantly, they were involved, and the fire burned hot.

The closer she got to Jack, the further she got from Rex...and her whole family, to be fair.

Jack was no fan of small towns or big families or legacies that were "handed to you," as he described her long-term plan to someday succeed her father in the business.

When she was thirty, they started Wallace & Wingate and the sky seemed to be the limit. At thirty-three, she started to desperately want a child, and Jack agreed to one—with a nanny, so she didn't step away from their thriving business—and she was pregnant within the year.

At thirty-five, she lost the first one at eight weeks. At thirty-nine, the second at ten weeks. The last one, when she was forty-two, made it to eleven and a half weeks before the cramps and bleeding and agonizing disappointment.

She sighed and looked around, sad for lost dreams and babies and businesses and—

"So you are the famous Raina Wingate." The voice made her whip around to face the doorway to Dad's office, where a man stood silhouetted by the light behind him.

"Blake?" she guessed, the light making it hard for her to see him.

"At your service." He took a few steps closer and she realized he was much younger than he sounded, somewhere in his late twenties, wearing what they used to call "preppie style" of a blue button-down and khakis. His hair was slicked back with plenty of product, his cheeks clean-shaven.

He walked across the hardwood floor like he owned the place. Like Raina used to when she was an intern and

Rex was out of the office. She liked to pretend, but this guy looked serious about his game.

"As I live and breathe!" he cooed, reaching out a hand. "Raina Wingate is real. I was beginning to think you were just folklore."

She smiled, not at all sure what that meant. It hadn't been that long since Dad's stroke. Was she that late?

"Blake Youngblood." He shook her hand with a power grip. "Assistant to Rex Wingate, big fan of your work."

Fan of...her work? "Thanks. I, uh, wanted to get in here sooner, but—"

"That's fine. All is well."

She stared at him for a moment, feeling scrutinized by his intense gaze. "Good to hear," she said. "I've promised him I'll take care of everything—"

"No!"

No? Did he just say...*no?*

"I mean, you don't have to. I've got it under control."

Did he, now?

"You just stay with your family, Raina. Can I call you Raina?"

"Of course." She regarded him, wondering why Dad would pick this young man as an assistant. Yes, he liked a go-getter, but there was a patina of something unreal about him, and Dad never liked a slick agent.

Of course, Blake wasn't an agent, he was an assistant.

"I'm spending plenty of time with my family and my dad—"

"Oh my gosh, I'm so blown away by meeting you I forgot to ask. How is he?"

Blown away by meeting her? Was he serious?

"He's improving every day," she said. "But he won't be back at work for a while. So, I'll be the resident Wingate until then." She looked behind him at the door to her father's office. "I think I'll get to work."

He didn't move. "Not necessary, Raina. There's nothing for you to worry about."

She wasn't sure if he was being super helpful or physically blocking her way.

"You have a big family! Go be with the girls and your stepmother."

"My..."

No one called Suze a "step" mother, even if the term was technically accurate. How would he even know that Susannah wasn't her biological mother?

"How *is* Susannah holding up?" He crossed his arms and shook his head. "That woman is a rock, is she not? I only met her briefly, but I get the impression she's a true steel magnolia. Am I right?"

Oof, she wanted to put this guy in his place. Send him for coffee or flick him out of sight. But, out of deference to her father—and Susannah "let's keep up appearances" Wingate—Raina kept a smile in place.

"That she is. And I thank you for wanting to be sure I'm with my family. I promise you, I am. But now, I'm here. So..." She gestured and started walking. "I'll use my father's office."

"Oh, I don't think he'd like that," he said so quickly

she jerked to a stop, giving him her best "are you kidding me" look. "I mean, he's fussy about who goes in there," he added. "I can set you up at a desk downstairs in the agents' cubes—"

"Blake." She narrowed her eyes. "I'll be in my father's office. Thank you."

He stared down at her, looking like he might give her grief, but finally backed away with a nod. "Of course. Do you need anything, Raina? Some coffee or water?"

"Just the files of every open project, any pending contracts, calls that need to be returned, and the password to get into his computer."

He opened his mouth, then wisely shut it again. "You bet. I'll have all of that to you in a few minutes."

With one more quick smile, she finally got past the gatekeeper and breezed into Dad's office, pausing at the doorway when memories, emotions, and sudden deep love for her father hit her.

She could practically smell his lingering aftershave, and hear the echo of his booming voice. She could sense his presence and his power. The heady sensation took her back to those days when she'd rush in here, so proud and ready to let him know she had an offer on a house or got a new client for the firm.

Even on their most successful and exciting day at Wallace & Wingate, she'd never replicated that thrill.

She dropped her bag on the sofa and rounded the desk to his oversized leather chair. Plopping down, she spun it around to look out the window, across Wingate Way to the water visible between the carnation-pink cottage that was Rose's florist shop and the two-story white stucco of Madeline's dress shop.

There'd been a time when all she wanted to do was sit in this chair and make her father proud. Then she'd given that up for Jack.

And now? Did she even have Jack? Had she sacrificed all this for nothing?

She couldn't even think about that. It hurt too much.

Raina was lost in the details of a complicated contract that had just come back from a lawyer when she heard the distinctive tone of a FaceTime call from her phone. Expecting a call from any one of her sisters, the name on the screen gave her a physical jolt and she couldn't tap the button fast enough.

"Hey there, stranger." She smiled at the sight of her husband's face, the first time she'd seen him since she left Miami. "This is exciting."

He gave a soft laugh and ran his hand through his hair, which still hadn't been trimmed.

"No excitement, just wanted to touch base and let you know we got offers on two units in the Jimenez brothers' Brickell property."

"Oh, that's great." Not as great as, say, calling because he missed her, but she took it.

Lifting the phone as she leaned back, she asked, "Guess where I am?"

He squinted, then she flipped the view on the phone and did a slow scan.

"Chez Rex?" he guessed.

"Bingo." She turned the camera back and eased into the chair, glad for the flattering backlight of the window. "Finally made it in here and I'm going through a stack of stuff. Congrats on the two offers. I'm sure Rodrigo and Emil are over the moon."

"Rodrigo is."

She laughed. "Don't tell me. Emil told you to counter at twenty percent higher.'"

He didn't smile at their longstanding inside joke about the client. "Only fifteen, but I think we have a deal."

"That's fantastic," she said.

"How's Rex?" he asked quickly. "Any change? Any news?"

She settled back to give him a report. "Definitely improving, but it will be a slow road. We can understand him when he talks now, though it's still slurred. But his doctor thinks he's on track to go home in a few days."

"Then are you coming back?" he asked, and she tried to read the tone. Was that hopeful or...not?

She took a deep breath and opted not to play games. "Do you want me to?"

"Raina," he chided. "Don't ask stupid questions."

"Well, I can't answer yours yet. I'm not sure how long I'll stay. I've just begun to dig through any and all Wingate business, so I don't know how much he really needs me here."

"I'm sure he needs you there."

And was that his way of saying he wanted her to stay up here?

She sighed in frustration. After sixteen years of marriage, she should know what her husband was thinking.

"I just don't know yet," she said vaguely.

"How's everyone else?" he asked.

"Suze is hanging in there, but this is hard on her. My sisters are all good, at least as much as can be expected. There's talk of Tori moving here."

"Seriously?"

"Well, Rose is talking about it. But I don't think it's that far-fetched. Chloe's getting married in...just over a month."

He gave a soft laugh. "I know, Raina."

She skipped the part about the bridesmaid dress fitting coming up, since he obviously wasn't interested.

"Well, I hope that wedding isn't the next time I see you," she said.

For a second—a flash, really—she thought she saw something in his expression that said...that would be the next time.

Then, he shook his head. "No, no," he said vaguely.

After an awkward beat, she switched the phone to her other hand and asked, "How are things at Dub-n-Dub?"

Again, she'd hoped for at least a whisper of a smile at their private nickname for the company, but he just frowned and dragged his fingers through his hair again.

"You know, the usual."

If she knew, she wouldn't have asked. "Any news on my listings?"

"We sold the one off Old Cutler."

"Oh, the house you were going to rent?"

His eyes flickered. "Yeah, Lisa got a fat offer over asking, so we jumped on it."

We, we, we. It was starting to irritate.

"But the McGradys gave the Pinecrest listing to Century 21, so there's that. And we had a closing yesterday that went...awry." He chuckled, maybe for the first time since they'd gotten on the phone. "We salvaged it."

She braced herself for another "Lisa saved the day" comment, but he looked away and muttered something to someone off-camera.

Then he turned back to her. "Dani sends her love."

At least someone did.

"Give her a hug." She shifted in her seat. Small talk seemed a little sad, considering the "big" talk they needed to have, but she didn't get the sense he wanted to get into anything now. "So, what's on the schedule these days?" she asked.

"What isn't?" he said, looking down at his desk. "We have an open house for the Key Biscayne property on—"

"Oh, Harbor Drive. Of course!" That was her major listing, and she and Dani had moved mountains to set up the perfect party for the open house. Good heavens, that all felt like a million miles away.

"We have it all covered," he assured her. "Lisa actually brought in her own staging company, an outfit we've never used, and you'd die at how gorgeous it looks. We'll have an offer before the end of the day on Sunday."

She managed not to respond. "The owner wanted a champagne tower. Did we—"

"No. It's not 2014, Rain. We went with signature cocktails."

"Oh, okay." She wasn't in the mood to fight for the champagne tower or to ask how he was able to get out of the staging contract she'd signed with her favorite vendor. "That all sounds good, Jack."

"Oh, and I have one more piece of amazing news." He smiled again and looked...at the camera or over the top of his phone at someone else in the room. She couldn't tell, but a low bubble of true discomfort rose in her chest.

"What's that?"

"Two words. Indian Creek."

She frowned at the reference to the area that was known as a "Billionaire Bunker" in Biscayne Bay. There were fewer than fifty homes, and not one could be touched for under twenty million. "What about it?"

"Well, we've been trying to crack that place for ages, right?"

"We got a listing there?" she guessed, sitting up a little straighter in shock.

"Lisa worked some magic, I guess," he said on a laugh. "And really enjoyed sticking it to Coldwell."

Her throat tightened, threatening to betray her true reaction to something that normally would have been cause to celebrate. She didn't care about Lisa's magic. Or beating the big conglomerate competitor. Or even getting a listing on Indian Creek Island.

She'd had enough. And whether he wanted her to or not, she needed to get home and claim her husband.

"Oh, I gotta run, Rain. I have to take this call."

"But, Jack, we need to—"

"I'll call you back!"

The screen went blank and all she was staring at was a list of apps on top of a picture of the man who'd just hung up on her.

She *had* to get home.

"Knock-knock!" Blake called brightly from right outside the door, making her wonder just how much of that conversation he had heard.

"Yes?"

He came in, holding a stack of papers. "This just got delivered by courier. An offer on a house near the Ritz-Carlton that Rex has been working on for a few weeks. Would you like to review it? I can handle it if you prefer."

"I'll do it." She reached out her hand for the contract. "There's nothing I love more than a good offer."

"You'll probably want to counter," he said. At her look, he added, "I mean, it's low and Rex—"

"Thank you," she said as she took the papers, just a little bit sick of other people doing her job.

"Sure, sure. Is that all?"

She looked at him for a moment. Was it that hard to find good help, or did Dad smell real untapped talent? He'd groomed many an assistant into fine real estate agents and used the position to build his pool of high performers. It was one of his most successful business strategies.

She gave him a tight smile. "Yes, that'll be—no, wait. I do have a question, Blake."

"Anything at all," he said.

"I've been looking for something my dad was working on at home, but can't seem to find the file."

"Sure, what is it?"

If only she knew. "A contract, I think. Or maybe a cancellation? It was definitely a debt cancellation." She didn't know why, but her gut instinct was to keep the "it was burnt to a crisp" part to herself.

He shook his head, genuinely baffled. "That is not ringing any bells."

"Okay. Well, maybe you could check his files? I'd like to look into it."

"Can't you just ask him?"

"No stress, doctor's orders. So I'm keeping all business away from him."

"Oh, good...good call, Raina. I'll go digging for recent cancelled contracts ASAP." He pivoted and exited, leaving her with a new offer and a heavy heart.

For some reason, even being in the office that she'd dreamed would someday be hers when Dad retired, work wasn't giving her any joy today.

Bet it was bringing Lisa joy, though.

She curled her lip at the thought and started planning when she could at least slip away for a quick night or two with her husband.

Chapter Eleven

Tori

Between the trip to the airport where she had to say goodbye to Kenzie, an unexpected late-morning rush, and the fact that Miguel, the line cook, had never made braised short rib tacos before, Tori's day was definitely derailed.

So when her phone buzzed with a text from Madeline reminding Tori that she had a bridesmaid dress fitting in five minutes, she almost cried.

"I can't leave now!"

"Sure you can," Miguel assured her. "I got this."

"But those specials? I didn't mean to throw the tacos at you, but I really think customers will like them."

"They will love them, and I watched you make them. I can do it." He grinned at her. "Maybe not with such flair, but I'll try."

"Good, good." It had been a long time since she'd worked a restaurant kitchen, having parlayed her culinary degree into a catering business many years ago. But she knew how a restaurant like the Riverfront Café should run, and with the right people? She could make it sing.

And it had been her contribution to the promise the sisters had made, so working here—like Raina picking up Dad's projects at his office and all of them pitching in to help Suze prepare for Dad's homecoming—made her feel useful.

And God knows she was needed, since the chef/manager, Jim Elliott, had fallen off the face of the Earth.

She grabbed her bag and hustled out to the front of house, spying Bambi seating two customers.

"Bridesmaid dress fitting," Tori mouthed to the hostess.

But Bambi scowled and shook her head, holding up a finger to ask Tori to wait, chatting with another customer for a second, then finally hustling over to Tori.

"You can't leave," she said.

"I can. Miguel has this. We're good, and I promised—"

"Jim Elliott is on his way in, acting like he hasn't been on a bender for the better part of a week."

Shoot. Now?

"What did you tell him?" Tori asked.

"That we had a new temporary manager and chef, and her name is Wingate." She cocked her head and gave a look like she just loved saying that. "I don't think he was happy about that. He kind of hates your dad."

"Excuse me?" Who hated Rex Wingate?

She lifted a shoulder. "He calls him T-Rex because, well, Mr. Wingate has given him a few stern warnings."

"How many?"

"I lost count."

"Then why doesn't my father fire him?"

"I don't know, Tori. He keeps giving him another chance. Good help is hard to get, I guess."

Tori just shut her eyes, thinking. Not that there was much to consider. A head cook on a nearly week-long drinking binge had to go.

"Okay. What's he look like?"

"That." She nodded toward the door, where a man with a weathered complexion and a serious scowl stood. His thin white hair was pulled back into a ponytail, his taut but thin arms covered in tattoos.

"Okay. I'm going to take this outside where it's private. Please do me a favor and call Raina at Wingate Properties and see if you can get his last check cut before I get back."

Bambi drew back with a nod of respect. "Sure thing. And good luck."

"Thanks. Do I need it?"

"He can be a pain in the butt and rough around the edges," Bambi said. "But he has to know this was coming."

"Here I go." Squaring her shoulders, Tori walked straight toward him but he instantly started off toward the kitchen.

"Mr. Elliott," she said.

He threw her a look. "Sorry, lady, I'm late for work."

As he took another step, she snagged his arm, and he froze, turning to pin beady blue eyes on her.

"Can I help you?" he asked with sheer disgust in his voice.

"My name is Victoria Wingate. Let's take a walk, Mr. Elliott."

A little bit of the color in his cheeks disappeared, but he nodded and silently walked with her out the front door. She paused for a moment, then eyed the wharf along the river. A tourist trolley was parked nearby with all the seats full and the tour guide starting a spiel. People milled about, waiting for a ferry to Cumberland Island, leaving no privacy anywhere.

"This way," she said, gesturing to where there were fewer people, just a lot of boats. "I want to talk to you."

They'd crossed a small bridge and reached the widest dock, and started walking when she realized that he'd yet to ask about Dad.

"Perhaps you haven't heard that my father is in the hospital," she said, giving him the benefit of the doubt.

He snorted. "Oh, I heard. That's all the talk was at the Palace," he said, referring to a popular bar. "He owns half the town, so I bet you'd get a sweet piece of Wingate pie if he kicks."

Revulsion rolled through her, but she maintained her composure. "He doesn't own half the town," she said. "Not even close. But he does own the business where you work and have seen fit to not show up for several days."

"Well, with Rex out..."

"You thought you could get away with not working?"

He turned and stared at the water, clearly avoiding eye contact. "Look, I know I been gone a few days, but there was a death in my family."

"Oh." She inched back, suddenly wondering if she'd been too hasty. "I'm so sorry," she said. "Who passed away?"

"Uh, my, uh..." He looked down at the dark water. "My fish." With that, he let out a muffled guffaw.

"Was your job a joke to you, Mr. Elliott?"

His eyes crinkled as if the answer to that was a big resounding *yes*. "Life's a joke to me, Vicky."

God, she hated to be called that. Probably as much as Rex would hate T-Rex.

"Well, the Wingate businesses are not a joke," she informed him. "We run them efficiently and with what we hope is a tremendous amount of understanding and flexibility for our employees."

"Oh, Rex has been understanding all right." He gave that snort-laugh again. "But I don't want to push the old SOB to another stroke, so if you don't mind, I'll just..." He tried to pass her and she shifted her stance to block him.

"I do mind. Look at me."

He finally did, eye to eye, since he was just about the same five-foot-six that she was. "What?"

They stared at each other for a moment, the only sound a soft clang of a metal clamp against a nearby sailboat mast and the splash when that boat rocked in the water.

"We're terminating your employment with the Riverfront Café, Mr. Elliott."

He curled a lip, looking left and right, then spit on the wooden dock. "Get out of my way, Vicky."

Her heart kicked up, but more in anger than fear. "Your last check will be waiting for you at the front desk of Wingate Properties," she said steadily. "You will no longer be welcome at the restaurant."

He looked hard at her now, giving her a chance to see his eyes were really red and his face pockmarked.

He drew in a breath so hard his nostrils flared, coming closer. "One push, Vicky, and you'll be in that water."

"You lay a hand on me and you will regret it until the day you die."

"Oh, you're his daughter all right." He started to go past her, purposely bumping her shoulder with his.

She didn't say a word, but held her breath and her ground, vaguely aware that the sailboat rocked again, as if someone were in the cabin, but she didn't dare take her eyes off the man retreating from her.

He took three more steps, then whipped around. "You can't do this!" he hollered, so loud his voice bounced off the water.

"I'm doing it."

"You can't!" His eyes tapered to slits just before he lunged toward her.

"Hey!" A man's voice cut into the air along with his body, jumping off the boat and onto the dock. He pounced on Elliott and pushed him to the wooden deck with a thud, his back to Tori.

"The lady would like you to leave," she heard him say. "You need help with that?"

Elliott shook him off and managed to struggle to his feet while the other man popped up with ease.

"Go!" the man ordered with a slight push to his shoulder.

Elliott threw Tori a dark look and took off, striding away while her rescuer watched to make sure he was gone.

"Thank you so—"

When he turned, she froze, blinked, and stared in complete shock. "Dr. Verona?"

"Justin," he corrected. "It's my day off."

"Not from heroics," she replied, brushing some wind-blown hair from her face with a trembling hand, still not believing...anything. "Seriously, thank you for the help."

"I heard the confrontation and came up from..." He jutted his chin to the sailboat docked next to him.

"Oh, that's your boat?"

"Also my home."

"Your..." She inched back, taking a moment to drink in the size of the two-masted sailboat, then looked back at him, a whole different "doctor" in a faded navy T-shirt and board shorts. "You live aboard?"

"I do," he said, shrugging broad shoulders, eyeing her. "I'd ask if that was a lover's quarrel, but I've spent enough time around you to know he's not your type."

"Oh! No, I was firing him from the Riverfront Café and he was none too pleased."

"Ahh." He nodded, a slow smile forming. "Well, good

timing then. You work at the café? I've never seen you there and I'm a regular."

"It's a Wingate property that my dad owns, and I've been subbing while..." She glanced over her shoulder. "Our regular cook decided to take some completely unapproved time off."

"I see."

But she didn't. "Wow, you really do pop up in the most unexpected places in my life."

He gave her a wide smile and it felt like the sun just came out for the second time. "Why do you think that is?"

"Um...kismet? Destiny? Serendipity?"

"Serendipity." He dragged the word out and crossed his arms. "I like that."

"As a reason we keep meeting?"

"For her new name." He gestured to the sailboat's stern, where a shadow of words was all that was left of whatever the beautiful boat had once been christened. "She was the *Carpe Diem*, but that's so cliché, don't you think? I was looking for something a little more..." He slid into another smile and melted her with a look. "Charming and unexpected," he finished.

Wait a second. Was he flirting with her?

Why, yes, he was, and she was here for it, as Kenzie would say. "Yeah, I get that. Charming is...good."

"Or I could just go with *Hottypants*."

She choked a laugh that came right from her belly. "Well, you might get trolled in the water, but, hey.

Captain Hottypants has a ring to it, and certainly meets the 'unexpected' criteria."

"Just like you," he said softly, the compliment almost caught in the wind.

"Well...Dr....Justin." She took a step backwards, unable to take her gaze off him. "Thank you so much for being my savior."

"My pleasure. But, um, Tori. I was about to give ol' *No-Name* a run in the wind." He gazed up at the tall mast, the breeze clanking metal against it with the same force her heart hit her ribs. "Would you like to join me?"

More than she wanted her next breath. But she couldn't blow off the fitting, since Chloe had come up from Jacksonville and Madeline ran a tighter ship than the handsome sailor in front of her.

Reluctantly, she shook her head. "I have a dress fitting for a wedding."

"We did establish that the family wedding is not yours. I hope."

He *hoped*?

"Oh, no, not me. I'm...single. Really single. Single as a Pringle, as the kids say." Oh, good God in heaven. *Shut up, Tori!* At least he had the good grace to laugh. "The fitting is for a bridesmaid dress. My little sister is the one getting married."

"I know, your mother told me. Or is she your stepmother? I get confused with your family."

"It's a confusing family," she assured him. "Susannah is my stepmother, but she's been around since I was a little girl, so we just call her...our mother."

"And Suze."

Wow, he was observant. "Yeah." She glanced behind him to really look at the scope of the boat. "You really live on it? I mean, her?"

"I do. I joined the neurology group near the hospital a few months ago and I just...I don't know. The idea of buying a house and settling down just didn't appeal to me. I bought the boat and thought I'd stay on it for a few weeks, and that was six months ago."

"Wow. That's...so free." The idea was utterly... romantic. Probably not practical, comfortable, or realistic, but quite dreamy.

"I am free." He added a smile and the breeze lifted up a few thick locks of dark brown hair.

"That's...nice." She took another step backwards. "I better go, but, really, thank you for swooping in and rescuing me. Considering I've spilled coffee on you and then hung a nickname you'll never lose around your neck, it was very kind of you."

"I would never ignore a woman in trouble. You were holding your own with the guy, but I didn't want to have to dive in and perform CPR."

Too bad. She might have liked that.

"And thanks for the invitation." She eyed the long white vessel, imagining the sound of the sails flapping in the wind as it cruised over open water.

"Maybe next time, Tori."

"Yes," she said. "Next time. I guess I'll...see you around."

"Well, your father's going home soon, so unless you come with him to the neurology appointments..."

She bit her lip, liking where this was going. "You can find me in the Riverfront Café, for now anyway."

"Okay, I'll look for you."

"Great." She gave a wave. "All right, then. Bye."

She took a step back, then turned and started to walk.

"Um, wait, Tori."

She turned, her heart doing really stupid things at the way he said her name. "Hmm?"

"Speaking of weddings..."

And then her heart darn near stopped. "Yes?"

"This is kind of crazy, but..." He took a few steps closer. "One of the other neurologists' daughter is getting married this weekend and I...I need a plus one. I think that's what they call it now. I'd just call it a date."

She stared at him, truly speechless.

"Would you consider going with me?" he asked.

"To a wedding?"

"It's right here on Amelia Island, at the Ritz, so if you don't have a dress or—"

"Yes." The word was out like it had a life of its own. "I mean, no, I didn't pack a dress but, well, I have a lot of sisters and one is a dressmaker, so..." She felt like she was melting in the sun and didn't hate one second of it. "I could go."

"Really? That'd be awesome. It's Saturday night."

"That sounds...great." It actually sounded like an absolute dream, but she managed not to say something stupid.

"Why don't you, uh..." He reached into his pocket and pulled out his phone. "Give me your number. Here you go."

Their hands brushed as she took the phone he offered and somehow managed to type in her cell number.

"Thank you again, Justin," she said when she gave it back. "I mean, for the save. That guy was a lunatic and you...you're...you're going to let me say something silly again and laugh at me, aren't you?"

He shrugged. "It's fun."

She laughed. "All right, then. Bye."

"Bye, Tori."

With a wave, she turned and walked away, doing everything in her power not to skip and dance down the docks. He already thought she was nuts. And she already thought he was...perfect.

Her own phone buzzed madly, but she didn't bother to look at the text. It was Madeline, she presumed, who was going to kill her for being late. But too bad. This was totally worth it.

Chapter Twelve

Rose

"Lizzie?" Rose called to her manager, currently arranging bouquets in the back of the shop. "I gotta run. Can you watch the front?"

Liz Cooper, a longtime employee, master floral arranger, and all-around great human, popped into the retail section in the front with greens in one hand and ribbons in the other.

"Yes, you do gotta run," she agreed, looking at the clock. "Your sister will not like it if you're late for the fitting."

"She slotted all the Wingate women in like the crazed schedule-making seamstress she is, so..." Rose opened the cabinet under the cash register and grabbed her bag. "You're on for the next hour or so."

"Go have fun," Liz said. "I've got one more order and the truck should be back for the rest of the deliveries any minute. I'll listen for the bell."

Rose blew her a kiss and slid around the counter to the front door, making that bell ding when she opened the door to hustle over to Madeline's studio.

But she hadn't gone twenty steps from her little pink florist shop when she spotted Chloe's car on the street. That was no surprise; she knew Chloe wanted to be here for the fittings and planned to go to the hospital and see Dad, since she hadn't been up here all week. But her sister was in the car, head down, shoulders moving.

Was she crying? Or talking to the dog on her lap?

Rose paused at the front of the car, and when Chloe didn't look up, she tapped the hood. "Hey, there."

Chloe's head shot up and even through the windshield, Rose could see the tears.

"Chloe!" Instantly, she was at the passenger side, reaching for the door. "Are you okay?"

Chloe stared at her, then turned away, looking straight ahead, visibly trying to get her composure while Lady Bug, her little Shih Tzu, scrambled off her lap to bark at Rose.

Finally, Chloe reached over, scooped up the dog, and unlatched the passenger door in a silent invitation for Rose to slide in.

"What's wrong?" Rose asked, taken aback by the streaks of mascara down an otherwise flawless face.

"Would you believe PMS?"

"I might," Rose said, reaching over to give Lady Bug's baseball-sized head a stroke. "But sitting in the car crying when it's dress fitting day seems like extreme PMS. I thought you wanted to be there to see every dress. Isn't Tori up there now?"

"Tori is late. So late, in fact, that I got bored and took Lady Bug for a walk."

"You're not walking. You're crying in your car." She gave a gentle touch to her baby sister's narrow shoulder. "Or is it wedding jitters?"

She finally looked up, her cornflower blue eyes overflowing with more tears. "I hope so."

"I don't understand. What made you cry?"

"A couple who walked by me. They were old, like eighty."

"Were they mean to you? Did they say something?" Rose was beyond baffled.

"They kissed," she sobbed the announcement so hard, Rose was sure she hadn't heard right. In fact, it was so absurd she almost laughed. "On the lips."

"*Oookay*. Was it offensive or something?"

"It was...real." She swiped at her nose, and Rose slid a hand into her purse for the tissue that all mothers of six-year-olds kept handy.

"Why did that upset you?" Rose asked gently, the first flicker of real concern in her chest as she gave the tissue to Chloe.

Her sister took a shuddering breath and dug for control, needing a good five or six seconds as she stroked the dog rolled into a ball on her lap. No wonder little Avery thought Lady Bug was a stuffed animal—she frequently acted like one.

"Because," Chloe finally said, "that's what marriage should be."

Rose stared at her, completely at a loss for how to respond. "Yes, kissing is part of it. Sweet for eighty-year-olds." She frowned and dipped her head, trying to get closer, trying to follow the crumbs Chloe was dropping. "Do you and Hunter kiss?"

She just swallowed.

"Chloe, is everything okay with you and Hunter?"

She sighed, shook her head, then blew her nose so noisily, the dog startled. "It's complicated. Never mind."

"Never mind?" Rose scoffed. "Nope. Sorry, sweet little sis, that won't work."

She searched Rose's face, still not saying anything, but good heavens, it was easy to see she wanted to.

"Really, Rose, it's truly PMS and wedding jitters and...you know. No, never mind, you of all people wouldn't understand. You and Gabe are like...on another level of married. We'll never be like that. Not even on our honeymoon."

Ohhh. Rose felt herself nod lightly. That's what was going on here. She took a slow breath and danced around all the options she had for responding.

"All married couples are different, Chloe. You will never be happy if you compare yourself or your marriage to other people."

Chloe stared straight ahead, silent. "It was the *way* they kissed that got me," she said after a moment.

"Like..." Rose prodded.

"Like they...belonged."

"Well, they've probably been married for sixty years. You get a rhythm." When Chloe didn't respond, Rose dipped her toe into dangerous waters. "You don't think things will be like that with Hunter?" she asked gently.

Chloe plucked at the nearly shredded tissue, letting

Lady Bug sniff it. "They're not now. Will they change with marriage?"

Rose wanted to say yes. Or no. Or, quite honestly, she had no idea. Her marriage had only deepened over the years. "Uh, well, Chloe, it's hard to say. I guess it depends on how much work you guys are willing to do."

"Pfft. Work? Being a resident at Mayo is the only work Hunter has time to do. I barely see him and when I do, it's..." She huffed out a breath. "It's not like that."

"You don't kiss?"

"Well, we do, but it has to have a purpose, if you get my drift."

"Yeah," Rose said. "I get it. And that part of a marriage is really important."

Chloe just shook her head, holding something back, but Rose didn't want to prod into places so private.

"Honey, you are at a very...difficult threshold," she finally said. "You're weeks from your wedding, and Dad's in the hospital, and Hunter has a lot of pressure at work. Don't put too much stock in one kiss."

Her sister just sighed. "I guess."

Rose reached across Chloe's body to snag her left hand, thumbing her knuckles, grazing the sizeable diamond resting on her ring finger, hoping it served as a reminder of why she'd accepted it in the first place, of how she felt—hopefully—every time she looked at it.

"I have an idea," Rose said. "What if you and Hunter could find a day or two to get away from everything—the wedding planning, the stress, your jobs—and just recapture the feeling you had when you were first in love."

"It's hard with Lady Bug," she said.

"I'll take Lady Bug," Rose insisted, reaching for the furball. "I love this little dog, and you know my girls just go crazy for her. We're keeping her for the honeymoon, right?"

Chloe nodded and let her dog climb into Rose's lap so she could compose herself and blow her nose again.

"Well, give us some practice time and take a weekend. Gabe and I love to do that. We talk about when we met, or go over our lives year by year. It's so important to reconnect emotionally. Then everything else falls into place."

She didn't answer right away, but swallowed. "He never has time."

"Yes, I imagine a residency at Mayo is extremely time consuming."

"It is," Chloe agreed. "And sometimes I don't know if it's the job or the fact that this is really the first time we've lived in the same city. Our whole relationship has essentially been long distance and now..."

"Now you're not sure you really know him?" Rose guessed.

"I don't know." Chloe sighed. "I really think it's the stress of being a resident for such a difficult specialty practice."

"When is the residency done?" Rose asked.

"The Monday before the wedding," she said.

So, Rose thought, no time to find out if it is the residency... or the real man with no distance that was causing the problems.

"And I put all my paid time off for the week of the wedding and the honeymoon," Chloe continued. "I had to sell my soul for that. Honestly, it's the worst job in the world."

"Working in the PR agency? I thought you loved it."

She made a face. "It's beyond boring because my accounts are a tax firm, a garage improvement company, and a non-profit that has no budget. Not the glam PR job I'd hoped for when I agreed to move to Jacksonville from D.C."

"But you were so happy he got selected for Mayo."

"Of course! It was close to home and the Mayo Clinic in Jax is prestigious for a young plastic surgeon starting out. But, honestly, the job I got? Let's just say it didn't align with my much bigger professional goals."

"You wanted to be a reporter," Rose said, remembering when Chloe got her Masters in journalism from Georgetown. "But I thought PR was closely related. You work with journalists, right?"

"I write boring press releases and brochure copy. I'm not reporting news or digging for stories." She gave Rose a sad look. "I have had to completely give up the TV dream, but that's okay. I knew that when I fell in love with Hunter."

Rose smiled, thinking of Chloe as a little girl who used to set up a table and stare at an imaginary camera to deliver the family news. It was the cutest thing, and Dad always called her the next Barbara Walters. She certainly had the looks and talent and drive to make it in that competitive arena.

"Why did you have to give that up?" she asked. "They have TV stations in Jacksonville."

Chloe snorted like Rose had suggested she work on the moon. "You don't walk into a mid-size market and get on air, Rose. A TV reporter has to be willing to move. You start in the smallest markets, and keep working your way up. And at twenty-nine? That ship has sailed, I'm sad to say."

Rose found that hard to believe, but she knew Chloe had done her research. "Well, what about a newspaper or even a news website? Can you get a job at a place like that? Not as glamorous, but you'd be reporting."

"It's still about moving and digging into a community. And, let's be real, Rose. Hunter's going to be a plastic surgeon. We'll go to whatever practice makes him the best offer, and that could be anywhere. And then we'll stay there and I will..." She sighed. "Be a doctor's wife."

"You'll be Hunter's wife," Rose said softly. "Married to the man you love. And, yes, marriage means compromise. But you'll find something that fulfills you. I know you will, Chloe."

"Chloe!" The echo of her name was accompanied by a thud on the hood of the car, making Lady Bug bark noisily.

They all reacted to the sight of Tori, who was practically dancing outside the car.

Chloe pushed the door open. "You're so late, you'll be part of Rose and Raina's fitting."

Tori's smile was wide, goofy, and unrestrained. "Yeah, I'm late. Too bad, so sad."

Chloe and Rose shared a look and a soft laugh.

"You'll be sad when you face the wrath of Mad Madeline," Chloe teased, reaching into the back to get her purse and Lady Bug's leash. As she turned, she snagged Rose's gaze. "Thanks," she said. "I'm sure it's just PMS."

"So am I," Rose said, reaching to hug her.

Except Rose wasn't actually sure of that at all, but she wasn't physically capable of bursting anyone's bubble, especially not her dear, darling baby sister.

CHLOE PULLED it together and half an hour later, she was her old self again. Raina showed up early enough to be right on Tori's heels, so the five of them got unexpected time together in the spacious loft studio, surrounded by mirrors and dresses in bags, with Lady Bug sleeping in a patch of sunlight pouring in through the second-floor windows.

And no one could be upset when Tori delivered her news that she was going to a wedding at the Ritz with none other than Dr. Hottypants, as he would forever be known. She was vibrating with happiness.

"It takes the sting out of the fact that Finn couldn't, wouldn't, or wasn't allowed to, by decree of his awful father, come down for his spring break. Now I am free to be...Hottypants's plus one."

They all laughed as she spun on the fitting stage.

"Don't dance those pins out," Madeline warned. "Also, what are you wearing?"

"I don't suppose you could whip a little something up for me."

"No," Madeline said, fighting a smile. "But I have some wedding guest dresses in the showroom downstairs, and I actually have something black and beaded in mind. Ideal for a wedding at the Ritz." She added a nudge. "You're done. Go take this off."

"Perfect!" Tori sang as she gathered up the bright pink silk of her gown and headed toward the dressing room.

Madeline gave them all a "can you believe her" look, making Rose, Chloe, and Raina move even closer on the sofa and chairs around the fitting stage, whispering their reactions.

"He's perfect for her!" Rose announced.

"And just what we need to push her over the edge," Raina added.

"What do you mean?" Chloe asked.

"I think she's playing with the idea of moving here," Rose replied softly. "Now she's working at the Riverfront Café, has a man in town, and if the kids are a yes..." She rubbed her hands together. "She's ours!"

"Wow, she'd move here?" Chloe's eyes got wide. "That'd be amazing."

"What will be amazing is having someone on that stage with a dress on that I can pin," Madeline said from her spot in the middle, only half teasing.

"Come on, Rosebud." Raina pushed up. "Let's go put

them on together and we can come out like a couple of flamingos."

"Flamingos!" Chloe cried. "You don't like the pink?"

Instantly, Raina put her hands over her mouth. "No, I love it, Chloe! We all do!"

"So much," Rose insisted. "And the flowers will be a nice softening point to—"

"I knew this pink was a bad idea." Chloe slumped into the velvet settee. "And it's way too late to change."

"Change?" Madeline practically choked.

"No!" Rose exclaimed. "The color is gorgeous! And I can match the shade on the tablescapes to bring a perfect pop of pink."

"Pop." Chloe made a face. "Like wearing bubble gum."

"Chloe!" The name came out in unison from all of them.

But Chloe let her lower lip stick out as she crossed her arms, clearly miserable. This *had* to be PMS, Rose thought. She was way too unhappy for this to be normal.

"Second thoughts will make you crazy," Rose said, stepping back to sit next to her. "It's a pretty, bright, lovely spring color, and you get to have whatever color you love at your wedding."

"It's a sickening color," she said. "And I didn't pick it. Hunter did."

"Hunter?" Tori choked as she came out holding her dress. "He picked *this*?"

"See? You hate it!" Chloe whined, tears springing to her eyes.

"No, no!" Tori insisted. "It's just so much more...you. That's all."

"Me? Have you ever seen me wear that color? No. He said his mother's bridesmaids wore pink and he had some picture in his house of her wedding, and thought that's the color they had to be." Chloe dropped her face into her hands. "I can't even stand it."

The other sisters all shared shocked looks, at a loss as to how to help. What kind of groom tells his fiancée what color the bridesmaids should wear?

"Well, then, I have an idea," Madeline said, getting all of their attention. "Why don't we take a break from bridesmaids and do a bridal fitting instead? I've added the final lace and buttons to your dress, Chloe, and I'd love to see how it looks."

She looked up, a spark of life back in her eyes. "But Mom isn't here. She wanted to come to that fitting."

"We'll do it again, with Suze and Grace," Rose said, instantly sensing that Madeline's idea was genius.

"But not Sadie."

Now she was just being petulant or looking for reasons to be miserable.

"Sadie's got her dress," Madeline reminded Chloe. "She's having it fitted in Brussels."

"Come on, Chloe." Rose gave her a nudge. "Raina hasn't ever seen the dress on you."

"And I'd love to," Raina said. "But someone get me a tissue, 'cause my baby sis is getting married."

"You?" Madeline scoffed. "I was almost twenty when this girl was born. I held her and loved her like she was my own. And now I'm making her wedding dress."

"Aww." Chloe bit her lip and looked lovingly at Madeline. "You were always like a second mommy to me. I thought everyone had two."

Rose tightened her grip on Chloe's shoulder. "Well, I was twelve when you were born. And you were my living, breathing baby doll who I could dress up."

"I remember," Chloe said. "You used to put flowers in my hair."

"And I will again, when you get married, sweet one."

"We were all so over the moon when the seventh sister came," Tori said, coming closer. "You completed us, Chloe."

"Seven is a perfect number," Raina said. "I remember Dad saying that the day you were born."

"What do you say, Chloe?" Madeline asked. "Let's see how those pleats came out on you."

She exhaled and glanced at Rose. "Will it make me feel better or worse?" she asked on a soft whisper.

Rose had no idea, but she said the only thing she was capable of saying. "Better. Much, much better. And we're all going to cry because we love you so much."

"You're going to cry..." Chloe pushed up. "Because you have to walk down the aisle like six bottles of Pepto Bismol."

They all cracked up, but Chloe and Madeline went off to the find the dress, and all Rose could do was say a prayer that this would help her mood. And that Hunter was the right guy for her little love of a baby sister.

Chapter Thirteen

Susannah

When Susannah pulled into the driveway of the beach house on the day Rex was being discharged, she wasn't surprised to see a number of cars she recognized, with some spillover in front of the bungalow.

Of course, some of her daughters would come home for the big day.

For a moment, all she could do was stare at the house without even opening the garage door, sinking into the pure relief of coming home. The creamy peach stucco always reflected the sun so beautifully, and she'd even come to love the large red brick chimney that ran up the side of the house.

Rex had insisted on it being brick "for balance and a nod to the history of this island," but she'd thought it was out of place.

He was right, of course. Always, always right.

She'd missed this place. She hadn't spent more than a few hours here since Rex had his stroke. She'd drop in to shower, change, pack fresh clothes, but then she went back to the hospital.

She'd slept in that miserable recliner every night, always grateful when one of the girls brought her breakfast, coffee, and begged her to take a break.

She had taken a few, during his brief PT sessions, but for the most part, Susannah had essentially "gone to the hospital" along with her husband. And now...it was time for a new normal.

The very idea made her want to let out a long, sad moan of unhappiness. The mountain ahead was so high, some days she wasn't quite sure she could climb it.

But she would. One step at a time. Starting with getting this place together so Rex could properly rehab here.

Raina assured her that all the equipment she'd ordered had been delivered, but Susannah had never even taken the time to figure out where to put it all.

And she certainly couldn't do that now. Rex was currently in a hospital transport vehicle being driven here. But all he'd need at the moment was his hospital bed, which Raina said the delivery company had set up, and maybe a little bit of space in the game room to work with a physical therapist.

Now that Rex was coming home, she could find the time to unpack the equipment and get Gabe and some of the other firefighters to assemble it, then figure out a way to make it fit downstairs.

One step at a time, Susannah. One step up the mountain.

On a sigh, she clutched her purse and overnight bag, then climbed out of the car. As she did, the front door opened and Madeline and Raina came out to the driveway. Behind them, Rose and Grace followed, and finally Tori and Chloe, who'd come all the way up from Jacksonville.

All of them? Every one of them. Well, not dear Sadie. But all of them who lived on this continent.

For a moment, she just stared, emotions welling up fast enough to make her speechless.

"Girls..." she managed. "How sweet of you to come."

They greeted her with a chorus of "Mom" and "Suze" and "Welcome home," all with arms outstretched for hugs and kisses.

"I honestly didn't expect all of you," she said, stroking Rose's blond hair and smiling into Chloe's eyes. "Didn't you have to work today?"

She wrinkled her nose. "I called in sick with pre-wedding jitters and they bought it."

"Thank you for being here," she said to all of them, glancing from one to the next. "I wondered why no one showed up at the hospital today. I figured you were all busy."

Grace and Tori flanked her, taking her arms.

"Mom," Grace said. "We have a little surprise for you."

"And we don't want you to freak out," Tori added. "Because we know you like things done a certain way, like a good control freak."

Susannah rolled her eyes, but didn't deny the charge.

"What did y'all do?" she asked, slathering the question with her sweetest Georgia accent, making them laugh.

"We did some things," Madeline announced, brushing her dark bangs over her brows, then gesturing toward the door.

"Some...*things*." Susannah narrowed her eyes at them, seeing that they were all conspiratorial and secretive. "You unpacked that equipment for me, didn't you?"

Raina and Rose looked at each other, beaming smiles.

"Thank you, girls. Let's go see where we can put it all."

They all walked through the front door, which led to an entryway on the first floor. She wasn't terribly surprised to see there were no boxes where she expected them to be piled up, and she gave Grace's arm a squeeze.

"I really appreciate that you unpacked all that."

"Mmm," Grace said. "Just keep going."

She paused in the entryway, then glanced to the left. Rex's office was dark. "Did you put it all in there?"

"Nope," Raina said. "That room is off-limits to Dad and if he tries to go in, I will personally change the locks."

"He won't," Susannah said softly. "He's still mastering that wheelchair."

"Come to the game room," Rose said quickly. "But close your eyes."

"Close my—"

"Yes!" they cried in unison.

"Okay, okay." She squeezed them shut and let two of them lead her through the open double doors to a room she knew so well, the site of so much family fun.

"Open now," a few girls said at once.

She did, blinking into the light pouring through the sliding glass doors. She could practically hear all of them holding their breath as she attempted to process what they'd done.

"Oh..." It was all she could manage. Everything was... different. And perfect. "How did you... When did you..." She put both hands to her mouth and fought back a sob. "I can't believe it!"

She closed her eyes and held out her arms, wishing, not for the first time, that her arms were big enough to hold all of these girls she loved so much.

"Believe it, Suze!" Tori squeezed in closer. "We've been at this for days."

How could she not know that?

"Come on in and look around!" Raina pleaded. "You're going to love this!"

"I do, I already love it." But they let her break free so she could carefully take in what they'd done.

First of all, the sectional was gone, along with the pool table, opening up a vast space in the middle of the room. "Where did everything go?"

"Gabe and a crew put the pool table at the fire station for the time being," Rose said. "Then they hauled the sectional to Wingate Properties storage. That's okay, right?"

"Okay?" Susannah bit her lip, but that didn't do a thing for the tears burning her lids. "More than okay. I'm...overwhelmed."

There was a small cheer among them as everyone

started talking at once.

"Do you like where we put the treadmill?" Raina asked. "It's so sunny in that corner, we thought it would be good. And the stationary bike works like a dream."

Not that she could even imagine Rex using that, but it did look good there.

"And look at the bar," Grace said, inching her closer to the long whitewashed countertop where Rex loved to serve drinks and tastes of his beloved wine collection. "No more booze, just gadgets. This is..." She picked out a large electronic instrument with slots for fingers. "The Neofect Smart glove."

"Yes, I remember someone at the hospital suggesting I order that."

"Well, we did. This monitor is not for work," Raina said, tapping a TV screen at the end of the bar. "This headset is for virtual-reality games like ping-pong, which will help him recover his hand-to-eye coordination. And this pegboard is for fine motor skills."

Again, Susannah vaguely recalled ordering that.

"How did you know to do all this?" she asked, sounding as breathless as she felt.

"We talked to the PT company," Madeline said.

"And I had one of them come out here," Raina added.

"And Kenzie Googled stuff," Tori chimed in. "She took a TikTok video of the whole thing being set up in fast motion. Wait until you see it."

"Not now," Madeline said, putting a steadying arm around Suze. "You're reeling, aren't you?"

She was. With love and shock and gratitude. "Oh my gosh, look at the massage table!"

"We'll all want a few of those," Chloe joked, sweeping a hand toward a workout bench next to an array of free weights and straps.

There was still a small seating area by the sliders, a mini living room so Rex could have company while he went through rehab and a place to relax and look out at the dunes and the water. So wonderful, because she had no idea when he'd be able to climb the stairs and get to the rest of the house.

"I absolutely cannot believe you did this."

"And that's not all!" Tori said in a fake commercial announcer voice, gesturing them into the hall that led to two other bedrooms. "If you order now, you get a... hospital bed!"

The others laughed but Susannah just stood in the doorway of the larger bedroom and pressed her hands to her chest, speechless.

Gone was the creamy blue headboard and king-size bed, and in its place, a hospital-style atrocity that took up almost as much space. But it wasn't cold and clinical like she expected. It was draped in a quilt that she recognized as one Madeline had made years ago, using selections of cloth she'd taken from dozens and dozens of dresses and clothes that had gotten handed down over the years.

The sheets were bright blue with cheery decorative pillows, and next to the bed was a raised nightstand on wheels with a beautiful bouquet that had Rose's finger-prints all over it.

"Look at the floor, Mom," Grace whispered.

She did, realizing that they'd covered the carpet with a rubber material so Rex could easily be wheeled in and out.

"The bathroom is all set up for handicapped access, too," Rose said. "We even put a chair in the shower if he needs it."

Would he be showering? Susannah blinked at her, not wanting to let them know that the occupational therapist had taught her how to shower Rex.

She tamped down the thought and focused on her beautiful daughters, awash in gratitude.

"Thank you," she whispered, but she wasn't sure they heard her as they each wanted to show off their gift to her.

"He won't have to sleep down here alone," Raina said, coming close to guide her to the next room. "The bunk beds have been moved to a spare room in Rose's house, and here's the old king-size bed. It's big for this room, but you can sleep here. See? We put your favorite comforter on the bed."

And on the nightstand, she noticed another bouquet, this one with her favorite, white roses.

For a long moment, she stared at the flowers, finally letting herself breathe and think.

"I honestly don't know..." Her voice cracked as a few loving arms wrapped around her.

"Suze, you don't have to—"

She held up a hand, quieting whatever optimism Rose was going to deliver. "But I do have to thank you. I am overwhelmed by my daughters." She touched a cheek, stroked some hair, held a gaze. "Every one of you are the most beautiful girls a mother could have. And for that reason, I am not going to cry."

"Mom, is there anything at all we've forgotten?" Grace asked.

"I'm going to guess you've stocked the fridge and did my laundry," she said on a laugh.

"Yesterday," Madeline told her.

"And Tori's running the Riverfront Café like a pro," Rose added.

"Oh, Tori." She reached for her. "Thank you. You know, Dr. Verona told me you ran into him down by the water the other day."

A soft flush warmed Tori's cheeks as she slid a glance to her sisters.

"I'm going to a wedding with him tomorrow."

Susannah felt her jaw loosen. "What else have I missed while I was holed up in the hospital? Has anyone been to Wingate House? Have you all given up your lives completely?"

Raina came closer. "Dad will be thrilled I handled two closings for him, but I'm going to sneak down to Miami tomorrow, if that's okay. Just for a quick trip."

"Oh, Raina, of course. You—you *all*—need to get your lives back on—"

They all froze at the sound of the front bell.

"That's the hospital transport," Susannah whispered. "Rex is home."

For a few heartbeats, no one said a word. Or maybe, like Susannah, they were sending up silent prayers.

It was time for the new normal.

But because of her beautiful girls, Susannah was ready for whatever it might be.

Chapter Fourteen

Raina

There was no way Raina could wait until tomorrow morning, even with the rain sluicing over her windshield. With Rex home and settled by Friday afternoon, she decided she had to go to Miami and surprise Jack tonight.

"You sure that's a good idea?" Tori's question came through the car speaker just as Raina hit Jacksonville traffic not an hour into her four-hundred-mile trek down I-95.

"Why wouldn't it be?" Raina asked. "The rain will stop by the time I get to Daytona."

"But, with everything else..."

Raina frowned. "You mean Dad? Susannah thought it would be fine with you next door and Madeline's staying with her all night for backup."

"Not because of Dad, but...you know."

No, she didn't know. Or maybe she didn't *want* to. "Rose thought it was sweet and romantic, just the gesture we need," she said, a little frustrated with Tori right then.

"Because Rose will tell you not just what you want to

hear, but with the most positive spin possible. Plus, Rose has, uh, never faced...disloyalty."

Raina's heart rolled around in her chest. "What are you saying, Tor?"

"Nothing, nothing."

Raina was silent for a few seconds and then knew there was no way *not* to address what Tori wasn't saying. "Just because your husband cheated doesn't mean they all do."

"Of course not, Raina, and you're right. I'm jaded. Beyond cynical. I have no right to even imply that. I'm sorry."

But she had every right. Raina had griped plenty about...Lisa. "Do you think it's possible?" she asked on a worried whisper.

"I think anything's possible, but it certainly isn't a pattern for Jack, is it?"

"No. Was it a pattern for Trey?"

"Not the first time," she responded dryly. "The second one makes a pattern."

"And you stayed with him after the first?" Raina asked in disbelief.

"No, I only found out about the first after the second. But my situation was totally different, Raina. We were at each other's throats. He didn't like any choices I made in life. It wasn't a good marriage like yours."

Raina exhaled slowly. Was hers a good marriage? She wasn't sure anymore.

"And that's why you think this is a bad idea?" Raina

pressed. "Because you think I'm going to walk in and..." She let her eyes shutter. "Oh, God."

"That only happens in the movies," Tori said.

"How did you find out about Trey?" she asked.

"I turned my head at an intersection and saw them kissing in the car next to me."

Raina grunted. "Brutal."

"Worse for Kenzie, who spotted them first."

"You never told me this!"

"It's not a story I'm proud of," Tori said.

"What did Kenzie do?"

"She cried. But if it happened today, she'd record it and go viral."

That made Raina smile. "Well, I'm going and if I find out..." She whimpered. "Then I'm going to..."

"Record it and go viral," Tori cracked.

"Very funny."

"Why don't you let him know you're coming?" Tori asked.

"Because then if he is cheating, I won't know." And even as she said the words, she realized that deep down, that was why she was on I-95 headed to Miami on this rainy Friday night.

"Okay, well, good luck. When are you coming back?"

"Probably Sunday evening after the open house. I set up a meeting with a possible new listing for Wingate bright and early Monday morning," she said. "I promise I'm not leaving the family now, or Dad's business. I just... have to go."

"I understand," Tori said. "So you won't be here to

make sure I don't have lipstick on my teeth before Hotty-pants picks me up tomorrow?"

"That's why God created mirrors. You'll be gorgeous in that dress we picked, Tor. I want all the gory details when I get back, from the way he kisses to why in God's name he lives on a sailboat."

Tori chuckled. "You got it. And good luck, honey. I hope he's—"

"In bed alone," Raina said wryly.

"I was going to say thrilled to see you. But, Rain, if you're really worried, then maybe you should call him now, and use this weekend to talk to him, openly and honestly."

It was good advice, but Raina didn't take it. The truth was, if her husband was cheating on her, she wanted to know. Then they'd talk. To lawyers.

The fact was, deep down, in her heart of hearts, she didn't believe Jack was doing any such thing. Business and deals got him excited, not other women. And, yes, Lisa was bringing plenty of that, so maybe they were connecting on the professional level and maybe that was cheating, of a sort. They could talk about that.

But if it was sex? She had to know.

The rain did let up in Daytona, but the traffic was heavy from Vero Beach down to Fort Lauderdale, and there was an accident just as she crossed the Dade County line.

It was almost one in the morning when she let herself through the security gate at Cocoplum and drove up to a very, very dark house. She pulled into the driveway and looked at the two-story behemoth that Jack had been so eager to buy.

He craved a way to tell the world they'd made it, and insisted that good real estate agents had the best houses. She understood that he'd come from a modest background, with none of the family, history, or security she'd grown up with. For Raina, a house with charm and character was so much more appealing than this McMansion in a style that agents jokingly referred to as "contemporama."

She didn't want to set off the alarm, so she turned it off using the app on her phone and let herself in through the side door that led to the drop zone and laundry room, just off the kitchen.

Once inside, she stood very still and took a deep breath, inhaling the familiarity of home. The kitchen was spotless, with one cobalt blue glass in the sink, which made her smile. Jack always had a glass of milk before bed, like a little boy, she liked to say.

One glass, not two wine glasses...like in the movies. There was no underwear strewn up the stairs, no sexy music coming from the bedroom, no laughter or sensual sighs.

In fact, the door was open and the room was pitch dark. She touched her phone for light to find her way to the California king, smiling again when she saw his bare back rising and falling as he slept on his stomach, the comforter on the floor because he hated it, the overhead fan spinning at high speed because she wasn't there to complain about the chill.

A wave of relief hit her, so strong it nearly buckled her knees.

Of course he was alone. Of course he was faithful. Of course she'd made this whole thing up in her head and she loved him and he loved her and all she wanted to do was crawl in that bed and show him.

The screen light of her phone went out and she stood for a second, wallowing in bone-deep joy that she'd been wrong. It had been worth the drive to find that out.

She didn't want to scare the life out of him by turning it back on, though, so she hung back and whispered, "Hey, Jack. Don't freak out."

"Mmm." He moaned and moved, reaching his hand over, the move so darn sexy that she took a few steps closer and touched his back.

"Baby, what are you doing?" He turned over, and his eyes popped open with a gasp, and he shot straight up. "Raina! Jeez! What the hell are you doing?"

"Surprising you."

"Holy..." He reached over and turned the lamp on, his hair a tousled mess, his eyes heavy with sleep. "You want to give me a heart attack?"

"No, no. I just..." She kicked off her shoes and sat down next to him. "I missed you so much, Jack. I couldn't stay away."

His eyes cleared as he blinked the sleep away, a storm of emotion she couldn't begin to read darkening them.

"Aren't you happy to see me?"

"Of course, yeah, yeah." He reached for her, giving

her a quick hug, which was not what she wanted, not at all.

"Then move over," she said seductively, adding a kiss to his warm lips.

"Why didn't you call me? This could have been...a disaster." He shook his head.

"How?"

"Well, if I heard you come in, I might have gone for the gun, for one thing."

"If I heard you move, I would have let you know it's me." She pulled her T-shirt over her head and wrapped her arms around him. "I love you, Jack," she whispered, still trembling with relief that all her weird and stupid worry was a waste.

"Baby," he murmured into a kiss.

Somewhere in the back of her mind, she thought about how he rarely—maybe never—called her that except in their most intimate moments.

And that just made her want to have one of those right now.

This was what they needed. *This*. Just this. After sixteen years of marriage, they could start here and fix anything.

RAINA WOKE to light pouring into the bedroom, freezing under that high-speed fan. The space next to her was empty and she didn't hear any sound from Jack's bathroom. Did he go downstairs and not turn off the fan?

Making a face, she pushed up and reached for the remote on his nightstand, tapping it to drop the blade speed, then falling back on her pillow with a sigh. And a smile. A big, fat, *I was so wrong and it feels so right* smile.

Where was he?

After a minute, curiosity won and she got up, brushed her teeth and peeked behind the door for her bathrobe, which was not hanging on its usual hook. Had she packed it? Maybe, but Susannah kept one in the guest room that she loved and had been wearing that one at the beach house.

Instead, she stepped into her closet, grabbed a T-shirt and sleep pants, and meandered down the stairs, hoping he'd made coffee. No such luck, but she heard the pounding beat of Rush, the untenable rock music he liked when he worked out. She headed to the gym to find him under the bench press, sweating and grunting.

"Morning," she called over the music.

"Seven...eight..." He clunked the bar with a clang and sat up. "You can turn that down."

She touched the button to the sound system and smiled at how good he looked in his shorts and tank top. "You've got a lot of energy today."

"I do." He almost smiled. "But I'm a little ticked at you."

Her eyes widened, certainly not expecting that. "Why?"

"You should've called, Raina. That was dumb."

"To come to my own home on my own schedule? Why was that dumb?"

"You really...surprised me."

She came closer, smiling. "That was the idea. And I think it worked out nicely, don't you?"

He just inhaled and let his eyes close. "Yeah, it was nice."

"Why are you in here so early?"

"The Biscayne Bay open house." He laid back down on the bench, reaching up for the bar, pushing it out of the hook that held it in place. "I'd like to get a good pump before that."

She frowned and shook her head. "It's tomorrow."

"No, Lisa moved it. She rallied a bunch of agents and this date was better."

"When were you going to tell me?"

He rolled his eyes and let the bar drop right back into its holder without lifting. "What difference does it make?"

"I don't know, it's...my listing. But that's fine. Is it still at noon? I can be ready."

"You're going?" he asked, his voice rising in surprise.

"To the open for *my* Biscayne Bay listing? Yes, I'm going."

He let out a noisy breath. "I don't think that's a good idea."

She stared at him, silent for a second, a little sick of him telling her what was or wasn't a good idea. "Why not?"

"Because Lisa has that listing now and if you show up, it's like you don't have confidence in her."

"Maybe I don't," she shot back. "I secured that listing and I have every right to be there."

He pushed out from under the bar and sat up. "Of course you do, Rain. And I want you there. So much. But you know how it is when you step into another person's listing. You want control and a chance to be the only contact with buyers."

"Well, you're going."

"Of course, because...it's a Dub-n-Dub deal." He grinned. "But you should do something else and skip the open."

"I didn't come here to do something else, Jack."

"You came all the way from Amelia Island for that open?" he asked with disbelief.

"I came for you," she said, exasperated. "To be with you, to talk to you, to..." To do what they did last night, even though he seemed to have forgotten it. "I just want to spend the weekend having fun with my husband."

He flinched. "Fun?"

"Yeah, you know, that thing people do when they're not working?" She tried to sound light, but even she could hear the low-key resentment in her voice.

"Fun gets planned, Raina. You popped in out of nowhere. I can't change this open and I don't want to insult Lisa by having another—"

"Insult Lisa? A month ago, she was a competitor. Now going to my very own listing that she got handed to her because my dad is sick is an insult?" She choked. "That's ridiculous, Jack. I'm going to the open house."

She pivoted out of the room and headed back

upstairs, bypassing the coffee for the shower she wanted more.

But as she opened the glass door of her walk-in shower, she eyed the empty shelf where her shampoo and conditioner usually resided. Now that, she packed.

Puffing out a breath, she wrapped herself in a towel and marched all the way out of her dressing area, through the bedroom, and into Jack's bathroom, reminding her of how dang stupid these must-have his-and-hers main bathrooms really were.

But he had shampoo and—

She froze as she stared at the freestanding bathtub that she knew for a fact he had never in his life gotten into. He only put one in here for resale and because it looked good under the window and the bathroom designer had persuaded them to include it.

There was her robe, draped over it. A used candle next to it. And a bottle of her favorite L'Occitane verbena bath gel.

All of her blood chilled in her veins and a slow, ugly tremble took hold of her.

Someone took a bath in here. By candlelight. With her bath gel. And her bathrobe.

Bile rose as she backed away from the tub in horror, her pulse slamming noisily in her head. Lisa? Was it Lisa? Had Lisa slept in that bed, used that tub, and worn her robe?

Was that enough evidence?

She turned one way, then the other, a crazed bolt of determination rocking her.

There had to be proof. Some kind of proof. How could she know? But everything just looked normal.

What had Tori said about catching her husband in bed with another woman? That only happened in movies. What else happened in movies? How else did women find out?

Jewelry in bed!

Yes, that was a classic. Finding someone else's earring in the sheets. She marched to the bed, lifting up pillows and fluttering the sheets.

"What are you doing?"

She startled at Jack's voice, digging for calm, because she did not want to be a hysterical, accusing shrew.

"Who took a bath in your tub?"

"I did."

"With my verbena bath gel?"

"It was all I could find. I pulled a muscle and needed heat. My trainer said a bath with—"

"With my robe and a candle, Jack?" she fired the words at him and watched him pale for one flash of a split second, then his complexion turned red with anger.

"My robe was dirty. I spilled red wine on it." He powered past her, practically mowing her down as he strode into his closet. "Look!" He came right back out with his white terry robe, a purple stain on the front. "Just what are you accusing me of, Raina?"

"Of..." She swallowed, unable to say the word. "But the candle?"

"It was next to your tub and it looked nice and it smelled like you."

Oh. Her heart folded. He sounded genuine but she felt...not right. Not good. Not happy.

"You see why I hate when you're around your sisters?" he spat the question and she just stared at him, stunned by it. "You get crazy. You get...different."

She let out a breath, her whole body, soul, and brain hurting. "I'm going back there," she said softly. "My family needs me."

She went back to her dressing room, only then realizing she hadn't even brought her overnight bag up here. She pulled on a T-shirt dress, stuck her feet in sandals, and grabbed a sweatshirt because she was so darn cold, inside and out.

He wasn't in the bedroom when she left, and she didn't bother to hunt him down.

Instead, she found herself driving on I-95 on Saturday morning after all—only she was going north, not south. She was going home.

Her sisters didn't make her different. They made her better. And she'd never needed them more.

Chapter Fifteen

Tori

"Another slow one." Justin took Tori's hand and led her to the large dance floor in the middle of a stunning ballroom at the Ritz-Carlton. "I can't resist."

She laughed, because...well, he made her laugh. She couldn't remember the last time a man did that—ever?—and she loved every endorphin-filled moment of this date.

"Then we'll dance again," she said, already too comfortable with his arms around her, swaying as he led them around, nodding to the few people he knew, but mostly his dark blue gaze was right on her.

"You know," she said, resisting the urge to unlock her fingers at the nape of his neck and tunnel them into his hair. "There's something incredibly liberating about knowing no one at a wedding. I can be anyone."

"Who would you rather be than Victoria Wingate?" he asked.

Right at that moment? No one. "Me, but without the baggage."

"Baggage makes people interesting," he said.

"Without any, you're just another bangin'-hot strawberry blonde in a sexy black dress."

She laughed at that, a little trill that bubbled up because...he thought she was bangin' hot and that made her feel...whatever bangin' hot was. She had an idea, and liked it.

"Thanks, but what I really am is a strawberry blonde with, you know, baggage."

"Kids? An ex-husband? That's just a carry-on, honey."

"Yeah, but I had to check all the insecurities in my heavy bags."

"What can you possibly be insecure about?" he asked, sounding like she'd genuinely baffled him, which was a compliment in and of itself. "I mean, you own your business, and I assume that means you are an accomplished chef. Your family adores you, you're smart, funny, and can hold your own with a clown on the dock. Both clowns," he added with a wink. "No pesky insecurities allowed."

"Well, when you put it that way, okay." She searched his face, lingering on every delicious detail. "What about you? No insecurities? I mean, I guess you can't when you're an actual neurologist who can stop hearts as well as brains."

He chuckled at that. "Trust me, Tori, I have my share of...stuff I'm carrying around."

"Kids and an ex-wife. That's just a carry-on...honey."

He smiled at the echo of his words, but then his expression grew serious. "I got dumped."

"No!"

He threw his head back and laughed. "I love how you think it's impossible."

"Well, duh. Who could walk away from Hottypants?"

"Oh, you'd be surprised."

"Then tell me," she requested.

"Okay. Out here on this lovely Amelia Island night." He guided her toward open French doors that led to the lush resort grounds, making Tori feel like the heroine in a historical romance sneaking off with a duke.

To the east, a not-quite-full moon rose over the water, but they stayed on a stone path that meandered around sweet-smelling honeysuckle and hibiscus bushes, coming to various patios and clusters of palm trees, all with soft up-lighting and plenty of privacy.

"Maybe you know this already," he started after they'd walked for a bit in a companionable silence. "But you can be married to someone for a long, long time and not know them at all."

She considered that, nodding. "I suppose. Although nothing my ex did really surprised me. He had—well, I'll say an appreciation of rather than weakness for—beautiful young women. Couple that with an occasionally malfunctioning moral compass? His cheating almost felt...inevitable, although that didn't make it hurt any less."

"But his appreciation of women was for, well, *women*."

She slowed her step, frowning and putting two and

two together and coming up with...seriously? "Ohhh. She's gay?"

"Yep."

"Wow." She let out a sigh, deciding that was the only reason a woman would leave this man. "That must have been a shock."

"To put it mildly."

"You had no idea?" she asked.

"None whatsoever." He exhaled, thinking before continuing. "She's the same person, and a pretty wonderful human being at that. Our kids are crazy about her, and are very accepting of their new second mom."

"Did they marry?" she asked.

"Not yet, but they will."

She looked up at him, admiring his cool demeanor about the situation, but wondering if maybe that was a cover for much deeper pain. "So you were completely blindsided? That must have hurt."

"I was...crushed." He gave a tight smile. "We were very happy, or so I thought. I fully expected to head into my, well, not golden years, since I'm only forty-eight, but my *later* years with Michelle at my side, but that was not meant to be."

"How did she tell you? I assume you were still married and you knew this was her reason for the divorce."

"Yes, and she told me with great tenderness, I must say. About a year earlier, she'd become very, very good friends with a new tennis instructor at our club. They were inseparable." He lifted a brow. "Literally. Anyway, after about a year, when our youngest was firmly in college, she told me that she was in love...with Jillian."

"That's got to leave you reeling even more than catching your husband kissing a thirty-year-old in the car stopped next to yours at an intersection."

He thought about that. "Not really. I mean, what your ex did was small and disrespectful and terribly cliché. But Michelle faced such a major change, and I know she didn't make the decision to divorce lightly. She followed her heart and took a massive risk that she'd lose a lot of people over it. I'm happy to say she didn't lose many, maybe not any, and we remain good friends."

"That's impressive," she said.

He just shrugged. "Like I said, she's a terrific woman and, honestly, the divorce was amicable. We both wanted to do the right thing."

An amicable divorce, Tori thought. There was a concept she didn't know.

"I tried to do the whole starting over thing while staying in Pittsburgh, getting a very cool condo in the city. I even tried some dating apps, but I just wasn't ready." He swallowed visibly. "I needed a fresh start, a new place, and no more pitying looks from the nurses at the hospital when I did rounds."

"Oh, they weren't *pitying* you," she teased. "They were circling in for the kill."

He laughed. "Fools. All they had to do was spill coffee on me."

"My signature move." She grinned up at him. "Just call me the master of the meet-cute."

They stopped at a stone balustrade at the edge of another patio, the distant music of the wedding floating on the warm evening air. "Is that what you call it? Well, everything about our meeting was cute, including..." He looked into her eyes. "The coffee spiller."

And there went her heart again. "So, what was the turning point that brought you to Amelia Island?"

"I had feelers out and heard about the opening at the neurology group. I'd never been here or even close. I thought Florida was teal buildings, palm trees, and nauseating humidity."

"It can get pretty humid in the summer, you'll see as many live oaks as palms up here, and Amelia Island has something rare for this state—history."

"And I get the impression the Wingates are a big part of that."

She nodded, a swell of pride rising. "We are."

They were quiet, the only sound the distant music from the wedding, the sweet smell of jasmine and honeysuckle hanging in the air.

"So, what was the worst thing that happened for you in that divorce?" she asked. "Have you lost all trust in womankind?"

"I lost trust in myself," he said. "I thought I should have been...enough."

"Justin! She didn't leave you because you weren't enough. I'm sure she made that clear."

"She tried, but it shook my...faith."

"In what?"

"Everything. Myself. Marriage. People you think

you know but realize you don't." He huffed out a breath. "Anyway, that's my sob story. Happy to never talk about it with you again. Unless you have more questions."

"Hundreds," she replied. "But they're mostly about you."

"Hit me."

"Why the boat?" she asked. "So you don't have roots or a mortgage and can sail away at any time?"

"Actually, yes," he said, quite seriously.

"And would that unwillingness to connect or commit be why you're charming a woman who lives a thousand miles away?"

His eyes flashed as though the idea surprised him. "I don't know," he said slowly, gaining points for honesty. "But despite my training, which can reduce human emotions to little more than bursts of neurotransmitters released in your brain, I'm still a firm believer in chemistry."

"Not the lab kind."

"The kind that inexplicably and unscientifically and magically attracts two people."

Chills danced all over her as she stared at him. "You, uh, felt that? With me?"

"Present tense." He put his fingertip under her chin and lifted her face. "Don't you?"

"Drowning in it," she admitted on a whisper.

He ran the pad of his thumb over her chin in a move that really ought to be illegal, it was so incredibly intimate.

"I want to know you more," he said simply. "I wish you weren't leaving."

And right that minute, she wished she wasn't, either.

"Well, I have that business I run, two kids who are entrenched in life up there, an ex who wants to see them every other weekend and holidays and coaches my son's baseball team. I'm rather...stuck."

"Then we should make the most of the time we have," he said. "Which is...how much longer?"

"I'm going to stay through my sister's wedding in a month," she said, putting into words the thought she'd been waking with every morning for quite some time. "They need me at the café. Plus, my staff has the business covered, my kids are with their father, and I'm..." She leaned into him. "Having a lot more fun than I should be, considering I came down to support my family in a time of crisis."

A slow, sweet smile that looked like victory lifted his lips. "Then I'll take every minute I can get."

Suddenly, she was lost in his eyes and in the myriad possibilities he presented. Some terrifying, some thrilling, all enough to make her just a little dizzy.

The distant music stopped, replaced by the indecipherable sound of the DJ making an announcement.

"I hear the music of the cake being cut," he said, angling his head in the direction of the wedding they'd just left.

"Yeah? Well, I hear the music of my life getting all kinds of jumbled and complicated."

He smiled and lowered his head. "I like that song."

He kissed her just lightly enough to make her want more, then wrapped his arm around her and led her back, probably unaware that she didn't actually feel her feet touching the ground.

WHEN THEY FINALLY SAID GOODNIGHT and finished one last kiss at the bungalow door, Tori waited until his car had pulled back onto Fletcher before unlocking the door. As she did, a light caught her eye from the beach house. Someone was awake at one in the morning?

She took a few steps to get a better look, surprised that the light was on the third floor, Raina's suite, which should be empty, because she was in Miami. Right?

Pulling out her phone, she tapped Raina's number, half hoping she'd forgotten a light on when she left for Miami. Hoping she'd let the call go to voicemail because she was happily in the arms of her faithful and still-loving husband.

"Hey." Her voice was thick enough for Tori to know she wasn't doing any of those things.

"Why is there a light on in your room?" Tori asked.

"Because I'm in here, halfway through a bottle of three-figure wine."

Tori could hear the sob she was fighting. "Oh, no, Rain. Was it a bad idea?"

Raina just sighed, tearing Tori's heart out.

"Want to bring what's left of Dad's wine to the steps on the beach?" Tori asked.

"I'll be there in five minutes."

It took Tori less than that to change into a sweatshirt and yoga pants and hustle toward the beach in the moonlight. She spotted Raina on the stairs of the walkway, staring out into the darkness of the ocean at night.

She joined her without a word, sitting down next to her, hand out.

Raina put a plastic glass in it, picked up the bottle and poured. When she finished, she got her own glass and lifted it to Tori.

"Tell me you had a better time than I did," Raina said.

"I had...the best time."

Raina's eyes flashed. "Really? Tell me everything."

"Nope. You first." She tapped her glass and sipped, scooting closer. "I'm here for you."

Raina shuddered and let out a soft whimper. "It wasn't quite like the movies, but I found some...things that gave me pause."

"Oh, okay. Tell me."

She did, sharing a story of bathrobes and candles and previously unused tubs that Tori had to admit didn't look great. But at least she didn't walk in on something unthinkable.

"Well, that's all circumstantial evidence," Tori said.

"Don't go Rose on me, Tor. You know and I know that it's...not good. And what's worse? The way he's talking to me, the way he's looking at me. Even when we made love—"

"You did?"

"I did," she said on a sigh. "When I got there. I was so stinking relieved and happy to see him alone, and he looked all sleepy and warm..." She gave a sad smile. "I guess I thought it was what we needed to get things started. To find that place where we always, always connected."

"Did you? Connect, I mean?"

"It was...cursory," she said sadly. "I blamed it on the fact that I woke him up and basically scared the life out of him when I walked in, but..." She shook her head. "Whatever. Except if I slept on the same sheets as that—"

"Don't," Tori said. "Don't make presumptions. Work on facts. What do you mean about the way he's talking to you and looking at you?"

For a long time, she said nothing, staring out at the blackness, the only sound the crashing ocean waves.

"I feel like I've lost him," she finally said. "Like a wall is just slowly building up around him, brick by brick, day by day. Is that another woman? A change of heart? A longing to move on? Midlife crisis? I don't know, but my marriage is officially on the rocks."

"Oh, baby." Tori dropped her head on Raina's shoulder, awash with sympathy.

"What should I do?" she asked in a strained voice. "Force the issue? Make demands? Seek counseling? File? I don't know how to solve this problem, Tor. But I feel like a failure."

"Which you are not."

"I never fail. And I don't want to fail at marriage. I don't want to."

"Why not?" Tori challenged. "What's really at the root of your determination not to fail?"

She turned and looked at Tori, a little surprised by the question, but clearly considering it. "I've always had a fear of failure. I never want to...disappoint Dad," she admitted with a self-deprecating laugh. "You think that's at the heart of this?"

"None of us likes to disappoint him," she said. "But it always has been deeper for you."

"Because I'm so much like him. I followed in his footsteps and I'm a natural problem-solver and I..." She stared at Tori, emotion whirling in her eyes. "I'm the reason he lost our mother," she admitted on a sob. "And I've spent my life trying to make up for that."

"Raina!" Tori spilled a little wine as her arms shot around her sister, determined to hold her and squeeze that thought out of her. "You can't blame yourself for an amniotic embolism. You were a newborn! You know that's crazy."

"I know, but I feel so bad. Who wouldn't? I wasn't even the boy he so desperately wanted. And, yes, I know that's stupid and doesn't make sense, but I still want to make it up to him."

Tori held her and squeezed a little harder, her eyes filling with sympathetic tears. "You made it up to him with a life well-lived, Rain. By being his student and such a success at his business."

"My own business. It hurt him when I left."

"It hurt him when I left, and when Sadie moved to

Europe, and when Chloe went to D.C. for graduate school. He likes us all nearby."

"But my decision not to stay and work at Wingate Properties was personal. I chose Jack over Dad, and now I really regret it." She blinked and a tear fell. "What should I do?"

"Well, you know, this might be a weird suggestion, but what if you talked to Dad about it?"

She leaned back, eyes wide. "He can't..."

"Would it stress him out to know you've carried this around for more than forty years?" Tori asked. "Probably not. Maybe it would help him heal to give you the forgiveness you so desperately need."

"I've never talked to him about it," she whispered. "I'm scared to."

"Why?"

"I don't want to make him relive that day. I don't want him to feel it all over or remember that giving me life took hers. I don't want to...face it."

"Well, I get that," Tori said. "But if you're most afraid of failure in life, and that's what's holding you back from either fixing your marriage or moving on, you might have to face it."

"I know. But not...yet." She eased out of Tori's arms and regarded her closely. "Now, can I please get the scoop on Hottypants?"

Tori laughed softly. "Well, his wife left him for a woman."

"No!"

"And he kisses like a god, makes me feel beautiful, and wants to spend every minute he can with me."

"Yes!" She laughed and leaned in. "I'm so happy for you, Tori. You deserve this. You so truly deserve this."

"Thanks. Anyway, I've decided I'm definitely staying through Chloe's wedding."

Raina looked at her on a soft intake of breath. "You are?"

"I am. Will you?"

Her sister blinked and inched back. "Well, it seems a little like avoiding the inevitable, but yes, I'd love to."

Tori offered a toast. "Then let's stay another month."

"Done and done."

They took deep drinks of the expensive wine and leaned against each other, quiet while they watched the moon sparkle on the water.

Chapter Sixteen

Rose

While a meeting with a bride and groom was always one of Rose's favorite ways to spend a few hours, today's one-on-one was even more special, because the bride was her baby sister.

Chloe had taken off the day in the middle of the week to come up to Amelia Island with Hunter, and they'd spent some time with Dad and Suze before their "floral design" meeting at Coming Up Roses.

They were three weeks and one day from the event, and Rose was ready to finalize every floral decision for her sister and future brother-in-law. Waiting for them to arrive, she scanned the open albums she'd spread across the table in the large design and décor room where they'd meet, and tapped the screen of a laptop to bring up more.

Having Hunter here was a bonus, since frequently the grooms skipped the floral design meetings. But Chloe's fiancé had definite ideas about the event, more than most grooms, so she wasn't surprised he'd be coming along.

A few minutes later, she heard Chloe's voice in the

front of the shop, so she headed out, smiling before she even saw her sister.

"I hear the bride," she called, coming around the corner with her arms out to find Chloe standing next to tall, chestnut-haired Hunter. "Hello, gorgeous."

Chloe gave her a brief hug, just long enough for Rose to sense her sister was tense.

"Was it hard seeing Dad?" Rose asked, hoping the morning had gone well. Dad was making great progress. His words were no longer garbled, he functioned well with his right hand, though the left was still weak, and he used that motorized wheelchair like a pro. But if they'd witnessed the struggle to get him from bed to wheelchair or watched him fight his way through an exercise, it might have been difficult.

"No. Yeah." She gave a soft laugh. "It's not easy, but he was in good spirits. Happy to see us, don't you think, Hunter?"

Hunter lifted a dubious brow. "He's had an ischemic stroke, not a neurological incident to take lightly. Hey, Rose." He reached down and gave her a quick hug. "Sorry, you know I'm going to go full doctor in a situation like this."

"Of course," Rose said. "Never apologize for what you do, Hunter. And we're so happy to have the gift of someone else who knows medicine in the family."

"Someone else?" he said with a quick laugh. "There's another doctor I don't know about?"

Rose kept her smile planted but Chloe answered first.

"Gabe's an EMT," she said. "Rose's husband. You remember him."

"Oh, an EMT. Yeah, but there's no substitute for the degree. I saw a lot of stroke patients before I entered my specialty study."

"Then you can give us some additional insight," Rose said, gesturing them both toward the back. "He has an excellent neurologist."

"Where'd he go?" Hunter asked as they walked into the design area. At Rose's questioning look, he added, "To med school, I mean. The neurologist. I wouldn't want old Rex with one of those quacks who got a degree in St. Barts or some such thing. Was it a Top Ten school?"

"I'm not sure," Rose said. "But he seems tremendously qualified."

"Oh, look at this!" Chloe cooed over a large white arch with some silk flowers wrapped around it for showroom purposes. "Is this for the ceremony?"

"It could be," Rose said. "Of course, I'll use real flowers for that, but lots of couples like that behind them as a backdrop. I don't think it's necessary at St. Peters, with all the stained glass and a sanctuary like nothing else for miles. I assume you've seen the church, Hunter."

He eased into a chair, placing his phone on the table face up. "Please. You mean Westminster Abbey?"

At his tone, Rose frowned. "You don't...like it?"

"He thinks it's too over the top," Chloe said, looking up from some candle holders Rose had laid out. "But I won that argument."

Why was there an argument at all, Rose wondered.

"Did you want to get married somewhere else, Hunter?" she asked.

"I wanted to get married in the church where my parents go in Virginia. It's a plain Presbyterian thing without any of the religious bling."

"Oh." Rose nodded. "Well, it's very sweet of you to compromise and choose our town and our family church. Every Wingate wedding for a hundred years has taken place on the sacred ground of St. Peter's, so it would have broken my father's heart for Chloe to marry somewhere else."

Hunter's brows flickered as he made an unreadable face and pretended to look at his phone, but Chloe came closer, and put her hand on his shoulder.

"Hunter," she said. "It's going to be fine."

He didn't answer, but tapped the screen.

Rose looked from one to the other, her gaze settling on Chloe, who was staring at Hunter with concern and uncertainty on her face. Rose waited for someone to elaborate, but when they didn't, she snagged the laptop and turned it toward them.

"Let's start with the big things—the church for the ceremony, then the tablescapes. This is the list of various arrangements and bouquets you requested from our original meeting," she said. "And some very basic décor ideas. Now that you have a finalized guest list—"

"It's not final," Hunter said. "A lot of my friends are up to their eyeballs in residency programs at top hospitals around the world. They're busy. They may not have had a chance to RSVP yet."

"Well, they better do it soon," Rose said gently. "Because you need to give a final list to the caterer and the Eight Flags Country Club ASAP, not to mention the calligrapher who is doing the table chart and name cards."

"We'll get it all," Hunter said dismissively, checking his phone again. Maybe he didn't care so much about the flowers.

"Hunter, come on," Chloe said, frustration in her voice. "We only have a little bit of time before you have to get back, so don't pout."

Was he pouting?

Uncomfortable with the personal nature of the conversation, Rose made an effort to focus on the laptop.

"Well, for argument's sake, let's figure about 150 for a final headcount, so that's fifteen tables of ten. Last time we talked, Chloe was leaning toward these tall vases, but we could still do candles with low flowers." She inched the screen toward Hunter so he could see the huge bouquets Chloe had loved so much.

"How can you see the person across the table?" he asked.

"These are very high," Rose said. "They are designed so you look under them and easily can see—"

"I think that's really awkward, don't you?" he asked Chloe.

"I think it's kind of beautiful—"

"But then 'awkward' might be the theme of this wedding," he added.

"Seriously?" Chloe asked in a harsh whisper. "You have to get over it, Hunter."

Rose inched back. "You guys want to take a minute? I can work in the front while you—"

"Ask her," Hunter demanded, gesturing to Rose. "Ask your sister who is a wedding professional if she thinks it's going to make people happy or uncomfortable."

Chloe's eyes shuttered with visible pain. "Don't bring her into it."

"She's kind of into it," he said sarcastically, turning to Rose. "It's about Rex," he said simply.

"Rex?"

"He can't *wheel* her down the aisle!"

For a moment, Rose just stared at him, breathless, speechless, and at an utter loss.

"I mean, be serious." He dropped his elbows on the table and lowered his voice. "He's got some real medical issues and it doesn't take a professional like me to see it. I don't want my friends and family to cringe when the doors open and she comes out."

"No one is going to cringe!" Chloe exclaimed, her face pale and her eyes already misty.

"Hunter," Rose breathed his name, trying to keep the judgment and shock out of her voice. "He's her father. She's his baby daughter. My family is standing on our heads to be sure he's there and none of us, I can assure you, cares how he gets down that aisle, just that he does."

He had the decency to look chided by her. "Yeah, sure. I understand."

But did he?

"The thing is, I'm the oldest in my family, first wedding," he said. "And I'm like, you know, a big deal to them, the Johns Hopkins doctor and all. They're expecting perfection. I kind of have a reputation for it."

Chloe's lip slipped under her teeth as she sat silent, looking at Rose, then cast her gaze down, clearly uncomfortable with the conversation.

"Of course," Rose said quickly. "And no doubt you've delivered over and over. And you are delivering again with Chloe, who, I'm sure we can agree, is perfection personified."

He gave a tight smile that didn't quite reach his eyes. "It's just going to be hard if he has...an incident."

"An incident?" Rose asked.

He gave her a stern look. "He's had a cerebrovascular infarction. He's suffering from hemiplegia. Do you know what that means? No, of course you don't. It means he's not in complete control of his body or his faculties. He could say something outrageous, or do something embarrassing. He could drool or fall asleep or—"

"I get the idea," Rose said, cutting him off as she dug deep for patience with this man. "And I know you've just seen him for the first time, but he's actually made tremendous pro—"

"I'm a doctor. I've seen a million stroke victims."

He was a resident plastic surgeon and not a day over thirty. A million? She swallowed, praying for the right words to smooth this out and take away the look of sheer agony in her baby sister's eyes.

He turned to Chloe, putting a conciliatory hand on

her arm. "Look, babe. We just have to talk this out and I think you'll see I'm making the proper recommendation."

Chloe shook her head. "I'm sorry, Hunter, but you're not the doctor here, and he's my dad. I will not tell him he can't walk me down the aisle."

"*Wheel* you," he corrected, making her wince. "Unless you want to push him."

"Chloe," Rose said, slowly standing up, because if she didn't get control, he was going to see one very rare thing indeed—Rose Wingate D'Angelo punching a man in the face. "I think you and Hunter need to work this out, with love and kindness and an open heart. I'm going to go out front and help with customers and arrangements. You two talk."

Chloe nodded, fighting tears.

Hunter looked at his phone.

And Rose clenched her fists and strode out to the front, quivering with anger.

Could she make it through this meeting without losing it? Heck, could she make it through the wedding?

And, more importantly, could Chloe make it through this marriage?

ON NIGHTS when Gabe was home from his shift and didn't have another the next day, Rose and her husband routinely slipped away to the greenhouse in the backyard for some quiet time when the girls were in bed and the boys were allowed their video game time.

It was a precious, important time and Rose loved their getaway in the greenhouse.

Gabe had set up a loveseat with a small coffee table in the glass enclosure so they could look up and see the moon, inhaling the heady fragrance of flowers, earth, and vegetables, and enjoy the serenity of time alone together.

Rose would bring a cup of decaf while Gabe poured his giant Coke over ice, and they'd catch up on each other's thoughts and feelings and families, since the Wingates and the D'Angelos were local.

Tonight, though, all she could talk about was the horrible hour she'd spent with Chloe and Hunter earlier that day. She filled him in, and also shared what Chloe had told Rose at the fitting about giving up her professional dreams for him. And all of it weighed heavily on Rose, who tried, but failed, to find the silver lining.

After she finished, she sipped her coffee and dropped her head on his shoulder, a little lighter for having unloaded it all. "I'm worried. I'm truly worried for her, Gabe. I'm just not sure she's doing the right thing."

"Could it just be wedding stress?" he asked. "It's three weeks away, and the guy is under pressure and those residents have agonizing hours, as bad as at a fire station."

"Yes, he's a resident at Mayo, but he's at the end of a three-year program," she said. "I don't doubt that he's had to do some very difficult surgeries and that it's not all boob jobs and facelifts."

"Not at all," Gabe said. "He does microsurgery rotations, pediatric surgery, and he has to write and publish at least one research paper or two. Honestly, Mayo's plastic surgery residency in Jacksonville is unquestionably one of the best in the world, and I bet he's leaving it all on the court every single day. Maybe he was just plain tired and a day of family and flowers wasn't doing it for him."

"Now you sound like me, finding the positive," Rose said with a smile. "I will tell you this—you have a lot more respect for his medical expertise than he has for yours."

He lifted one impressive shoulder, unfazed. "Hey, I'm a firefighter EMT. I don't expect him to be in awe of me."

"You save lives. He fixes noses."

He laughed, eyeing her. "You *are* ticked off, babe. It's a rare night when you're as snarky as Raina or Tori."

"I'm not...okay, yeah. He brought out my bad side."

"That's quite a feat, since you don't have one." He reached for her hand. "And I don't mean to make light of what is obviously troubling you. I'm just saying that there could be a lot going on behind the scenes and I don't think Chloe would marry a jackass."

Rose wasn't so sure of that. "I just don't want her to wake up one day, roll over and look at him, and realize he wasn't worth it."

"Do you think she will?"

"After today? My money's on that happening on the honeymoon."

"Ouch." He took a deep drink, thinking. "So what are you going to do?"

"Me? Nothing."

He drew back, surprised. "You don't want to give her

some sisterly advice? Fire a warning shot? Give her a chance to reconsider?"

"Reconsider?" She groaned at the thought. "I can't tell her not to marry him now! And that's not who I am, anyway. My job is to find the light and guide her into it. I couldn't begin to tell her what I thought today, and I'm freaking out just thinking about what I would say. I don't do *mean*."

He squeezed her hand as her voice rose in anxiety. "It's not mean, Rose. It's loving to tell her the truth."

"Except...she'll hate me. And what if I'm totally wrong?"

"How about if Tori does your dirty work?" he asked. "She's brutally honest."

"Tori didn't see it. Plus, she's all wrapped up in her own doctor. She is officially having a thing with Hottypants."

"I don't know what a 'thing' is," he said dryly, "but that poor guy shouldn't have that callsign. It's brutal."

"Too late."

"What about Raina talking to her?"

"I haven't talked to her about what I saw today. I called, but she's up to her eyeballs in Wingate Property stuff and I don't know if she's the best person to talk to about this right now. Things are not good with Jack these days."

"Jeez. Wingate women having some problems with their men."

"Not this one," Rose whispered with a kiss on his chin.

He tunneled his fingers into her hair and guided her mouth up to meet his, taking a longer kiss, then holding her close to him. "So, back to Chloe. What's going to happen?"

"Um...she's going to marry him. And Dad's going to go down the aisle with her, either in a wheelchair or on a walker. If Hunter doesn't like it? He can just...not like it."

"He'll get used to the idea," Gabe said. "The bigger question to me is whether or not Rex *wants* to go to that wedding."

She looked up with a gasp. "You don't think he does?"

"I hung out with him a little bit today after my shift ended." He gave her a dubious look. "He's getting better physically, there's no doubt. But he seems distant and...I don't know. Down? Maybe scared?"

"Of course he's scared," Rose said. "His life looks... different. He has to know that Suze is fluttering about protecting him from the least little bit of tension, and so he knows he's vulnerable. And he's not...Rex, the great and powerful."

"So true," Gabe agreed. "What's another solution? Maybe Chloe would postpone. Not cancel, but maybe she could use the excuse of Rex's illness to get all the deposits moved back, or eat some of the cost. And she can take a few more months to be sure she's doing the right thing, then re-set the wedding date in six months or so. Rex would be better and she'd be more certain of her decision. You think she'd go for that?"

"She'd *abhor* the idea, as any bride would," Rose said. "It would also cost a lot, although I'm not sure how much.

I certainly wouldn't charge her. The country club and all the vendors might have cancellation fees, but they could waive them if she reschedules. But taking apart a wedding at this point? With invitations out, and flights and hotels booked, and all the details done? Oh, it's a nightmare. But..." she added with raised brows. "Not as much of a nightmare as marrying Horrible Hunter."

Gabe chuckled at that. "In fact, she'd be giving Hunter what he wants," Gabe said. "Which is a chance for Rex to be healthy—well, healthier—at their wedding. And her father's stroke is a legit reason to have to reschedule."

"I don't think he's terribly concerned about my father's health," Rose admitted. "I think his issue is how Dad 'appears' to other people. *His* people."

"Well, then he can kiss my—"

She reached out and stopped him with two fingers to his lips. "My sentiments exactly."

He smiled under her fingertips, then kissed them lightly. "Would you be able to make the suggestion to her, Rose? It's not too far out of your wheelhouse of improving, helping, assisting, and generally making things nicer."

She laughed softly. "No, it's not. And I'd prefer that to what I really should say, which is, 'Run, don't walk, away from this man.'"

He looked hard at her, his blue eyes narrowing. "Honey, even though it would be a miserable conversation, you do owe your sister your best advice."

"I know," she murmured. "But I don't think I could

stand the hurt and sadness in her eyes. She's my baby sister, Gabe."

He took her hand and brought it to his lips, saying nothing, but that was fine. It was exactly what she needed.

"But," she continued, "I could suggest she consider delaying the whole thing...*for Dad*. Maybe it would be enough time for her to see Hunter's true colors."

"Good idea."

"It sure was." She smiled. "Yours."

He shrugged. "You married a genius."

"A gorgeous, wonderful, sweet, loving, sexy genius." She leaned into him. "So tell me about work. How's the probie? What's his name? Or are you just going to call him Probie like you did poor Clayton Waring for a year?"

"Probably. His name is Travis McCall and he's not bad. Decent head on his shoulders, takes direction, he can cook—passably—and drag a hose, so we'll keep him."

"Is he married?" she asked.

"Why? You looking for a new husband?"

"No, but Chloe might be," she said on a laugh. "I'm just curious how young he is."

"Actually, not young at all. Early thirties, which is old for a freshman firefighter, but he's got the bug. Left some big corporate job to train. He's actually a cool guy."

"See? And you were so worried about breaking in a rookie."

"I still hate breaking in rookies, but this dude isn't bad. And my dad came in today, so the whole place was happy." He grinned. "The man is one magical chief. The entire station still jumps to attention when he walks in the door."

"You'll be a magical chief one day, too." She leaned into him. "The second magical Chief D'Angelo."

"Babe, I'm not even captain yet, and I don't do magic."

"Are you kidding?" She looked up and kissed him. "I'm certainly under your spell."

And just like always, they spent the last of their moments in the greenhouse wrapped in each other's arms, sharing coffee and Coke-flavored kisses, and forgetting everything and everyone but each other.

This is what she wanted Chloe to have, Rose thought as she rested her head against his chest and listened to the heart she loved. This is what she wanted for everyone in her family, in the world.

If she said that out loud, she'd be accused of rampant positivity and optimism. She didn't care. Everyone should love like this. Especially her baby sister.

Chapter Seventeen

Susannah

"You could surprise your physical therapist and be standing behind that walker when he arrives," Susannah said lightly, tempering the suggestion by putting a hand on Rex's arm. "You're ready, you know."

He just sighed and turned from her, staring out at the dunes and the ocean beyond.

"What's the matter, Rex? Yesterday was such a good day."

"Not today."

She leaned in. "Not walking today, or today isn't going to be a good day? I'm not following."

He shook his head, silent, and frustration zinged up her spine. Wasn't this supposed to get easier every day?

In some ways, it had. They could converse and he had more mobility and energy. He'd been home more than two weeks and he was a different man than the one that had been wheeled in here that day. For one thing, he could work that chair himself. In fact, it had gotten easy. Maybe too easy.

"I don't want to press, Rex, but—"

"Then don't."

She slammed her mouth shut and stood up, busying herself with picking up his dishes and cup, swallowing against a lump in her throat that always seemed to be here.

"I'm just going to run these upstairs," she said. "I'll be right back. You okay?"

"Yes, Suze. I can be alone for five minutes. I'd like to be."

She flinched at the comment, but chose her battles—and this certainly wasn't one of them. Anyway, fighting with him would just cause stress, and she'd made an art form out of avoiding that.

She took the dishes up to the kitchen, taking a moment to stand still in the sunshine that poured in over the whole living area. It wasn't dark downstairs, but it certainly wasn't like this, bathed in brightness that warmed the sea and sky outside every window.

Before this happened, she'd only gone down to the first floor when the kids were playing games or they had family movie night. She lived up here, in light and happiness, but some days she forgot what that felt like.

Tamping down the inner pity party, she rinsed the dishes and put them in the dishwasher. Stealing another minute, she walked to the bank of French doors and stared at the water, exhaustion pressing on her whole body. Did he have any idea that—

"Suze!"

He barked her name loud enough to make her whole

body startle, then she darted toward the stairs. "I'm right here. Is everything okay, Rex? Are you—"

At the bottom of the steps, she froze at the most unusual thing—the light was on in his office. He'd wheeled himself in there and was now in front of his desk, looking around.

"Where is it?" he demanded.

"Where's what?"

He didn't answer, but heaved a breath, and her own got caught in her chest. "Rex, stay calm now. What are you—"

"Who's been in here?" he demanded.

"Raina, I guess. That's it. No one."

He looked around, his eyes a bit frantic. "You found me...that day? Right?"

"Yes. Don't you remember?"

"Not...clearly." He sighed again, then closed his eyes. "But some things...yes. Oh, God."

She rushed in at the way he moaned the last two words. "Rex, what is it? What's upsetting you?" Whatever it was, she had to fix it, remove it, or get him away from it.

He was silent, staring at the desk, then the window, then the floor. "Only Raina?" he asked. "No one else?"

"I've kept everyone away, Rex," she said, coming closer. "If you'd like to meet with one of your agents or your assistant—"

"No. No." He held up his good hand.

The doorbell rang and she stepped away. "That's

probably Phillip, here for your PT," she said gently. "Maybe he can get you on that walker."

He looked up at her, nothing but sadness in his eyes. "I'm sorry, Suze."

"For what? Not running around here on a walker? I should be sorry for putting so much stress on you. You can stay in that chair as long as you like, including at Chloe's wedding."

"Oh." He whimpered. "When is it? I've lost all track of time."

"Two weeks."

He just closed his eyes. "Go get Phillip. I'll try."

"That's my man." She kissed him on the head and walked to the front door, smiling back at the friendly PT who was here every day at the same time.

"Hello, Mrs. Wingate," he said. "How's our patient today?"

She sighed, thinking of all the ways she could answer that. *He's sad, frustrated, sick of this, and feeling miserable.*

"He's fine and ready for you," she said instead. "Good luck. I'll be upstairs."

With that, she headed back to the sunshine of her living area, just in time to meet Raina coming down from the third floor, her eyes downcast. She'd been quiet these past few weeks since she'd gone to Miami for that quick overnight, and seemed to spend more and more time at Wingate Properties.

"Good morning, Raina."

"Oh, Suze." She looked up, surprised. "I didn't even see you."

"You're deep in thought," Suze said, tipping her head toward the kitchen. "Time for coffee before you run off to slay the real estate dragons?"

She gave a soft laugh. "Sure. How's Dad today?"

"As well as can be expected," she said, searching Raina's face. "How are you?"

"As well as can be expected," Raina echoed.

"You don't seem happy," Susannah said as she went to the coffeemaker. "And I take it Jack isn't coming up anytime soon." She sighed as she put in a K-Cup. "I hate that you're apart from him so much."

"It's not your fault, Suze. Things just aren't great right now."

She turned, not that surprised by the words, which she'd suspected, but the defeatist tone was a little alarming. "Do you want to take another trip down there? You can. You should."

"I don't," she said.

"Oh, honey. Do you want to talk about it?"

Raina just stared straight ahead, silent while the coffee brewed and Susannah put a cup in front of her and got the creamer from the fridge.

"You have a great marriage," Raina finally said. "Did you and Dad ever have, you know, troubled times?"

"Other than right now?" Susannah asked on a dry laugh.

Raina poured the creamer. "If this is the worst you have, count your blessings."

She nodded, agreeing with that. "Well, you take those vows, you know. Better and worse. Sickness and health. Richer and poorer. Till..." She didn't want to say the rest. He was better, but she still went to bed every night hoping they had another day.

"I remember," Raina said. "I think there's a line in there about...forsaking all others, too." She took a sip and then sputtered. "Eesh! Check the date on that creamer."

But Susannah was stuck on what Raina had just said. "What do you mean?"

"It tastes awful." She picked up the creamer and squinted at the top. "Huh. It's okay, but..." She pushed the cup away. "I don't really want anything this morning."

"Are you going to just drop that comment and not expect me to ask for more?"

Raina looked at her, her dark eyes sad. "Yeah," she finally said. "It's all just the wild musings of a woman who is far from home. I don't want to talk about it."

"But are you saying—"

"Please."

Susannah nodded, knowing exactly how far to push any of her girls.

"So how is he, really?" Raina asked, clearly changing the subject.

"He's..." Susannah pushed the button to make her own coffee. "Troubled," she finally said.

"I noticed that," Raina agreed.

"It could just be the situation or the wedding or... well, something." Susannah brought her coffee to the island, standing across from Raina. "He was in his office a few minutes ago and he did seem bothered by something, but I don't know what."

"Mmm." Raina lifted her brows. "I might."

"What is it?"

"A surprising shortfall of cash."

"What?" Susannah drew back, certainly not expecting that. A big contract that fell through or a major listing going to a competitor, a building he wanted that someone outbid him on? Those were the things that bothered Rex at work. But never...money. "Cash? How much?"

"I don't know," Raina said. "I can't figure where the hole is, but I would have expected quite a bit more on hand than I can find in any of his accounts."

Susannah looked at her, the conversation she just had with Rex playing over in her head. "That must be it," she said. "That must be what has him so troubled."

"It's troubling, but only if he knows. He's been out of the loop for more than a month now."

"Is it a lot?" Susannah asked.

"I'm not sure. I found a lot of money moved from accounts I can access, but I can't figure out where it went. Maybe he's made a big investment that we don't know about."

Susannah couldn't think of one, but Rex didn't always tell her everything about his business. "Can you pay the bills?" she asked.

"Yes, payroll, closing costs that need to be advanced, we're fine. But it's concerning."

"How can I help?" Susannah asked, then quickly added, "Without stressing him."

"I know, I know," Raina said. "I would have just asked him and still would like to, but I don't want to upset him. Do you know all his bank accounts? Every single one?"

Susannah grimaced, a little ashamed of how far removed she was from the business. "Not really. But can't you find that kind of thing at his office? In his files or on his computer? Doesn't that new boy know?"

"Blake the Fake?" she snorted, then held up a hand. "Not to be mean, he's a fine assistant, but whoa, he's full of himself."

"I've only met him in passing," Susannah said. "Rex only hired him a few weeks before his stroke."

"He won't be an assistant for long," Raina said. "He's itching to get out in the field and make sales, so it doesn't matter that I'm not crazy about him. But you know what I can't find is a password program, which might help me find any other bank accounts and how to get into them. Do you happen to know which one Dad uses?"

"A program? I don't think he uses one."

"How does he keep track of all his passwords?" Raina asked.

"I think he writes them in an address book." At her look, Susannah laughed. "He's seventy-five, Raina. He's conquered all the technology he wants to for one lifetime."

"Gotcha. Where might one find that book?"

"Probably in one of his offices, either downstairs or in town."

"Can I go down now and look downstairs?"

"Yes, let's sneak in there and look. I know it's a brown book that says 'World's Greatest Grandpa' on the front. Ethan gave it to him one Christmas. Although my guess is that it's in town. But..." She cocked her ear. "It sounds like they're doing some exercises and he won't even see us. I'll help you look."

"Is there any reason we can't ask Dad? It makes perfect sense that I would need that to do his job, so it shouldn't stress him out."

"Eh, okay, but..." Susannah curled her lip. "If he knows about this money problem and it's what's bothering him, then it could stress him out. He might not want you to look."

"Or he might want me to find it," Raina said. "But we don't have to tell him why I want the password book. Every website he goes to has a password. It's normal that I'd need it to fill his shoes at Wingate Properties."

"You're right," Susannah said. "And if this is what's upsetting him and you solve the problem, then that's a good—"

A clunk and a loud exclamation made them both jump, and Susannah gasped.

"He fell!" she whispered, whipping around and tearing down the stairs at record speed. "Rex! Rex, are you okay?"

"He's fine," Phillip called just as she swung around the corner to see Rex on the floor.

"Fine? He fell! What happened?"

"Tried to...walk," Rex muttered.

Phillip held up his hand to keep Suze from coming any closer. "I'll get him back in the chair, Susannah. And we'll stick to other exercises today. Let us have a little privacy."

She nodded, backing out of the doorway right into Raina. She turned to see the concern on Raina's face, knowing it must mirror her own.

"I'll look for it later," she said. "You can look in town."

Raina nodded and Susannah turned around just in time to see Rex being hoisted into his chair, tears on his face. Her heart cracked and fear rose. Swallowing her own tears, she took Raina's hand and walked to the stairs.

Chapter Eighteen

Raina

When Raina arrived at Wingate Properties and walked up the stairs, she was furious to see Blake Youngblood sitting at her father's desk.

"Excuse me," she said, breezing in. "Pretty sure you're in my seat."

He laughed and instantly pushed up, grabbing papers that were spread all over the desk. "Sorry. I had to spread this contract out and this is the biggest surface I could find. But I'm so glad to see you."

Somehow she found that hard to believe but she dropped her bag on the guest chair and asked, "Did you need something?"

"Your brains, experience, keen eye, and Wingate genius."

Whoa, he was laying it on thick. "Oookay." She laughed. "On what?"

"This offer for a beach condo. I just know I'm missing something that's going to come back to bite my—er *our* —client."

"Which one?"

"I—er, *we*—got an offer on the Sheridan condo," he said.

"We did?"

"Whoops. I guess I should have led with that. I showed the property yesterday and the buyers loved it."

She gave him a sharp look. "Are you licensed to buy and sell real estate in the state of Florida, Blake?"

"No, but I swear, Raina, I did not falsely represent myself as a licensed agent. I didn't do much else than unlock the door and show them around. I certainly don't expect commission."

Good, because without a license, he wasn't getting one.

"What's the problem on the offer?" she asked.

"I don't know. There are contingencies, so..."

She rounded the desk and squinted at the sea of papers, skimming the familiar words of an offer and the list of reasons why it could fall through.

"Why do they have a title contingency?" she asked, pointing to the fifth one.

He shrugged. "They asked for it. Red flag?"

"Bright red. If the title's in question, which is why they'd put it in there, no lender will close on that mortgage and you can't waive this with traditional financing. That's the problem. Strike it."

"Oh, of course! Why didn't I see that? That's why you're the genius." He finished gathering the papers, tapping them into a neat stack. "Should I just leave this here for you to review?"

"I'll take it from here, thanks."

"Sorry for squatting," he said. "I'll be at my desk if you need anything."

What she needed was the password book and privacy. "Thank you. Can you close the door on your way out?"

He left, and the minute the door clicked, she dropped into the chair and pulled out the only desk drawer, along the top of his Parson-style table. It was neat, like everything in this office, with separate spaces for office supplies and a few odds and ends, like his nail clippers and a bottle of multivitamins that had expired a year ago. Those had Susannah's fingerprints all over them, she thought with a smile.

But no brown address book that said, "World's Best Grandpa."

"Come on, Dad. Where do you keep your old-school password book?" She took everything out, felt along the edges, but found nothing.

Glancing around, she turned to the computer table behind her and started on the drawers in it, taking out every single file and reaching inside.

Frustration grew as she lifted every single knick-knack on his shelves, pulled out books and looked behind pictures.

It had to be in the top drawer...unless someone who sat here frequently had taken it.

Throwing a distrustful glance in Blake's direction, she pulled the drawer out again and got down on her knees, peering inside the top, sliding her hand up there and touched... something. Paper? An envelope? A small password book?

Her heart kicked a bit as she tried, and failed, to grab hold of whatever had been jammed into the bottom of the desk. If she pushed too hard, it would end up inside the desk and the only way to get it would be to remove the wood panel under the desktop.

She pulled out her phone and pointed the flashlight beam into the dark back of the drawer and, yes, indeed, there was an envelope. Could the book be inside the envelope?

But the only way to get it would be to...break the drawer. Destroy what was surely a very, very expensive antique desk that she recalled being part of the historic hundred-year-old bank. And whatever this was, what were the chances it would be the password book?

Not very good, but determination shot through her as she jimmied and shook and pulled and—

"Crap," she muttered as half the drawer snapped off the metal runner on the side.

Okay, dang, she'd have some explaining to do, but nothing compared to the satisfaction of reaching into the now four inches of space and closing her fingers over an envelope hidden from the world.

What was it?

Her heart dropped when it looked like an old card with the Hallmark imprint on the back. It was unsealed, but the flap was folded into the envelope. Man, if she broke a valuable desk to read a ten-year-old birthday card from a client that somehow got stuck in this desk, she'd be mad.

She flipped the envelope open and pulled out a silver card with a single heart on the front and black script that read, "Happy Anniversary to my Husband."

Oh, Suze. Raina smiled, chuckling softly at her idiocy for thinking that she was going to pull out anything that would help her. She almost slipped the card right back where she found it without opening it, but then she saw something handwritten, very small, along the side of the heart.

August 21, 1980

She stared at the date as some blood drained from her head, because this card was dated exactly one day before she was born.

"This isn't from Suze," she murmured to herself, only half aware that she was still kneeling on the floor holding a card written by her mother.

With a soft exhale, she eased herself all the way down, thudding softly on the dark silk rug that gave Dad's office such a rich, masculine feel. Her fingers trembled as she ran them along the edge of the card.

Yes, somewhere in the recesses of her mind, she knew that her parents' anniversary was August 21, and that Charlotte Wingate had actually gone into labor while they were out to dinner celebrating the date. The twins—although no one knew there were twins—came three weeks early on August 22, 1980.

Her mother had died the day after giving this card to her husband.

Letting out a soft moan, Raina stared at the card, a little terrified at the emotion that would rock her when she read it. This wasn't the first thing that Charlotte had touched, made, loved, or left behind that Raina had handled.

She'd held jewelry that Dad had given to Madeline, Tori, Rose, and Raina over the years. Some clothes that had been important to her, some keepsakes and treasures and pictures.

No one had tried to wipe her memory away, but time and a very loving and treasured "new" mother had certainly dimmed what was left of Charlotte.

Raina didn't remember one day in her life before Dad remarried. She didn't know if she was a sad, motherless toddler, although there were some pictures and a few videos—very few, until Suze arrived—that gave Raina the impression that Madeline, who was only six at the time, had done her best to help Dad give Raina and Rose the love and attention babies needed.

Was there a hole in her heart that belonged to her biological mother? Or just a big fat steaming pile of guilt?

Maybe she'd know if she sat down with a shrink and dug into her psyche, but even then, Susannah Wingate was her mother. And this woman...

She sighed again and opened the card, which was signed, "Love, Char," but it was the long note on the inside left flap that got her attention.

My Sweet and Darling Rex,

These have been the fastest and happiest eight years of my life. Thank you for making me feel loved every day, even now when I'm the size of a house! It's okay. Our boy will be big and strong and smart, just like his daddy.

She closed her eyes and breathed out, trying to forgive her father his dream and determination to have a son. It was natural, she supposed, especially considering his father and grandfather and all the importance placed on a son.

They didn't have clear ultrasound technology in the early 1980s. A sonogram was done "if something was wrong," and while it might have warned them they were having twins, it certainly could never have told them the genders of those babies.

Rex had been hoping for his boy...and he got two more girls.

He rarely spoke of the day, but Raina had done a little research. Maybe more than a little during those weeks when she'd been pregnant.

Charlotte's heart rate must have spiked, probably moments after Raina was born. Her breathing would have become labored and she probably grew agitated and had chills and pain and...

Raina closed her eyes, picturing a patient suffering from a blood clot from her amniotic fluid. There would have been a seizure, and panic that must have ensued, the doctors, the nurses, the two crying babies...and Rex watching while his wife's heart stopped beating.

She shuddered, hating the string of thoughts she'd had so many times. It was like a song in her head that played over and over, all those years when she was trying to get pregnant, she kept thinking about...that.

Tears made the words move on the page, as if Charlotte were still alive, and sending her a warning not to get pregnant or that could happen to her, too.

Wiping her cheek before a teardrop fell on the card, Raina forced herself to keep reading.

But even if it's not a boy, I will hold you to the promise you made last night. We'll name her Regina and trust that God has a bigger plan for this family.

I love you like raindrops on roses.

Yours forever,

Char

She stared at the last line, something she didn't think she'd ever heard before except in a song.

Raindrops on roses.

Was that where he got their names? Or had they named the babies before the embolism? Had he decided on "Raina" and "Rose" because of a sweet little saying they shared? Had they made that decision before she died? And why wouldn't Rose have been named Regina, since she came first?

Was that her mother's doing...or her father's?

Holding the card against her chest, she let the tears spill in earnest, wondering—not for the first time—how different everyone's lives would have been if she hadn't been born.

She had questions, so many questions. But she wasn't even able to ask her father where his password book was kept, let alone how he felt the day she was born and her mother died.

Chapter Nineteen

Tori

T *rey?*

    Tori stared at her phone screen and let out a grunt. Her ex-husband was the last person she wanted to talk to when she was walking out the door to take a late afternoon sail with Justin. Usually, if he had something to say, he used Kenzie as the go-between. At the very least, her daughter would warn her to watch out for an incoming missile of misery.

But she wasn't prepared and didn't want to take this call. Except she'd never ignore it, just in case something was wrong with Kenzie or Finn.

"Hey," she said casually as she climbed into her rental van. "What's up?"

"Big news, that's what's up. You got a minute, Tor?"

Tor? Oh, boy. He wanted something. "A minute, sure."

She put the phone in the console on Speaker, bracing herself for a request, a change, a favor, something.

"The AAU tournament schedule is set and, man, it's a good one."

Okay, a schedule change. And since it involved the travel team that Trey coached, he was probably looking for an extra weekend to drag poor Finn out to the wilds of western Massachusetts so the kid could stand in left field and pray a line drive didn't come his way.

She'd told Finn he could be honest with his father—he could tell him he didn't love the sport. He could admit that the thought of getting hit in the face with a ball kept him awake at night, and he could take a stand and say he'd rather spend his weekends some other way.

But that would disappoint Trey, and Finn never wanted to do that. So he played on the fourteen-and-under AAU team that Trey coached, even though he was not quite the caliber of the other boys on the team. Even in middle school, it was obvious that some of those kids were going to play ball through college and maybe beyond. Finn? His father might have made it to the minor leagues, but Finnie got his athletic abilities from the Wingate side, which was to say...not much.

But God bless the kid. He did it for his dad.

"Great," she said brightly. "I guess that means there's a trip to the Berkshires in the future. Isn't that where the tournament was last year?" She was sure of it, because Finn's team had lost in the finals and he blamed himself for missing a "can of corn" flyball, as Trey called the easy catch—which had only made Finn more miserable.

"Actually, because I'm on the AAU Massachusetts board, I was able to get the Cougars in an elite series that, uh, lasts for a full six weeks."

She blinked into the sunshine. "Every weekend for six weeks?"

He had to be kidding. He wasn't supposed to have Finn that frequently. Every other weekend, and she'd been so generous moving those around to account for baseball.

"Actually, no, that's not how this tournament works."

"Good, because—"

"It's actually six solid weeks, and the travel is up and down the East Coast, not just Massachusetts. It's a national circuit, and we'll be playing the top teams from New York, Pennsylvania, Delaware, Virginia, and Georgia. It's a huge deal, Tori."

She just shook her head, not following. "Where are these games?"

"I just told you. New York, Penns—"

"Does he have to go there?" She heard her voice rise with disbelief. "How many games are you talking about? And has Finn agreed to this?"

"Finn is right here, if you will just calm down and listen to me."

She clenched her teeth, as she always did when he told her to calm down. The words not only had the opposite effect, they were delivered with typical Trey Hathaway superiority.

"Then let me talk to him and—"

"Will you please hear me out before you start shooting poison in his veins and trying to talk him out of something because it doesn't involve you?"

She squeezed the steering wheel.

"I'm listening," she ground out, vaguely wondering when Trey had gone from being the tall, handsome, charming baseball player she met playing Frisbee in the Boston Common to a controlling, obnoxious, unfaithful jerk who brought out the worst in her. And did all men change like that?

Would Justin?

She glanced at the clock and saw she was already late, of course.

Turning the car on, she waited for whatever golden wisdom and unassailable information Mr. Always Right was about to impart.

"It's a six-week travel tournament," he said. "We'd be on the road from the week school gets out until the end of July."

She slid the gear into reverse and almost laughed out loud. "You think you can take him that long, Trey?"

"Well, you're gone this whole month and I have him."

"Because he's in school and…"

Her voice faded out. He was right, technically. Good heavens, *why* would anyone ever get married and have kids with this unholy complication looming in the future?

"Here's the plan," Trey said, his tone leaving no room for argument. "You know David and Marcie Devine. You've sat with her at games, really good people, and Christopher was our MVP last year?"

"Oh, I know them," she said dryly. Marcie was insufferable, David put beer in his water tumbler, and Christopher thought the sun rose and set on his spoiled little self.

"Well, Heidi's gotten close with Marcie. Those two are like our lead cheerleaders, you know?"

She closed her eyes when she stopped at the light, patience waning. "And?"

"And we're thinking about renting an RV for the six of us and just going from tourney to tourney up and down the East Coast."

What did he say? She stared straight ahead, a hundred questions swirling until the person behind her tapped on her horn and she noticed the light had changed.

She went with the first question. "You want to take him on the road with another family, and live in an RV, for the entire summer?"

"Just six weeks."

Which left the hellacious two weeks before school started for her. "And what about Kenzie?"

"Oh. Yeah."

What a shocker. He hadn't even *thought* about Kenzie.

"I figured she'd hate it and want to stay with you."

What he figured was that she would be perfectly happy to be away from him and Heidi- Ho for a summer and who cared about Tori's life? She'd just pick up whatever crumbs he dropped and take care of everything and sew the dang AAU tournament patches on the uniform like a dutiful ex-wife.

"So, what do you think?" he asked after a long pause. "'Cause, um, we put the deposit down on the RV."

Of course they did.

"Let me talk to Finn," she said. "Privately, please."

He didn't answer and it was quiet for a second, and while she waited, she finished the one-mile drive from the beach to town. There was a festival of some sort, so traffic was a little heavy on the main drag, and she turned to take a back street toward the wharf, waiting with her breath held to hear Finn's voice.

"Hey, Mom." Was it lower? Was it changing? Was she missing a lot by staying down here so long?

"Hi, honey. Are you alone? Can you talk?"

"Yeah, yeah. Dad's in the kitchen with Heidi."

"Do you want to do this, Finn?" she asked, already knowing that it was really up to him and not her.

He sighed. "I guess."

"That's not very enthusiastic," she said.

"Well, I think it would be fun and, you know, different."

"But is that how you want to spend your summer? Sleeping in an RV? Living on the road? Playing baseball all summer long?" Because it sure sounded like hell to her.

"Chris Devine is cool," he said. "And I don't really know what an RV is, but—"

"Small," she said. "And you get claustrophobic in small places."

He laughed softly. "You mean in the pillow fort you and Kenzie used to make when we were little? I'm over that, Mom."

Actually, that was exactly what she was thinking of. "Well, does that sound good to you?"

She turned into the parking lot, glancing at the River-front Café, which was quiet and closed for the day, the umbrellas closed on the patio, the festive awning fluttering in the breeze. Her gaze moved to the water beyond...and to the sailboat moored at the wharf.

Her heart lifted, not just at the idea of seeing Justin, but the whole peace and beauty of this little piece of paradise. She loved it here.

And if Finn were gone for six weeks...she and Kenzie could spend the summer here.

She almost gasped out loud at the thought.

"It doesn't sound awful," Finn said, his tone the very embodiment of the phrase "damning with faint praise."

"Are you sure? I mean, you haven't really even liked playing ball this year."

"I know," he said glumly. "But it makes Dad all jazzed and stuff, and this team is really good. They're making me hate it less."

And more of that faint praise.

"There's, like, four new guys who are going to be in the summer league and they joined the Concord Cougars just because of Dad."

She wasn't surprised. Trey was not just a great coach, he came with true baseball credentials. He'd almost made it to "The Show," but even without MLB on his resume, parents wanted their kids playing under someone with Trey's background. They all thought their little darlings would get scholarships to big colleges and go on to be the next Derek Jeter.

"Well, if you really want to go..." she said, scanning

the view again and feeling a little bit guilty for almost wanting him to go so she and Kenzie could be here until August.

Was that wrong?

"Yeah, I do, Mom."

"And you're not just agreeing to this because Dad wants it?"

"No, well, you know. A little. But it's cool."

She let out a sigh, trying not to think of all that time without him. "But you have to be here for Aunt Chloe's wedding in two weeks, remember?"

"Oh, yeah, sure. I want to do that." He snorted. "I'd rather go to Amelia Island, but I guess that's not an option."

She let out a grunt. Why wasn't that an option? Because Trey would never allow it. He could take Finn for six weeks and haul him in an RV with another family, but she couldn't have him down here all summer with his actual family, including his favorite cousins.

It would cause a world war, and she didn't want to put the kids through that. Plus, she'd lose.

"Well, you'll be here soon," she said. "And maybe we'll come back after your tournament trip for a visit."

"Yeah, I want to see Grandpa Rex. How is he?"

"Much better and he would love to see you." Maybe that was a compromise she could get from Trey. "Let me talk to your father, honey."

A few seconds later, Trey was on the line. "So it's a yes?" he asked.

"Qualified," she countered. "Kenzie will be down

here with me, and when the tournament is over, I want to bring Finn here, too. Oh, and they're both here for Chloe's wedding, don't forget."

"I didn't, it's on the calendar. We got the tickets. But what about your job?" he asked.

"What about it?"

"Don't you run a business up here?"

"It's all under control, Trey." She hated talking to him about her catering company. He never liked the idea of her having one; then, when she did, he wanted to tell her how to run it. "I have staff and everything's covered. Plus, I'm running my family's café down here. And Kenzie can work there all summer."

"Great, great. Okay, we're all set then. Really appreciate it, Tori."

"Sure."

After hanging up, she gathered her bag and jacket and locked the car, walking toward the water and thinking about the sudden change in her life.

Divorce had been miserable, single-parenting was hard, and building a business was brutal. Not to mention, her father was recovering from a stroke.

As she neared the boat, Justin appeared on the deck, waiting for her. He wore cargo shorts and a soft T-shirt that accentuated his lean, strong body, his hair fluttering slightly in the breeze.

Truth was, except for the weeks away from Finn, she didn't hate this plan. Not at all.

$\approx$

THE CALL WAS JUST ABOUT FORGOTTEN two minutes after she got on Justin's sailboat for the first time. She'd only seen the vessel from the dock, and then, she'd been about to go to the mat with her former cook. In the few times she'd seen Justin, he either drove or they met at the restaurant, so this was her first boating experience with him.

"Welcome aboard the *Serendipity*," he said, taking her hand and guiding her onto the deck.

"That's what you're calling it?" she asked. "I thought you were kidding."

"I like it. Unless you come up with something better. I haven't commissioned the name to be painted on the back yet. Would you like a drink or a tour first or both at the same time?"

"Definitely that," she said, looking around at the gleaming teak details, the sitting area around the cockpit, and the two towering masts with cranks and canvas and all manner of boating things. "This is really amazing. Have you always been a sailor?"

"A dabbler," he said. "And I'm honestly in way over my head, but I've taken some sailing lessons and I'm getting better. Red or white?"

"Whatever is open or easy," she said, turning and taking it all in. "You live downstairs?"

"Below deck," he corrected with a smile.

"Ah, yes. The boat vernacular. Help me with that."

"The kitchen's a galley, the bathroom's a head, the front is the bow, the back is the stern, the right is starboard, the left is port, and you..." He handed her a glass of wine. "Are beautiful."

She laughed softly at the unexpected compliment, although she was growing used to them from him. "Thank you." She tapped the other glass he held. "And you had me at kitchen. You really cook down there?"

"Come on, I'll show you."

He guided her through an undersized doorway and down a few stairs to the living quarters, which somehow managed to not feel cramped, despite how much was squeezed into the space.

A step ahead of her, he tapped on one large door. "Closet, gear on the starboard, the head is right there." He gestured toward a small bathroom that she could see doubled as a full-room shower, too. "And there's the galley."

"Not bad." She took in the three small counters, cook-top, and cabinets, neat as a pin, but clearly used. "You cook?"

"Not as well as you, but I get by."

Beyond the galley was a sitting area, with two comfy couches facing each other, both under bookshelves, one with a small table raised high enough for eating. "These open up for more sleeping, but the main stateroom, if you can call it that, is in the stern area."

He let her by to peek into the room that held nothing but a large bed, with doors on either side for, she assumed, storage. He flipped one open and all that hung in it were scrubs in various colors.

"My wardrobe needs are light," he remarked. "And

only one is coffee-stained."

"It never came out?" she asked.

"Not completely, but it's my Tori Top, so I'll save it."

"Are you for real?" she asked, only half kidding.

His smile faded at the question. "Do you not trust me?" he asked.

"I hardly know you," she said slowly. "But you do say things to make a woman swoon."

"That's the boat rocking," he teased. "But what can I say? I like you. I'm a simple man and I say what I think."

"Simple? You're a neurologist."

"Who lives in a tiny house with no foundation and..." He led her back up to the deck and pointed to the sunset-washed sky. "No actual roof."

"But do you really need one?" she quipped.

"Not on a night like this."

She followed him to the cockpit, still absorbing the scale and size of the boat, the gleaming wood, and the heavy scent of the river. "Do you think you'll ever live in a house again?" she asked.

"I don't know. Have a seat and I'll get us ready to get underway."

She settled on one of the covered benches near the cockpit and he picked up his own wine, raising the glass for a toast.

"To simplicity," she said. "This makes my three-thou-sand-square-foot house seem like a mansion."

"It is a mansion," he said. "And I know the joys of living like that. But, I told you, this time, I just wanted...freedom."

"Speaking of freedom..." She took a sip and eyed him over the rim. "Looks like I'm getting a little of my own."

"How so?"

While she relayed the gist of her conversations with Trey and Finn, he started working with the boat, unzipping a large cover over one of the sails and pulling some lines and ropes.

When she finished, he got behind the wheel at the helm, listening to every word, which, she was starting to learn, was something she really liked about him.

"So, that means..." She took a deep breath and braced for his response. "I may stay here for the entire summer."

He snapped one of the ropes. "Seriously?"

She studied his expression, seeing nothing but happy surprise on his face. "Yep. How do you feel about that?"

He took a few steps closer. "Like I was just given...a chance."

Her toes curled in her sneakers and her heart slammed against her ribs and her lips rose in a smile she couldn't hide if she had to. "A chance at..."

Leaning over, he kissed her lightly. "You."

The answer was so simple, so real, so from his heart that she couldn't speak. So she sat silently while he returned to the wheel—which probably was called something else—and stood with his legs braced, hair blowing in the breeze.

"So, you think it's a good idea?" she asked.

"I think we could have the best summer of our lives." He started the motor, grinning at her. "Let's get underway and then unfurl our sails, matey."

Forty-five minutes later, they'd motored to open water on the Amelia River. There he raised one sail, then the other, each of them snapping to life and tipping the boat just enough to make her want to squeal in delight.

He'd downplayed his sailing skills, which were masterful, getting them under sail and flying along in a stiff breeze that carried them along the intracoastal waterway between Amelia Island and much smaller ones to the west.

"Look!" He pointed to the water, and a second later, a dolphin rose and fell next to them, making her laugh at the sheer beauty of it.

Bathed in late afternoon sunshine, the light spray in her face and hair, Tori sat back and tried to absorb the sheer glory of the moment...and the man who had given it to her.

Her gaze shifted from the navy blue water and the green land on either side to Justin, who stood like he was born on a boat, the wind in his hair, his face tanned and confident.

Yes, of course she and Kenzie could have the best summer of their lives. But surely she'd fall head over heels in love with this man.

And then what?

Trey would never let her move Kenzie and Finn to Amelia Island. So, she couldn't live here in this dream, not permanently. Was it worth the inevitable ache if she stayed until August?

Hard to say. But right now, she wanted to enjoy every wind- and water-sprayed moment of heaven.

Chapter Twenty

Rose

Chloe and her little pup, Lady Bug, showed up early enough to go to Sunday service with the entire D'Angelo family. They left the dog at home and trekked to the church, but the entire ride over and through the whole sermon, all Rose could think about was what she had to say to Chloe.

Instead of praying, she looked around the glorious sanctuary bathed in color from the stained glass, listening to the sounds of the ancient organ rising up to the vaulted ceiling that had been standing for well over a hundred years.

So many people were counting on this wedding, and Chloe had put her heart and soul into planning it. Susannah, too, who'd poured love and attention into her youngest daughter's nuptials, but all that had been sidelined by Dad's stroke.

Another reason to postpone the wedding—for their mother.

She looked to her side to see Chloe down the row with

Avery and Alyson on either side of her, each holding a hand. They'd skipped Sunday school just to sit with their beloved Auntie Chloe. And their hearts would be broken if she postponed, because they were official greeters at the reception, with special dresses and a guest book to manage.

But Chloe didn't look...rapturous as she gazed at the altar. She didn't look like a woman imagining herself standing there in her beautiful white gown. Not at all. A frown tugged at her arched brows and she chewed at her bottom lip, a habit that Susannah had, as well. It always meant stress.

Was it the wedding or the *marriage* stressing Chloe out?

Could it be that, deep inside, Chloe already knew she was making a mistake and didn't know how to stop the train?

There was only one way to find out.

After church, they hauled the entire family to the beach house. Raina was hanging in the kitchen with Tori, who was cooking a feast of a brunch that would be served to whoever showed up.

On one hand, it felt like a normal Sunday afternoon, where some, most, or all of the branches of the Wingate family frequently gathered, ate, and hit the beach. They were cooking on the main floor, but mostly gathered where Dad was, down in the old game room, now his domain.

When Chloe slipped out, Tori grabbed Rose's arm and tugged her around the counter with Raina.

"Well?" Tori asked. "Did you do the deed? Did you talk to her about possibly postponing?"

"In church?" Rose blinked at her. "No, I just prayed for the strength to do it...the right way."

Raina shook her head, still having not said a word other than a quick greeting when they arrived.

"You think it's a mistake?" Rose asked her.

"I don't know."

"Raina." Rose came closer, searching her twin's face. "What's wrong?"

"I'm worried about her, too. And I'm worried about some stuff at Wingate Properties. And...and..."

"Jack?" Rose guessed.

Raina blew out a breath. "I haven't talked to him in days, Rose. We've done nothing but exchange meaningless texts since our big fight, sometimes not even that. I'm scared."

"Oh, Raindrop." Rose went to hug her, but Raina shuddered as if she did not want to hear the nickname.

"It's fine," Raina insisted. "He'll be here for the wedding. We'll pound it out then." She inched back and eyed Rose. "Unless Chloe postpones. You're going to talk to her, right?"

Rose nodded. "I'm dreading it."

"I can imagine," Raina said. "But if you need backup to tell her not to marry the wrong guy—"

"Raina! You and Jack can work this out."

"Not if he's cheating," Tori chimed in.

Rose looked pained at the very idea. "You don't think—"

"I don't *know*," Raina said with a soft whine. "That's the worst part. If I knew, I'd walk. No, I'd run. But just having these doubts keeping me awake at night, making me sick to my stomach? I'm literally nauseous over the possibility."

Rose rubbed her back. "I hate that you're going through this."

Just then, they saw Suze and Chloe coming up the stairs, deep in conversation. Rose looked hard at Chloe's expression, trying to gauge what had happened downstairs, but Chloe and Suze just hugged tight, silent.

"We still have time, sweetheart," Suze said, putting a hand on Chloe's cheek. "He might use a walker."

Rose knew that Dad had been trying to make the shift to the walker, and she knew why—he wanted to walk his daughter down the aisle, not wheel her. But so far, he hadn't been comfortable enough to do it.

The reasons to postpone this event were mounting and Rose knew that only one of them could broach the subject. If they double or triple-teamed her, Chloe might feel like they'd ganged up on her.

Rose had to do this alone.

Her whole body vibrated with the thought of having the conversation. She despised conflict. She loathed making someone unhappy. And she loved Chloe with her whole heart and soul and only wanted her to be joyous and at peace.

Well, she wasn't going to be either of those things if she had to postpone her nuptials, but Rose had no choice.

MORE FAMILY ARRIVED, lunch was served and shared with Rex, until he got tired and wanted to nap. Susannah swept them all up to the main living area and out to the deck, so Rose took the opportunity to sidle up to Chloe.

"Want to go talk, Chloe?"

"Oh, yes. Do you have that centerpiece thing you were going to show me?" she asked. "Let's show it to everyone and see what they think."

"Let's, um, talk privately first. I want to...talk."

Chloe grimaced. "You can't get the cut-glass votives? Dang, I'm heartbroken, Rose. I wanted them so much."

Oh, honey, Rose thought as she put her arm around her sister. *Brace for more disappointment.*

"Come on. Let's walk down the beach."

A minute later, they were crossing the boardwalk from the deck to the dunes, watching Rose's boys slide on skimboards, while Avery and Alyson flanked Nikki Lou and all three of them ran after little Lady Bug, who barked at the waves.

Gabe was not far away, keeping an eye on all of them for safety, talking to Grace, who never veered from her little one.

"This feels normal," Chloe said, pausing at the top of the stairs to take it all in. "Even with Dad still working so hard to get better, this feels like a good Sunday."

"It *is* a good Sunday."

"I just wish..."

When her voice trailed off, Rose waited, holding her

breath. "You wish what?" she asked when Chloe didn't finish.

"I wish Hunter and I could stay here. On Amelia Island, I mean."

Her heart dropped. "No chance of him finding a position with a plastic surgery group in Jacksonville?" Rose asked. It was not local, but less than an hour's drive, so there could be many Sundays like this.

"Oh, he could have a job with one of the best surgeons in the county tomorrow," Chloe said. "They've all tried to recruit him."

"Really?"

"But the siren call of L.A. is strong."

Rose nearly choked. "Los Angeles?"

"Did you think I meant Louisiana?" Chloe asked dryly. "Yes, Los Angeles. As you can imagine, plastic surgery is top-notch out there and one particular group is a favorite of the Hollywood stars."

"Yikes." She tried, but Rose had a very hard time imagining Chloe in that world. "How do you feel about that?"

She shrugged. "They haven't made the offer yet, so I'm secretly praying he doesn't get it. California is so far and so...different."

"Yeah." Rose was still trying to wrap her head around Chloe possibly being three thousand miles away. "It's... wow. Have you told Suze?"

"No. I haven't told anyone but you. I'm waiting for some Rose magic here. Like why moving three thousand miles away is so awesome and how Hunter will shine and probably make oodles of money..." She looked at Rose, waiting. "Lady Bug will like it? Anything, Rose? Any good thing about moving that far away?"

Rose swallowed. She had nothing.

"Um, at least we'll have that first year of marriage in a new place," Chloe said when Rose was quiet for a little too long. "Right?"

Rose barely nodded and gave up on the idea of a walk, plopping down on the landing of the last three steps to the beach. "I need to, uh, suggest something to you, Chloe. About the wedding."

Eyeing her, Chloe eased herself onto the wood, understandably wary. "What is it?"

Rose took a deep breath, fisting her hands. "Would you ever consider postponing it for Dad?"

She braced herself for the response—the expected explosion and full-out rejection of such a costly, terrible idea. But Chloe stared straight ahead. Could she be considering it? Rose's heart lifted at the thought.

"Do you really think I didn't already suggest that?" Chloe asked, her voice emotionless.

Oh. Rose hadn't considered that. "Did you?"

"The day after he had his stroke," Chloe said. "I begged—well, I don't like to beg, but I did make a compelling argument."

"And Hunter—"

"Acted like I suggested he cut off both his arms." She gave a dry laugh. "The inconvenience, the cost, the disappointment for his friends and family...everything."

"But doesn't he want Dad to be healthy for your

wedding? I know you would lose some money, but it's not unheard of to move the date."

Chloe nodded. "I didn't love the idea, obviously, but Hunter lost his mind."

Rose looked at her sister, once again at a loss to find anything good in this situation. Didn't that response tell Chloe everything she needed to know about the man she was marrying? Gabe would move Heaven and Earth to make everyone, especially Rose, happy.

She dove in and tried her best. "You know, Chloe, marriage is a...partnership. One person doesn't get to make every decision."

"Easy to say when you're married to him." She jutted her chin toward Gabe, who'd just run after Lady Bug and snagged the tiny dog before a wave touched her precious paws.

"It doesn't change with who you marry," Rose said. "But how you...arrange your marriage."

"Hunter is strong," Chloe replied. "Strong-willed and strong-spirited. I've always found life is easier if you let the stronger ones take charge. Maybe that's the curse of being the youngest, but I'm not used to my opinion carrying as much weight as everyone else's."

Rose made a face. "Did we make you feel that way? I'm so sorry, Chloe."

"No, no one did, not intentionally. But it's a comfortable place to let the older one call the shots. Hunter's a firstborn and he owns that role in every way. He is always right." She laughed softly. "Always."

Rose cringed at the idea of marrying someone like that. "But no one person calls all the shots in a marriage."

Chloe stared straight ahead, not speaking.

After a few minutes, Rose put her hand on Chloe's back, hating what she had to say but knowing she had to say it. "It's not too late to change your mind," she whispered.

"About the date?" Chloe asked, with fear and uncertainty in her eyes.

"About...anything."

Tears welled in her eyes, which was no surprise. "You think I shouldn't marry him, Rose?" Her voice cracked with the question, along with Rose's heart.

"No, no. I don't know. Chloe, only you know the answer to that. But the fact that you even think it... Well. I don't know what to say, except it's not too late until you take that vow and put that ring on."

Chloe blinked and a tear meandered down her cheek. "I don't want to give up. I don't want to walk away. I love him, Rose. I do. I know he's not perfect—he's certainly not Gabe—but we've had wonderful times together. The stress of the wedding, finishing his residency, applying for these massive jobs, even the idea of moving. Throw in Dad's stroke, the last-minute planning, everything is just hard right now. Really, really hard."

Rose sighed. "All of those things, every single one of them, are good reasons to postpone."

"No, no. I think we have to power through. Once we're married, everything will be fine." She turned to Rose. "Won't it?"

It was time for Rose to say the most positive and uplifting thing she could. Time for her to tell Chloe that marriage had its ups and downs and change was a constant. Time for her to assure her sister that everyone had moments where they were less than perfect. Yes, even Gabe.

But she couldn't. So she just folded her arms around Chloe and held her tight, but she didn't say a word.

After a minute, Chloe stood. "I need to take a walk." She hustled off, calling for Lady Bug, who bounded over with unabashed love.

That's what Chloe needed. A man who loved her unconditionally and wholly and put her first above all.

But that's not what she had, and that made Rose's heart hurt so much. All she could do was sit in the sun and let the tears roll down her cheeks.

Chapter Twenty-one

Raina

Raina tossed, turned, moaned, threw the covers off, brought them back up again and finally climbed out of bed in the middle of the night. Blowing out a breath, she went to the spiral staircase that led up to the turret at the top of the beach house, longing for air and a new perspective on life.

Of course, she took her phone.

Not that she expected Jack to call her at two in the morning. But the last time he'd even texted was, what? Two days ago? Yes, he was busy, since work was "wild" and they were "crushing it" with new listings.

When did he start using words like that?

Since he started working so closely with Lisa Godfrey, she thought, hating that it was the obvious answer. Hating that was all she'd been thinking about for weeks.

She pushed open one of the massive windows, sucking in the salty beach air. She loved it up here, where the moon seemed closer and the stars were bright. It cleared her head instantly, which was great. The only problem was now she was wide awake and the only thing she could do was worry and wonder.

Although that wasn't the only thing she could do.

With Dad and Susannah sound asleep, she could find that password book Susannah kept forgetting to look for. As every day ticked by, it became more apparent that money had to be squirrelled away in an account Raina simply didn't know about.

She ran a business exactly like Wingate Properties and, understanding the cash flow was second nature to her.

Maybe, if she could solve this one problem, she'd sleep again.

On her way downstairs, she pulled on her robe. Well, the guest robe. Hers was at home, next to Jack's bathtub, being worn by...

Don't go there, Raina.

Barefoot, she padded down to the living level, then quietly down the stairs to the first floor. She stood for a moment, making sure she didn't hear anyone talking, although Suze didn't sleep in the same room as Dad.

Soon, she hoped.

She stepped into the darkened office and closed the door to block the light, leaving it open an inch so she could hear if her mother got up. She reached for the desk lamp, spilling a soft golden glow over the room.

"Password book, password book," she whispered. "Where would you be?"

Very slowly, so as not to make a noise, she opened the top desk drawer. The contents were much like the drawer at Wingate Properties, minus the cigars...and the sad card from Charlotte. She lifted a pocket calendar that they gave away to Wingate clients every year, flipping through the empty pages, but finding nothing that could help.

On a sigh, she tried the first drawer on the side and spied a desk organizer tray full of small office supplies. She was just about to close it when she saw the small corner of something brown under it.

"Oh, what do we have here?" She picked up the tray and stared at the small, flat book under it, fighting the urge to let out a soft shriek of success. "We have the World's Greatest Grandpa, that's what."

As she picked up the book, she ran a finger over the cheap gold embossing. She had a vague recollection of Rose's son giving this to him at Christmas. Dad had held up the cheap book that had been purchased at a school fair and raved like he'd been given a copy of the Gutenberg Bible.

How she wished she could make him a grandpa to yet another adoring child, she thought wistfully. The very idea brought tears to her eyes, making her shake her head. She had to stop being an emotional mess. This was all Jack, who had her worrying about something that probably wasn't true.

Probably? It *couldn't* be true. Jack wasn't a cheater. She knew that in her bones.

Swallowing, she opened the book and started her search, hoping for a bank account she'd never previously found. Or an investment firm, maybe. Something odd, something out of place, something...

The Iowa City Credit Union.

Something like *that*. What the heck was he doing with a credit union account in Iowa?

Instantly, she touched the mouse next to the keyboard, bringing the desktop computer to life. While it fired up, she studied the entry itself. Even that seemed to be different from the others, not scratched in over the years, but fresher somehow. Every other word and number had been written in Dad's precise, flawless printing style. This one was, too, but not neat. This one seemed...shaky.

Or was that her imagination?

She hit the keys, found the credit union website, and logged in with Dad's email and a string of numbers and letters.

It took a few seconds, but she was in and able to access account information with one click. In a second, she could see that there was...just under two hundred dollars?

"Well, that's a disappointment," she muttered, skimming through recent transactions.

And that's when her heart skipped a beat. Withdrawal, withdrawal, withdrawal...

How much money had gone out of that account? She added up the amounts in her head, vaguely aware of her jaw dropping with each hundred thousand.

Half a million dollars.

Well, there was the cash flow...but...when did it disappear?

One glance at the dates and she gasped out loud. Dad

didn't make these staggering withdrawals! The first one was...the day after her father's stroke with several more while he was in the hospital and then recovering at home.

"What the hell?" she whispered.

"Good question."

On another gasp, she whipped around, stunned to see her father sitting in the wheelchair in the open doorway. "Dad—"

"What are you doing?" he demanded, working for clarity in each word. But he didn't have to work for anger —that she could hear loud and clear.

"I'm...trying to run your business and I've discovered—"

"What?"

She inched back at the word. "An anomaly," she finished, suddenly remembering the stress that he was not allowed to endure.

Even in the dim light, she could see him pale, and she instantly stood, wanting to get as far away from what she just found as possible. *She'd* figure it out. *She'd* deal with it. But he could not know someone had withdrawn all that money while he was in the hospital and here, recovering from a stroke.

"What are you doing up, Dad?" She came around the desk. "And how on Earth did you get from your bed into that chair? I heard a rumor you could do it yourself, but—"

"Raina."

She came in front of him, crouching down, needing to physically stop him from seeing what was on his computer screen. "You want me to get you back in bed? You want anything at all, Dad?" Her voice cracked as she pressed her hands into the armrests of his chair. "I can get you some tea or—"

"Don't."

"Okay, no tea. Can I sneak you a snack? Suze is asleep and I know you like—"

"You know now," he said.

She stared at him, making sure she understood what he'd said. Based on the dark, knowing look in his brown eyes, she'd heard him right.

Instead of answering, she just stared at him, waiting.

"Don't you?" he demanded.

On a shaky breath, she leaned forward, feeling somewhat relieved. Okay, he knew about the money. That was...odd. But one wrong word could send his blood pressure skyrocketing.

"I do," she said very slowly. "And you didn't move that money. So...who did? And why?"

He breathed so hard, his nostrils flared. "I need..."

She waited breathlessly for him to finish the sentence, knowing he could be searching for a word he'd forgotten or maybe just fighting his mouth to form it. What did he need? Answers? An explanation? Proof?

"Replace it," he finally said.

"Replace..." Her brows furrowed, not quite sure what he meant.

"The money!" he barked.

"Dad." She managed a breath, then put a light hand on his leg. "It's gone. And I don't know who—"

"No!"

She drew back. "No, it's not gone or no...what?"

He just stared at her, no stroke powerful enough to take away the effect of his glare. "Don't ask, Raina. Never ask. Never!"

"Okay, okay," she said quickly, hating the two spots of red on his cheeks. That was stress, and she swore she wouldn't cause any. "But, Dad, can you understand—"

"Replace the money, Raina."

Did he mean find the person who took it...or what? "I would need to know—"

He let out a noisy sigh and closed his eyes, his voice quivering. "I need you to do this for me, Raina. Please."

She pressed her hands on his lap, trying to calm him with soothing hands. "Dad, I will do anything for you. You know that. But I have to talk to—"

"Make it rain, Raina."

She rocked back a little at the words he used to say when he'd send her out to get a listing, close a deal, or sell a property as she learned their business.

"Make it rain, Raina."

It meant make money, plain and simple.

"Dad, are you asking me to...somehow replace that money with half a million *different* dollars?"

He nodded very slowly. "Please. For me."

How the heck was she supposed to do that? "Dad, I can't—"

"Yes, you can." He leaned closer, putting his hand on her cheek. "You can fix this for me, Raina. Only...you."

His jaw started quivering, then his whole face bobbed up and down helplessly.

"Dad?" She stood up to reach for his hand. "It's fine. We don't even have to talk about—"

He shuddered and grew even paler, and his left eye started to twitch.

"Dad. Dad, please. Let me get you back in bed." She stood to push his chair, but he made a garbled, incomprehensible sound. "Dad?"

The twitching intensified, making him angle his head awkwardly.

"Dad? Are you okay?"

"It's...happening...again."

"Don't move, Dad. Don't—" Panicked, she yelled out the door. "Suze! Susannah! Call 911!"

Her mother appeared in a nightgown, running from her bedroom. "What? Why?" She froze in horror, looking at Dad. "What happened? Rex!"

Taking a breath, Raina willed herself to hold it together. *Phone. Call. Get help. Now.*

She yanked the cell from her bathrobe pocket and forced her fingers to press 911 on the keypad.

She kept her voice dead calm as she gave the address and described his symptoms, staying on the line while Susannah pushed Dad out to the hall, kneeling in front of him, talking and crying.

"He's having a seizure," Susannah muttered over and over again, as much to herself and him as to Raina.

Time seemed to stand still, frozen in the terror of the

moment, slowly rolling from one heartbeat to the next until she heard the siren and ran to the front door.

It opened before she got there, and Gabe came barreling in with two more EMTs behind him.

She watched them file in, followed by two firefighters carrying a stretcher, the entire team surrounding Dad and peppering Susannah with questions.

As they worked, she and Susannah just stood arm in arm, watching, hands pressed to their mouths, both of them trembling as adrenaline and fear cascaded through their veins.

"I don't know what happened," Raina said. "I just—"

"Shhh." Susannah squeezed her. "It's not the first time he's come in here. I found him here the other night. I don't know why."

But Raina did. Dad—or someone—took half a million dollars from Wingate Properties and now he wanted her to *replace it*? Had she heard that right?

She pushed the trouble away, more concerned as the EMTs marched out the door with Dad on the stretcher, his eyes closed, his face bloodless, his hands hanging useless at both sides.

Raina let out a sob as Gabe passed them. He shot her a look and put a hand on Susannah's shoulder. "'Sokay," he mouthed.

But it wasn't okay. It was so *not okay*.

"Meet us at the hospital," he added.

When he left, Susannah broke down and sobbed, but Raina ran to the bathroom and threw up.

MADELINE WAS WAITING when they got to the hospital with Tori. Rose was on her way after waking up her oldest son and leaving him in charge. Grace stayed home with Nikki Lou, but was as active on the 7 *Sis* group chat as Sadie, who was up and at work in Brussels. Chloe was on her way from Jacksonville, even though Suze had told her to wait until morning.

Raina understood the desire to be here, at the epicenter of the crisis, regardless of the time.

And speaking of time...she stared at her phone. She'd texted Jack four times and called twice, and both those calls went straight to voicemail without ringing. Which meant Jack had either turned his phone off or...he was on a call. At two in the morning, she went with the former.

Even though he left his phone on, charging, and sitting on his nightstand every single night.

"Justin's with him now," Tori said, breezing into the waiting room.

"Is he the neurologist on duty?" Madeline asked.

"No. I called him and he got right up and drove over here."

"That's good," Susannah said from her seat, flanked by Madeline and Rose. "He's good. He's a good man, Tori."

Tori nodded. "Who'da thunk Dr. Hottypants would be our savior?" she joked.

But the mood was too glum to laugh.

She took a seat and dropped her head on Raina's

shoulder. "I can't believe that Dad got up in the middle of the night to work. Thank God you were there, Raina." When Raina didn't answer, Tori lifted her head. "Talk?" she asked.

Raina nearly jumped up. "Let's go get coffee."

"For a second," Tori said. "I want to see Justin when he comes in to talk to us."

"In the hall, Tor," she whispered. "I have to tell you something."

With that, Tori was up, reaching for Raina's hand. "We'll be right back," she called to the others, then they stepped out of hearing range. "What's going on?"

"Brace yourself," Raina said. "And please, don't blame me. I tried and tried—"

"What happened?"

Raina swallowed and led her a little further away, then told Tori everything, including Dad's reaction.

"Wait. What?" Tori shook her head. "Half a *million*? Are you serious?"

"I'd say as a heart attack, but this seems like the wrong environment."

Tori didn't smile. "And it got withdrawn since he had the stroke? Then someone stole it. Maybe that new assistant of his. Or someone found the password book. One of the PTs that are always going in and out of there. This is a serious crime, Raina. We have to—"

"No, don't you understand? Dad *knows* about it. He told me to replace it. To *save* him. What does that mean, Tori?"

"That he made a bad investment or something and he

wants help recouping his losses. Not like him, but it happens."

Raina exhaled. "Then why wouldn't he say that? And why a credit union in Iowa? And why did this have to happen? I shouldn't have gone down into that office."

"Stop. Don't blame yourself."

But Raina did. She was wallowing in blame, strangled in guilt, and furious that she was in any way the cause of making her father relapse. "I'm going to help him. I have to."

Tori searched her face, then reached up and touched her cheek. "Honey, don't take this the wrong way, but whoa, you look like hell."

"Thank you." Raina gave a dry smile. "Been a rough night. Not to mention that my husband is ignoring me and I threw up after the EMTs left."

"You threw up? Why?"

"I don't know. Stress. I did the other day, too. Because my husband is maybe having an affair, I might have just given my father a stroke, and, oh, I need to pull half a mill out of my—"

"Maybe you're pregnant."

Raina gave a soft laugh, but it got caught in her throat. "Shut up."

"Been dizzy lately?"

Raina just stared at her, unable to even nod.

"Are you late, by any chance?"

She honestly had no idea, but...maybe. "I was in Miami that one time, and...there was one morning the day before Dad—"

"Hold on, I see my man." Tori shot off, right into the arms of her very own doctor on call, who greeted her with a kiss. Normally, Raina would witness that and grin, maybe tease her sister, or just thank God that this wonderful thing was happening in her life.

But right now, all she could think of was...

"Maybe you're pregnant."

Holy, holy—

"Raina!" Tori called, waving her over. "Come here! Good news!"

Raina hustled closer, greeting Justin and following him into the waiting room where the others stood. He went straight to Susannah and gave her a hug. Even in her mind-numbed state, Raina had to give him props for being a class act.

Heck, she couldn't even get her husband to answer his phone, and this man got out of bed in the middle of the night and rushed to the hospital.

When they were all gathered, he put his hands together and went into full doctor mode. "He did not have another stroke. In fact, he didn't have a serious seizure."

"Really?" a few of them asked in shock and hope.

"It's not unusual. Sometimes scar tissue in the brain, damaged by the original stroke, can send out abnormal electrical signals. This can trigger different kinds of seizures, and his was very mild, not a setback for his recovery, speech, or mobility."

"Oh, thank God," Susannah exhaled.

"Could it happen again?" Raina asked.

"They've run all the tests and I've combed his scan and blood work, but there are no signs of neurological change. His blood pressure was very high in the ambulance, but it's normal now. Something upset him, but certainly didn't push him over the medical edge."

Raina felt that now familiar wave of dizziness roll over her. That was not pregnancy. That was *guilt*.

"Can he go home?" Madeline asked.

"Absolutely, I want him home. Susannah, the discharge team is with him now, and you can go in and sign the paperwork."

"And when he's home?" Susannah asked. "Special treatment?"

"The same, but..." He breathed out. "Give him whatever he wants. He's right on the edge of either spiraling south emotionally or pulling himself out of this. It's a tricky time for a stroke patient. His brain is trying to decide if he wants to go on and fight this fight, or just give up."

"Give up?" Tori choked.

"This is Dad, he doesn't give up," Rose added.

"That's what he needs to hear," Justin said.

And he wouldn't give up if Raina could...*save him*. Cold sweat tickled the nape of her neck.

"Doctor." Susannah put her hand on his shoulder. "You know we have this wedding in a week. I'll take your advice and counsel. Should we urge him to come or just let him miss it?"

"Miss his youngest daughter's wedding? Not a chance. Rex can be there and do his fatherly duties. He just needs all of you to rally support and let him know that you don't care if he gets carried down the aisle by the bridesmaids. Just that he makes the trip."

They all gazed at him like he was a bit of a god—none more than Tori, who looked downright lovestruck.

"I'll let you all finish up here," he said. "I have rounds in..." He glanced at the clock. "Three hours. I'm going to try to get some sleep."

He accepted a round of thank-yous and hugs, then walked off with Tori.

They all gathered in a group hug and sent Suze off to see to Dad, all of them a thousand times cheerier than when they got here.

When Tori floated back in with a big old grin on her face, they all just cooed over her amazing Dr. Hottypants.

"Come on," Tori said, grabbing Raina's arm after Rose and Madeline said goodbye.

"What? We have to wait for Suze and Dad, remember?"

"Discharge takes forever. Come with me for a second."

Too tired to argue, she followed her sister out of the ER and into the hall to a small shop that was the only thing open in the hospital.

"What are we doing?" Raina asked.

"We aren't doing anything. But you..." She dragged her to the back and picked up a pink and blue box. "Are going to put me out of my misery and take this test."

"Tori! I'm not—"

"Prove it."

Raina just closed her eyes.

"Fine. I'll pay for it." Tori marched to the counter, swiped her card, and declined a bag. Then she walked back to Raina, who was waiting in the doorway, and stuffed the box in her purse. "Let me know."

But Raina already knew she wasn't going to take that test. She couldn't handle it, no matter what it said.

If she wasn't pregnant, she'd merely taste the bitter, inevitable disappointment of a negative test.

If she was? Well, that was a problem, since her marriage was in shambles and a baby was literally the last thing she needed. Plus, she didn't want to endure a fourth miscarriage.

"Oh, by the way." Tori slid into a wide smile. "I forgot to tell you. I'm staying all summer and having my fling. Maybe you should stay, too."

Maybe she should. After all, she had to...save Dad.

Chapter Twenty-two

Susannah

What was that noise?

Susannah lifted her head from the pillow, sleepy disorientation pressing down as she blinked into the pre-dawn light.

Was that Rex? Was he talking to someone?

She flipped back the covers and slid her feet to the floor, picking up her phone to squint at the time. Seven a.m.? A little early for a physical therapist, but...then she recognized the woman's faint voice.

Chloe had stayed upstairs in Susannah and Rex's master last night, having made that surprising decision at the end of the rehearsal dinner last night. She had her dress and everything packed for the wedding day, and her dog was at Rose's house for the weekend, but instead of going home with Hunter for their last night before the wedding, Chloe had announced she was staying at the beach house. She'd shared the king-size bed with Sadie, who'd arrived from Europe a few days earlier.

And now, before sunrise, she was talking to Rex?

Making her last plea, no doubt. Of all the people who

could change Rex's stubborn mind, maybe his daughter—the bride he'd disappointed by not even going to the rehearsal, let alone the dinner that followed—could sway him into attending her wedding.

But after the seizure, he'd refused. In fact, he hadn't gotten out of bed on his own anymore, either. Dr. Verona said it wasn't a setback, but it sure felt like one.

Susannah slid into her slippers and tied her robe, not rushing, because she wanted to give Chloe a chance to make her case. After a moment, she stepped into the hall, but stayed out of sight next to Rex's door, eavesdropping on the conversation.

"I don't know who else to ask, Dad."

Ask to...walk her down the aisle? Susannah had offered, almost insisted, but, oh, that didn't fly with Hunter. If she'd learned anything last night, it was that her future son-in-law was a stickler for tradition. A mother walking the bride down the aisle did not work for him.

He hadn't said as much, not to the wedding party who'd waited in St. Peter's sanctuary while the bride and groom had a private conversation in a back room. And not to the gathering of friends and family at a local restaurant last night, either. But when the night was over, Chloe said she was perfectly happy to walk down the aisle alone.

That couldn't be true, Susannah thought, leaning in to pick up more snippets of the conversation. Yes, she should and would make her presence known, especially if Rex sounded upset, but now...she wanted to hear them.

"You know the answer," she heard Rex say gruffly.

"If I did, would I be here asking you?"

Rex responded with something Susannah didn't catch, but she heard Chloe give a dry laugh.

"If I could do that by myself, without you, would I have sneaked in here while the gatekeeper is still sleeping to have this conversation?"

Emotions swirled at the question. Yes, she was a gatekeeper, but for Rex's health. But should she have let Chloe have this conversation sooner? Would that have been enough to get Rex to walk or wheel his daughter down the aisle this afternoon? Was it too late?

"I can't say what you want to hear," Rex said. "You have to do this alone."

Susannah's heart kicked at the response, enough to get her to stride into the room and do what had to be done—beg him.

"Why not?" Susannah demanded, her voice sharp for the first time since he'd had the stroke and she started to baby him to avoid another.

"Mom, it's okay. We're not—"

"No, Chloe, it's not okay." She crossed her arms and came around the bed to stand next to her daughter. Rex merely turned his head in the other direction.

"Rex, why won't you try?" she pleaded. "Pride? That seems a little foolish on your youngest daughter's wedding day. Shame? You'd be a *hero* if you rolled down that aisle. Fear? I've never known you to be afraid of anything. What is stopping you from pushing up from that chair, grabbing the walker, and *trying*? Dr. Verona said there is no reason you can't."

"Pain," he finally said.

"It hurts?" She leaned forward. "It hurts to try and walk? Where does it hurt? Your legs? Your back? You've never said that before."

His eyes shuttered as he lifted his right hand and put it on his chest. "Right here."

She sucked in a breath and stood. "Your heart? You're having chest pains? I can call—"

He snagged her arm with that hand, stopping her with a flash in his dark eyes. "No. It hurts...like a father hurts."

"Dad!" Chloe shot closer. "I don't want you to hurt. Not because of what I just told you. Please." She leaned over to kiss him, whispering something in his ear that Susannah didn't catch. "I'm going to be fine," she said as she straightened. "And all you need to do is get better."

For a moment, Susannah just stood there, looking from one to the other, sensing she'd definitely missed something in this conversation.

"Thanks, Mom," Chloe said softly. "I appreciate you taking up the fight, but Dad's right. Some things I have to do alone."

Like walking down the aisle? Susannah just gave a tight smile, and nodded. "Why don't you get a few more hours sleep, Chloe? You have a big day today."

"I know. The biggest ever." She blew a kiss to her father, gave Susannah's arm a squeeze and left the room.

"Oh, Rex," Susannah said on a sigh, taking the chair

that Chloe had been in next to the bed. "I wish you'd reconsider."

"I wish she would," he murmured.

"If you don't want her to walk alone, you know what you have to do."

He didn't answer but turned away again, a tear meandering down his cheek. A tear of resignation and regret and frustration and probably that pain in his heart.

"Why don't you try?" she asked again, this time in a soft, soft whisper.

He opened his eyes and looked at her, then he closed his eyes and held up one hand, his signal that he'd had enough and needed to sleep.

All she knew was that her daughter was getting married today, and she prayed that it would be a wonderful day, with or without a father of the bride in attendance.

"ONE MORE, with Susannah holding the veil. In the light, just step to your left, Chloe. Both of you look in the mirror. Okay, hold that smile..."

As the photographer barked orders, Susannah posed, trying to look happy and smile, but it was hard. Darn near impossible to hold a smile on this happy, happy day. Because it didn't feel happy. Not when she looked into her daughter's eyes reflected in the ornate mirror where they were posing for pictures and saw...agony.

"I'm sorry he's not here," she said through her smile,

giving Chloe's narrow waist a squeeze. "Don't let it ruin the day."

Chloe shot her a look that Susannah hoped the photographer did not capture. Because that look was not a blushing, joyous, excited bride.

How could Rex be so cruel as to disappoint his daughter so profoundly on her wedding day?

But then, he'd had a stroke. He shouldn't have to be here, and Chloe knew that. Still, she was deeply and genuinely unhappy. Despite being the most beautiful of brides. Despite having her sisters gathered around in their bright pink dresses, getting the most incredible weather imaginable, and having a packed church outside of this dressing room. None of it mattered, because Rex wasn't here.

"Can we take a break?" Susannah asked the photographer. "Can we just have...five minutes alone?"

"Of course." The woman lowered her camera. "I'll run over and see how they're doing in the groom's dressing room."

"Do you want us to leave?" Rose asked, coming up behind her, her eyes shimmering with the professional makeup that had just been applied.

"We can," Raina added. "If you want a minute with your daughter before she gets married."

"I need to call Justin and check on Dad anyway," Tori said. "It was so sweet of him to offer to stay with him today."

Susannah looked from one to the other, then at Madeline and Grace, currently in the chairs getting their makeup done, while Sadie fussed over what a big girl Nikki Lou had become while she was living in Europe.

For a moment, Susannah was awash with emotion, so strong it rocked her.

She put a hand on her chest and let out a soft moan.

"Are you okay?" At least three of them asked the question in unison.

"I'm fine," she assured them. "I've spent the last month teetering on the precipice of losing it completely, but I'm going to make it. I will not cry off all this beautiful makeup."

"Don't do that, Mom," Chloe said gently. "But, yes, if you guys will just give us five minutes. I do want to talk to Mom."

It was all they needed to hear, the room clearing out quickly. In a minute, Susannah heard the click of the door behind the makeup artists and she was completely alone with Chloe.

"Honey," she said, putting her hands on her shoulders. "I can sense how upset you are. I know it's a huge disappointment not to have Dad here—"

"It's not that, Mom. Really. I've accepted it. The man had a stroke and even you, the controller of all things in this family, cannot make him rise up and walk with me."

Susannah gave a sad smile. "I tried."

"I know you did, and I love you for it."

"But is it nerves, then?" Susannah asked. "Why do you not seem...happy?"

For the longest time, Chloe just stared at her, silent as

her chest rose and fell against the smooth satin bodice of her wedding gown.

"Mom, I'm not—"

Before she could finish, the door clicked open and Susannah made a face. "Not yet," she called over her shoulder. "I'm talking with Chloe."

"Well, I'm *walking* with Chloe. And I need to practice."

A thousand chills exploded all over Susannah's body at the sound of Rex's gruff voice. She froze, her gaze locked on Chloe's, whose blue eyes grew and grew with shock and joy.

"Dad?" she croaked, still not moving, as if that would break the spell.

The door opened a few inches and the first thing they saw was the metal leg of a walker. Then a foot—shiny in tuxedo shoes—then, very slowly, with his weight on the bar in front of him, he entered the room.

His hair was slicked, his bowtie perfect, and his tux made him look like...well, like Rex again.

"Is that okay?" he asked, coming into the room. Justin Verona stood a few feet behind him, a victorious gleam in his eyes.

"Rex," Susannah whispered. "Oh my gosh. How? What... How?"

"Try who." He tipped his head toward the doctor. "He caught me...at a weak moment." He gave Susannah an eyeroll. "You know I hate to cry."

"Oh, Daddy!" Chloe gently reached for him. "I didn't want you to cry because you couldn't be here."

"That's...that's not why," he said. "I just didn't want you to do this...alone."

"Thank you," Chloe whispered.

"I can take her, Suze," he added. "But I'd like you on the other side. Is that going to upset...anyone?" he asked, shifting his gaze to Chloe.

"Not me," she said. "And like you said, Dad, I'm the one who matters most."

"Amen," he muttered. "It's going to take a while for us to get down that long aisle, but we will." He waited a beat and gave her a very meaningful look. "If that's what you want."

If that's what she wanted, Susannah wondered. Was he crazy? This was everything Chloe wanted! She turned to her daughter, who was dabbing unshed tears from under her eyes as she hoisted up her yards of dress and made her way to Rex.

She hugged him gently, both of them holding each other while the photographer slipped back in for pictures and all the girls circled the two of them, cooing over Rex's dramatic entrance.

Raina elbowed Tori in the circle. "We've officially renamed him *Saint* Hottypants."

As they laughed, Rose slipped out of the group. "Wait, wait!" she said. "I can make this better!"

She disappeared for a moment and returned with a white and green garland draped over her arms. "I stole it from the back row, but..." She kneeled in front of the walker and wrapped the flowers around it, getting a huge cheer and some of the best pictures of the day.

The air was still vibrating from that excitement when they came out the side entrance and lined up outside the closed doors of the sanctuary, ready to enter the church. The sisters got into the proper order, oldest to youngest, and Madeline walked into the church first.

As the doors opened, Susannah could hear the historic organ filling the church with a familiar hymn as she slid her arm into Chloe's.

Tori was next and before she took her mark, she stole one more glance at Justin, who stayed close to Rex, like his very own neurological bodyguard, who'd promised to stay close.

Rose was next, blowing a kiss to Chloe before she stepped into the church and disappeared. Then Raina, who stopped to kiss her father as she passed. "You're a king, Dad," she whispered.

Then the younger girls surrounded Susannah, all trembling just a little with the excitement of the moment.

"I can't believe how much I miss all this," Sadie whispered, her green-gold eyes dancing. "And I love you, Chloe." She air-kissed her sister, and started her walk.

Grace was last, finally letting go of her daughter's hand.

"I'll see you down there, Nikki Lou," she whispered. "Stay right here until Grannie Suze tells you when to walk. Just like we practiced."

"We got her," Susannah assured her.

"Thanks. Best wishes, Chloe!" She stepped inside when one of the wedding planner's assistants opened the door, and Nikki Lou looked up at her Aunt Chloe with wide eyes.

For a moment, Susannah braced for a typical Nikki Lou meltdown. But even she seemed to understand the concept of rising to the occasion. *She must have inherited that from Rex*, Susannah thought with a smile.

"You're next, sweetheart," Chloe said to the tiny flower girl. "Just like yesterday, only drop the flower petals on your way."

She nodded solemnly and stepped inside on her cue, toddling away. Before the doors closed, they heard a collective, "Aww," from the guests.

That left the three of them, standing side by side by side. Rex gripped his flower-draped walker and glanced at Justin, who just nodded and whispered, "You got this, my man."

But next to Susannah, Chloe let out a shaky, nervous sigh.

"You got this, too," Susannah assured her.

Chloe looked at her, pale and stricken. "Do I?" she asked. "Because I'm just not sure about that. I'm not sure of anything."

Susannah drew back. "Chloe—"

"If that's true," Rex said, still fighting to make every word clear. "Then you still have time."

The two assistants grabbed the doors and pulled them open with matching nods for the three final people in the procession to start. The organ bellowed Pachelbel's *Canon in D*, the classic piece Hunter had insisted she use for the entrance.

"No more time now," Chloe said.

"There's time," Rex said on the first step. "Until you say, 'I do.' There is time."

What was he suggesting to her? Susannah frowned, trying to figure this out. Was he telling her *not* marry Hunter? Had he fought—and won—the battle to be here for her wedding only to tell her—

"I don't know what to do, Dad," she murmured under her breath as she slid one hand under Rex's arm and held her bouquet with the other. Susannah walked next to her with a lace handkerchief that had been made from her own wedding dress.

In a few slow steps, they reached the back of the church and every single person—all one hundred and fifty of them—turned to stare at them.

Susannah looked down the aisle, her gaze landing on Hunter, whose smile absolutely evaporated at the sight of his bride flanked by her parents. Oh, boy. He was *not* happy. How could he not be happy? He was marrying Chloe Wingate!

A punch of fury gripped Susannah's chest as the organ hit a high note that echoed to the rafters.

"Still time," Rex said.

What was he talking about?

She stole a glance past Chloe, only able see the right half of her husband's face, which was not smiling, and in his eyes, she saw nothing but...anger. Why?

And then she saw something different in the set of Chloe's expression. Something that looked like...resolve and fortitude. Not blissful love, but...determination.

"I think you know what to do," Rex muttered to her. "Walk."

"Yes," Susannah said to both of them, painfully aware of how long they'd been standing frozen in place at the back of the church. "Let's walk."

"I don't think..." Chloe said as they finally took a step. "That's what he means."

Then what *did* he mean?

They moved at a glacial speed due to Rex's walker, but that just made everything more surreal.

All around them, people grinned, wiped tears, and looked on with joy and awe. But why didn't the trio walking down the aisle feel that way?

Susannah's heart crashed against her ribs as confusion ricocheted through her head. What were they talking about? What was this secret communication she knew nothing of? What the heck was going on at this wedding?

They reached the midway point, then a few more rows of pews, and finally they were just a few feet from Hunter, who was actually frowning as his gaze moved from Rex to Susannah.

"Who gives this woman in marriage to this man?" Pastor Samuel asked, beaming at Rex.

Rex took a breath, shot a look to Chloe, and Susannah just held her breath.

"No one," Chloe said, breaking free of them and taking one step closer. The entire church gasped, but Hunter just turned the color of Chloe's dress.

"I'm not..." Chloe shook her head, fighting for every word. "I can't. I'm worth more. I can't."

Susannah swayed as she realized what was happening. Her blood ran cold as she tried to speak, but nothing came out.

"Chloe," Hunter said in his clipped voice. "You will not do this to me."

"Oh, yes, I will. I tried, Hunter, I really did. I wanted to. No one wanted it more. But I can't marry man who doesn't value me. I can't marry a man who doesn't put me on a pedestal. I can't marry a man who isn't as good as my father."

For at least three endless seconds, no one said a word.

Then Chloe took a deep breath, turned around, and stood stone still. Next to her, Rex put his good hand on her shoulder, the other clutching the walker.

"That's my girl," he murmured. "Now run free and find a man who deserves you."

The whole church burst into a noisy response of gasps and, "What?" and a chorus of, "Oh my God!"

But Chloe didn't wait to hear it, tossing her bouquet on the floor, scooping up her miles of white silk and lace, and tearing down the aisle at four times the speed they'd come up it. Her veil fluttered all the way to the end, and two shocked wedding coordinators opened the doors for her.

She disappeared outside and, without thinking, Susannah gave Rex a supportive arm.

"What just happened?" she asked, aware that their six other daughters were gathering like an army of flamingos ready to do battle for the one who just ran away.

"Good question!" Hunter exclaimed. "What the hell happened, Rex?"

Rex turned and sliced him with a look. "What happened was my daughter came to her senses. C'mon, Suze. Girls. Let's go have a party at the beach house to celebrate."

They circled him, around, front, and back, and very slowly walked down the aisle and out of the church, grabbing some more family members along the way.

Outside, in the late afternoon sunshine, they surrounded Chloe who looked shockingly at peace with her decision.

Chapter Twenty-three

Raina

"Only your family can make a party out of a complete disaster." Jack shook his head, looking around the fairly crowded deck.

"It's not a disaster," Raina said. No, it wasn't the Eight Flags Country Club with dancing, a band, and a hundred and fifty delighted guests. It wasn't a wedding, not at all. She forced a smile, one of the first she'd mustered since he'd arrived late last night, missing the rehearsal dinner completely. "Dad's in great spirits, for one thing."

Raina's gaze settled on her father, who was now back in his wheelchair after valiant duty on the walker. All around him, the beach house had filled up with friends and family...from the bride's side. Susannah had contacted the country club and offered to send people to pick up all the food, a job that Tori spearheaded in her rented minivan, with the ease of the top-notch caterer she was.

They'd brought it all but the cake, which Chloe suggested the country club employees and guests enjoy.

"Maybe not a disaster," Jack conceded. "But still a typically weird Wingate...thing."

What the heck was a Wingate *thing*—other than fun, fabulous, and comfortable? Except Jack didn't look comfortable. He never did with her family. He looked a lot like...Hunter.

Not quite deer-in-the-headlights, but definitely not like Gabe, who was sitting between Dad and Sadie, telling a story with his arms draped around both of them.

Sadie laughed, her wild caramel curls bouncing as she dropped her head back. She'd barely left her father's side since she'd arrived, trying to make up for the weeks she'd been in Europe while he was convalescing, and Gabe stayed close to his father-in-law, too.

All around, the family gathered in small groups, friends and relatives all talking in not quite hushed tones, fitting for the occasion. Which was, okay, a *little* weird, but at least they made the best of a bad situation.

"Want to go talk to Rose?" she suggested, suddenly hating that she wasn't in any of those conversations, but on the outskirts of it all, trying to make sure Jack wasn't bored or miserable.

"Sure, sure, one sec." He pulled out his phone and glanced at it, a shadow of a smile lifting his lips.

"Something amusing?" Raina asked. "Or some*one*?"

His eyes shuttered. "You know what? I'm going to make a call. 'Scuze me for a bit."

He pivoted and headed down to the pool, his phone at his ear before he reached the bottom of the stairs.

On a deep sigh, she headed to Rose by herself, but

didn't make it across the patio before Tori snagged her, sliding an arm around Raina's waist.

"Did you take the test?"

Raina just closed her eyes.

"Did you get your period?" Tori pressed.

And kept them closed.

"Raina!"

"Stop it, Tori. Haven't we had enough drama for one day?"

"Never enough. How proud are you of our little sister?"

Raina drew back. "Proud? I'm sad for her. She doesn't exactly look elated over there."

On the other side of the deck, Chloe, Susannah, Madeline, and Grace stood in a close cluster, talking, hugging, smiling, and generally drowning each other in much-needed support.

"Proud that she dodged a bullet," Tori corrected. "Even though it took her to the bitter end, she knew in her heart he was a bad choice. Better one lousy day and the cost of a wedding than a lifetime of lawyers and custody battles."

"I guess." Raina glanced toward the side steps, looking for Jack, but he was walking around the pool, deep in conversation. She knew who he was talking to. She *knew*.

"Chloe's moving here," Tori announced with a smug smile.

That yanked Raina back to the conversation. "Here? To Amelia Island?"

"Yep. I offered her a job at the café and she pounced, ready to start her life over. Maybe I'll make a chef out of her and she can run the place when I go back in the fall."

Raina felt her jaw loosen. "Oh, wow. You're both going to be here."

"And you? Dad's not ready to run that business, and with what you found—has he said anything to you since that night, by the way?"

She shook her head. "I'm terrified to upset him again and trigger another seizure. So, we've kind of let the subject drop."

"You can't let half a million dollars *drop*, Raina. Does Suze know?"

"Nobody knows anything except you. I made a few calls to the credit union, but I'm stymied without power of attorney. I can't bring myself to ask Dad for it, but I will. After the wed—after today," she corrected.

"And how are you going to go about 'replacing' it?"

She gave a dry laugh. "He couldn't have been serious, but if he was? I have a few ideas, but no one is going to like them."

"Sell a property?"

"Bingo, but I'd rather not go there. And especially not today." She turned and looked down by the pool again, letting out a soft groan. "That man is killing me."

Tori looked hard at her. "Look, I know I'm jaded and divorced and have been cheated on, so take this with a grain of salt, but..." She swallowed. "You deserve everything Chloe announced she wanted at that altar today, Raina. You should be treated like a queen."

"Please, Tori, everyone's situation is different."

"I'm just saying that bullets can be dodged by more than one Wingate woman today."

"What are you suggesting? I file for divorce because he doesn't like it here?"

Tori lifted a brow. "Have you talked to him? I mean, really talked. Openly and honestly?"

"He blew in last night at eleven. We were a little preoccupied today." She took a shuddering breath. "And now he's talking to...someone else."

Raina hated that Tori's look was pure pity, but then, she probably deserved it.

"Honey, talk to him. Today. Now. But first take that test."

"I'm not pregnant!" she said in a hushed whisper.

"Are you sure?"

Raina bit her lip. The fact was...she was utterly uncertain. She'd been sick again, felt dizzy when she was in Publix with Susannah the other day, and had definitely missed her last period. All that could be chalked up to stress.

But if she was...

"Go upstairs to your room right now and take that test," Tori insisted. "You want me to come with you? I will."

"No, I..." Suddenly her throat was dry and her whole body felt shaky and...yes, nauseous. That was the power of suggestion. It had to be.

"Come on." Tori gave her a nudge. "Let's do this."

"Will it shut you up?"

Tori snorted. "For a little bit."

Raina let herself be ushered off the deck and into the house, the two of them slipping up the stairs to the guest suite.

"It's in the bathroom," Raina said. "Sit here. Unless you want to watch and make sure I'm not cheating."

Tori rolled her eyes. "You're not a cheater, Rain."

But maybe, Raina thought as she went into the bathroom, maybe her husband was.

She was shaking when she came out, the way she always did when she took a pregnancy test.

"I need air while it cooks," she said, walking toward the spiral stairs that led to the turret. "I'm going up to the lookout to pray."

"What for?" Tori asked. "What do you want most, Rain? Positive or negative?"

She slowed as her foot touched the bottom step, considering the question. "I don't know," she said. "What I really want is for my husband to come in here, tell me my suspicions are wrong, beg me to come home, and profess his undying love for me."

But even as she said it, she knew it was a foolish fantasy. And that was the saddest thing of all.

Without waiting for Tori's response, she hustled up the spiral staircase to the turret, pushing open the window that faced the water and sucking in a breath. She was nauseous, no doubt about it. Only one other pregnancy had made her feel like this. The one she kept the longest—eleven and a half weeks.

A Cuban lady in Miami once told her in an elevator

that girls made you nauseous, but boys made you beautiful.

She closed her eyes and remembered that brief conversation. She'd been so happy, just coming from the doctor, she'd announced to a complete stranger that she was pregnant. The lady had praised God in Spanish and spewed a ton of old wives' tales about pregnancies. Heartburn meant it would have hair, and that you knew a woman was pregnant by looking in her eyes.

Strange how that whole conversation came back to her, a split second in time, but so—

"What are you doing up here?"

With a gasp, Raina turned around to see Jack at the top of the spiral stairs. "Oh, I didn't hear you come up." And why hadn't Tori warned her?

"Are you hiding from the party...or me?"

Raina leaned back against the wall for support and so that he didn't see she was shaking as she waited *for results from a pregnancy test.*

Now. She should tell him that right now.

"Jack, I...I have to—"

"No, let me go first," he said, his voice almost as strained as hers. "I'm gonna take off, Raina."

"Today? Now? You're going back to Miami in the middle of this—"

"Please don't call it a wedding. I don't need to be here and there's a, uh, an issue at work, so—"

"Don't lie," she whispered. "Don't make up some problem that doesn't exist on a Saturday afternoon. You're going back for her, aren't you?"

In the time it took for her heart to slam three beats in her chest and his face to pale a shade or two, she knew the answer. Her whole world shifted sideways so hard and so fast, she nearly buckled. She *knew*.

"Raina, I'm so sorry."

"Oh, God." She pressed her hand to her mouth, her pulse thumping in her head as she tried to accept that this was happening.

"I haven't slept with her," he said, the simple statement startling her. "But..."

"But you want to," she finished.

"It's more than that. It's...worse than that."

He visibly worked to swallow, shifting his weight from one foot to the other, then standing very, very still, silent.

"What could be worse?" she demanded in a tight voice.

"I'm in love with her, Raina."

Oh, yes. That could be worse. Blood drained from her head with a whoosh, making her lean harder against the cool stucco wall or lose her balance completely.

"I don't know how this happened," he continued, his voice stretched reed thin. "But it did. It took me by...*whoa*." He laughed softly, just amused enough that she wanted to lunge at him and claw his eyes out.

"This is funny to you?"

"No, no, no," he insisted, losing the smile. "It's not funny. It's not, well, sometimes it doesn't feel real. Surreal, that's the word."

"No, surreal is when a woman walks down the aisle

in front of a hundred and fifty people and runs away. This is more like a nightmare. Yes," Raina said, nodding. "I'm sure this is a nightmare."

"Raina, I'm so sorry. And I swear, somehow I've managed—we've managed—not to act on it."

She recoiled. "You've *managed*? You and Lisa have somehow mustered the strength to keep your clothes on even though you're married to another woman?"

"Oh, she's had her clothes off, but we didn't—"

"Jack!" She shouted his name, totally understanding what was meant by having your head explode. Because hers was. Her head and heart and maybe her whole body.

"I'm begging you, Raina, don't make this hard or ugly."

"Too late. Very hard. Very ugly."

"I'm going to work this out. We'll figure it out."

"There's nothing to *figure out*, Jack. You just said you're in love with another woman you've seen naked and I'm...I'm..."

Waiting for a pregnancy test. She clamped her lips to keep from saying it out loud.

"It started even before we made the acquisition," he said. "We became friends and she thinks like I do and then—"

"Stop." She took a step closer, pointing at him, not caring that he could see her finger vibrating. "Stop right there. I do not want to hear one detail of your emotional infidelity. I do not want your apology, your explanation, your figuring it out. I want you to leave. I want you to leave and never come back. I want you to get the lawyers, split the business, sell the house, and get as far away from me as a human can be. We are done."

"Raina, I—"

"Leave, Jack," she ground out the words, anger sliding through her teeth and hitting him square in the face.

He winced, nodded, and walked down the stairs noisily, then she heard his footsteps fade on the next steps. Two minutes later, she saw his car pull out of the driveway and turn into traffic.

Gone. Gone forever, she hoped. Gone to—

"Hey." Tori appeared at the top of the steps where Jack had just been, tears glistening in her eyes. "I hate to say this, but I went into the bathroom—the curiosity killed me—and he got right by me. And I heard the whole thing."

Raina whimpered, the first sob choking her.

"And I'd throw my arms around you now, Rain, but..." She lifted her two hands, holding a tissue wrapped around...her test. "I brought this to you instead."

Raina stared at her hands, at the tissue, at the fate of her life literally in Tori's hands.

"Oh," she whispered. "Can you just tell me?"

"Look at it, Raina. Look at it."

But she didn't have to. She *knew*.

She knew her life had just shifted to another dimension. She knew her future was as bright as it was uncertain. She knew that she would be moving to this very island to start all over.

And she knew that she would never be alone again.

Because this baby? This one? This baby was going to make it to the end.

Don't miss the next book in the Seven Sisters series, *The Café on Amelia Island*.

While her life shifts to a brand-new normal, Raina must devise a plan to recoup the missing money, and the opportunity presents itself in the most unexpected way. Tori sails into love, all the while knowing there's a ticking clock on her new romance. Chloe finally has a chance to test her journalism skills, but it comes at a cost. And an answered prayer gives Grace the piece of her heart she's been missing since the day her husband died.

Join the Seven Sisters of Amelia Island as they come together in good times and bad, embrace second chances, laugh in the face of adversity, and discover daily that they are stronger together no matter what they face.

Visit www.hopeholloway.com for release dates, covers, and sneak peeks into the series!

The Seven Sisters Series

Love Hope Holloway's books? If you haven't read her first two series, you're in for a treat! Chock full of family feels and beachy Florida settings, these sagas are for lovers of riveting and inspirational sagas about sisters, secrets, romance, mothers, and daughters...and the moments that make life worth living.

These series are complete, and available in e-book (also in Kindle Unlimited), paperback, and audio.

The Shellseeker Beach Series

Come to Shellseeker Beach and fall in love with a cast of unforgettable characters who face life's challenges with humor, heart, and hope. For lovers of riveting and inspirational sagas about sisters, secrets, romance, mothers, and daughters...and the moments that make life worth living.

The Coconut Key Series

Set in the heart of the Florida Keys, these seven delightful novels will make you laugh out loud, wipe a happy tear, and believe in all the hope and happiness of a second chance at life.

A Secret in the Keys – Book 1
A Reunion in the Keys – Book 2
A Season in the Keys – Book 3
A Haven in the Keys – Book 4
A Return to the Keys – Book 5
A Wedding in the Keys – Book 6
A Promise in the Keys – Book 7

About the Author

Hope Holloway is the author of charming, heartwarming women's fiction featuring unforgettable families and friends, and the emotional challenges they conquer. After more than twenty years in marketing, she launched a new career as an author of beach reads and feel-good fiction. A mother of two adult children, Hope and her husband of thirty years live in Florida. When not writing, she can be found walking the beach with her two rescue dogs, who beg her to include animals in every book. Visit her site at www.hopeholloway.com.

Made in the USA
Columbia, SC
06 August 2023

21329969R00195